Totally Bound Publishing books by Sara Ohlin

Graciella
Handling the Rancher

Rescue Me
Salvaging Love

D1296497

Rescue Me

SALVAGING LOVE

SARA OHLIN

SALVAGING LOVE

Dedication

For my gorgeous friend and writing partner in crime, Sara, who rescues all the animals.

Chapter One

Ellie was a soggy, soapy mess of bubbles and puppy fur. By some miracle, a few strands of her hair had survived the battle to bathe Chewie, one of the litter of four she'd found at the front door of her clinic, dirty, scrawny and huddled together in a cardboard box.

It wasn't the first time since she'd opened her vet clinic four years ago that animals had been abandoned at the door. Once, she'd even found a lovebird waiting for her. One lovebird. Everyone knew lovebirds were a pair. Ellie couldn't stand to see animals abandoned or put down, not if there was the slimmest chance someone could love them and give them a home.

Fortunately, these four babies would be adopted soon. Puppies always were. They were part Lab and part a whole bunch of mutt. Chewie was chocolate brown, like his namesake, and his hair was velvety and curly, more retriever-like. His shimmery brown baby eyes filled with longing every time he gazed at her. *I might have to keep this one.* As she poured water over him, he launched himself into her arms trying to cling to the large rubber apron she wore. Before she could disentangle him and put his butt back in the water, the bell over the front door rang. *Damn!* She'd meant to lock it. She kept Chewie attached to her chest with one hand, grabbed a towel to wrap around him with her other and headed out front.

Holy cow! "Can I...ah, help you?" The man stood by the front window, silhouetted by the fading evening light. Huge and gorgeous with rugged tan skin, black hair curling over his collar and the coolest blue-green eyes she'd ever seen. Ellie almost sighed, but that flash of beauty disappeared in an instant. Anger radiated from him.

"What the hell is going on, Ken?" he said into his phone, but he pierced her with his gaze.

His anger vibrated over them. Chewie started shaking in her arms and buried his head in the towel. "I'm sorry, sir, but can I help you? This is my —"

"What do I mean?" he ignored her to yell into his phone. "I'm standing here on my property that still has tenants in it. Explain!"

Sheesh. She leaned back with the force of his words. "It's okay, baby," she cooed to the shivering puppy in her arms. "Sir," she called louder this time, "we're closed right now and you're scaring the animals. If you wouldn't mind taking your phone call outside, I —"

He sliced his hand up to silence her.

Excuse me? She was not about to let this foul-mouthed jerk boss her around, but before she could say anything else, he hung up. "If you were closed, why was your door unlocked?"

"What?" It wasn't merely his size or harsh tone that had her brain malfunctioning. She couldn't keep up with his line of questioning.

"Your door," he said, his tone singeing her. "Why would a woman like you leave her door unlocked while she's here by herself?"

'A woman like you?' Ellie flinched. She didn't even want to know what he meant by that comment. She'd spent eighteen years of her life with people putting her down. No way in hell she was going to listen to more of it, not after she'd clawed her way out of that filth so long ago. She chose to focus on only part of what he said.

"I'm not alone." She scrubbed the soft puppy.

"Jesus." He closed his eyes.

She certainly didn't know what *that* meant. His swearing said a lot, but at the same time it didn't really say anything.

"Would you mind not swearing?"

"Excuse me?"

"I said, would you—"

"I heard you."

Okay, now she was getting angry. "Listen. I don't know who you are or what you're doing here, but, like I said, we're closed for the evening and I need to get home. You can make an appointment or come back in the morning when we open." God, she hoped he didn't come back.

"You should have been closed for good a week ago. Closed and vacated."

"What? What do you mean? This is my clinic. I signed a lease through the end of the year. That's seven months away."

"I know when the end of the year is."

The man had a degree in condescending behavior. His tone, his attitude, his entire demeanor said power and money, and the tailored gray suit, black dress shirt and shoes all bragged of wealth. The way he tried to silence her with his hand in the air. She couldn't stand people thinking they were better than everyone else. It got her hackles up. That and the way he studied her, assessing.

"I was stating the terms so you could realize your mistake and apologize for barging in here with your atrocious behavior and yelling at me."

He stared at her again. His features transformed from a pissed-off beast to a quiet, controlled predator. As if he carefully leashed his temper, and instead saw her as a problem to be solved. His eyes were calculating. It sent a nervous tingle up her spine.

"Well?" she prompted, trying to act braver than she felt. Chewie's heartbeat raced against hers. He wiggled to get loose from her tight hold.

"Terms have changed." He raised an eyebrow. Those eyes of his were a mysterious blue-green, like a deep pristine lake surrounded by mountains. And when he wasn't yelling, his voice soothed. He took a step toward her which jarred her out of her observations. She leaned back.

"What terms? Who are you?" She had to look up now. Jesus, he was well over six feet tall.

"Jackson Kincaid. I'm the new owner of this block. I'm tearing the entire thing down. Everyone was supposed to be vacated last week at the latest," he finished, delivering the blow to her gut just when the wriggling mass in her arms threw himself onto the floor and shook his sudsy, wet puppy body all over the man. Unable to find traction on the slippery floor, the pup flopped over on his back and clung to Jackson's pants with his tiny claws.

"Christ!" He reached down and plucked the pup up into the air, holding him away from his body.

"The new owner? Of the whole block? And you're tearing it all down?" She was surprised she could even find her voice at the shock. "You can't."

"I can," he said, glaring at her with that raised-eyebrow thing he did that made her feel ten instead of twenty-seven.

"Can't." She'd found her voice again, getting pissed.

"Can," he said, leaning in.

"You're a bully!" Anger heated her blood. "You don't even know me or the Heelys, or Carl and his daughter. I know your kind. And I won't let you come in here and intimidate me."

"You won't?" He looked at her questioningly. Or was he teasing her? She'd been so busy yelling, it almost sounded now as if he were fighting back laughter.

"No, I won't."

"And how do you plan to stop me?"

But she didn't get a chance to speak because Chewie let loose and peed all over Mr. Bully, drenching his perfect-fitting suit and his expensive leather dress shoes.

Ellie watched, frozen in place while he blinked. *Oh, shit!* "I…I am so sorry. He's just a, well—"

"Puppy. Got it," he clipped.

"Someone left a litter at the door and I had to get them clean. He's not trained."

"Yeah. I got that too."

"Here," she said quietly, trading him a towel for Chewie.

"Fuck! This day keeps getting better. Slime of the earth in my office earlier. Get over here to check out my buildings, find the tenants still here, an ignorant blonde and now I have puppy piss all over me." He wiped at his wet shirt and jacket with the towel.

She soothed Chewie and bristled at the *ignorant blonde* comment.

"Look, I'm sorry about what happened, but there's no need to be rude. You don't know me, which means you don't get to call me ignorant. What *I* know from *your* behavior is that you're an arrogant jerk who needs lessons in manners."

His eyes met hers, and the heat in them made her suck in her breath. Okay, maybe she'd gotten carried away and should *really* learn when to stay quiet. He acted like a jerk, but it wasn't like she had to point it out to him. Belatedly she realized it was kind of like teasing a hungry lion.

"Not ignorant?" His voice had turned low. Yup, definitely poking a lion. "You're here alone. It's dark. Every store along this street is closed. It's a sketchy neighborhood at best, and you leave your door unlocked?"

"Why do you care?" Ellie was confused by this entire conversation.

"Why?" He prowled closer. Okay, she should definitely be more careful about locking her door. "You. Here. Alone. Any cracked-up junkie could come right in and take what he wanted." He waved his hand up and down her body to indicate what that might mean.

"Now you're freaking me out *and* being rude." Her voice wasn't above a whisper, but he heard it.

"Good!"

"Good?"

"Yeah, maybe you'll be freaked out enough next time to lock your fucking door."

Okay, she was exhausted, and hurt by his words, although she didn't understand why, since he was nothing to her. She wasn't good in situations like this—

no matter how many years and miles away she was from her childhood, nasty people still affected her ability to be strong. It was painful to realize she hadn't gotten better at handling it at all. "Right. I understand," she began without any of the anger or passion lacing her words. "And I, ah, appreciate your concern, even if it's delivered in a yelling, jerky way, but you don't need to worry about me."

He braced back as if she'd slapped him. "You're kidding me?"

"No. Anyway, my night vet tech should be here any minute. Plus, I have Buffy. She's a great judge of character."

"Buffy?"

Ellie pointed toward the corner where her ten-year-old, one-hundred-pound Rottweiler slept on her dog bed, snoring away.

"Right, I can see how Buffy, who hasn't moved a muscle except to snore since I got here, is a perfect guard dog."

Ellie brushed back the curls that had slipped out of her ponytail. "If we continue this conversation tonight, you're going to throw your stuck-up disbelief and insults in my face, and as pleasant as it seems to be for you, it's not for me.

"I've been here since six, on my feet all day, which normally I don't mind because I love my job, but I had a horrible surgery on a dog. My assistant left at noon. I still have to get this little guy and his siblings settled for the night, which means fed, taken out to pee, shots and crates. I haven't eaten since breakfast. Dinner is a peanut butter and jelly sandwich before I face-plant into bed. You come in and threaten my clinic, no correction, my *dream*, which I worked my butt off to open. Maybe you could come back tomorrow, or we could meet for coffee and you can tell me, if you really are the new owner, what I have to do to convince you not to tear this block of buildings down. Then we can both go our separate ways and never see each other again."

It almost hurt her to say those words, because even though he was a total jerk, he was beautiful to look at. But horrors could hide behind beautiful appearances, something she was all too aware of. After all, her mother was a gorgeous model, but underneath she was crazy mean, and Ellie was the one who had taken the brunt of it.

He studied her while she spoke, silent and assessing again. Then he reached by her to grab one of her business cards from the counter. "Dr. Ellie Blevins, you think you can convince me not to tear this bag of bones down and build up a new condo development that will make billions?"

Billions? Did every battle she fought in this life have to be so outrageously difficult? This block was special. It wasn't only her clinic. It was the bakery, the hardware store that Carl and his daughter ran, her friend Ruby's spa, Lachlan's pub. This neighborhood burst with potential. And the park at the end of the block right along the river was lovely. The bonds she'd formed here, the true friendships, would make her fight back, even if she didn't feel brave enough for herself.

"It's not a bag of bones. It's a block of old, historic buildings that need love and care," she began. But standing there, taking in his polished rich-man strength, it was futile to convince him of anything. "You know what? Deal me the death blow now. I'd like to review the lease I signed before I throw in the towel and start looking for a new space and a new home, because I can tell there's no way you and I will ever be on the same page."

"New home?"

"What?" she said.

"You said, 'a new space and a new home'?"

"I live in the apartment above the French Connection Bakery. Mr. and Mrs. Heely have owned it for twenty-five years." There she was, exhausted-sharing again. And there he stood intense-staring. She closed her eyes at the craziest, weirdest conversation she'd ever had, and realized Chewie was asleep on her chest with his tiny head nuzzled in her neck. *Oh, soft love,* she thought, *if only people were more like dogs, so trusting, kind, and loving.*

"One month," he said.

"One month to be out of —"

"I'll give you one month to try to convince me."

"I... What?"

"You spend time with me for the next month. We get to know each other, and you can state your case."

"Spend time with you?" *Is he insane?*

"You said you wanted to try to convince me to change my mind."

"Oh," she whispered, confused again.

"You open tomorrow?"

"Yes," she said quickly, thinking maybe they'd tested each other's patience enough for one evening.

"Right, then. Tomorrow. Lock your door." Then he was gone, leaving her more confused than ever.

"Lock your door!" he yelled from outside, startling her out of her spot.

She went to the door, locked it, drew the blinds down and blew out a breath. "What in the heck just happened? I feel like a tornado blew through here and tossed us sideways into outer space. And what does 'tomorrow' mean? Is he coming back? Am I supposed to appear before him like a magician?"

She looked at Chewie and spoke into the empty waiting area with Buffy chasing squirrels in her dreams. *Holy cow! Holy freaking cow! This place is everything to me, more than my hopes and dreams – it's my safe place.* One single month to convince an angry lion not to eat her up? She might be an awesome veterinarian, but there were absolutely no instructions for how to communicate with a beast like Jackson Kincaid.

Chapter Two

Jackson walked through his silent kitchen to the huge great-room and into his study. He poured a bourbon and walked to the wall of windows facing the secluded back yard that stretched for half an acre before it butted up against the towering fir trees beyond.

Luminous. Her skin—he'd never seen anything so luminous and beautiful. Pale until she blushed, which also made the light freckles on her checks and nose more charming. A nose with a slight hitch. It had been broken at one time, which made it no less cute. Priceless skin that most women would pay a mint to have. Pale blonde hair with a hint of red throughout. Wet curls had fallen from her high ponytail and curled seductively around her face. Un-fucking-believable fiery eyes, a type of hazel that switched from coppery green to emerald with gold highlights when her temper got up. They were even more gorgeous with wet lashes. Jesus Christ, had she fallen right out of a fairy tale into the bathtub with her puppies?

And she didn't have a fucking clue how gorgeous she was.

He'd been in a foul mood before he even got to the site to see no demo happening and all the tenants still there. They weren't even aware the buildings had been sold.

Foul was an understatement. He'd come from a meeting with his client, Anthony 'Slimeball' Lucciano. Not simply a man wanting a good defense, but one sick fuck whose wife had been beaten nearly to death. She claimed Lucciano had done it. Lucciano said he had an alibi and someone else had attacked his wife in their home. Lucciano wanted Jackson to make sure he got off. And Jackson Kincaid, best criminal defense lawyer around, could do it. It was a game, playing the jury. And the lawyer who played the smartest won. Jackson always won.

He'd read the report. He'd seen the pictures of the wife that the prosecution had sent over. *Unrecognizable with the bruises and swelling and blood on her face.* Someone sure as hell had beaten her. Jackson had an ongoing hatred for any man who beat a woman, but when it came to defending his firm's client, he had no choice.

What pissed him off was that Lucciano seemed more concerned about himself than his wife who lay bloody, bruised and unconscious in a hospital. He already had little respect for Lucciano as a client they'd been defending against tax fraud and mafia-type crime for years, which now tipped over into disgust. He was damn tired of feeling like shit because of his job.

He stared out at the silent, dark yard that would be great for a dog. He'd never gotten around to getting a dog. Throwing back his bourbon, he knew he could win

Lucciano's case. And it didn't give him one ounce of pride.

Giving the wrongly accused a fair chance was how he'd started on his path as a lawyer. His penance. Defending sick, guilty dirt-bags with enough money to afford him was what he'd become. His prison.

Jackson's foul mood simmered under his skin at having spent too much time in the company of a psychotic bastard. When he'd realized Ellie was at her clinic, at night by herself, with the door unlocked, he'd lost his shit.

He should have been embarrassed. He'd never treated a woman so poorly, but she hadn't cowered, which brought a smile to his lips. She'd been offended and unconcerned about her own safety, and she might have appeared confused as hell, but she hadn't backed down from his temper.

He wanted out of his prominent partnership, out of defense, out of the fucking stink he'd gotten lost in. Which was why he and his buddy Connor Duggan, owner and general contractor of Duggan Construction, had purchased the broken-down block of buildings. Jackson wanted a challenge. Duggan liked to build. Both men won in the deal.

At some point, winning and power had become a way to keep the monumental failures of his past hidden. Now, looking out at the empty back yard, picturing Ellie with that gentle brown pup curled up asleep on her chest, he wanted to be surrounded by her warmth. He'd watched her stroke that puppy to calm it. The pup had yawned and nodded off into her neck. Fuck, he was hard again just thinking of her touch. He was jealous of a fucking puppy.

Ellie Blevins was eons from the sewer he worked with. He should shut this down, this whatever-the-fuck, one-month deal he'd thrown at her, but he wanted to be close to her again. He poured himself another drink and called Connor.

"This better be good, Kincaid."

"You busy?" Jackson asked his friend. Then he heard the woman's voice in the background. "Dumb question."

"Can we save the commentary for later, jack*ass*?"

"Closing's been postponed on our Corvallis property."

"You're shitting me."

"Nope, our idiot of a real estate agent conveniently forgot to explain it was a ninety-day closing, not thirty."

"He didn't forget. He wanted the deal and did whatever he could to get us to sign. Could see the drool coming out of his mouth."

"Right, which was stupid on his part because we were going to sign no matter what."

"You gonna rip him a new one?"

"Already done."

"What's with the midnight chat, brother? You know I love you, but right now there's something else I'd much rather be doing."

"Tenants don't even know it's been sold. Went by tonight. You working tomorrow?"

"I'm always working, except when I'm playing, which I'd like to get back to," Duggan said. "Except now she's asleep. Time to make my escape and get home anyway."

"Can you be at Corvallis before you get to your job site?"

"Sure thing. What's up?"

"Change of plans, my friend. Change of plans."

"How's that?"

"The tenant I met tonight, Dr. Ellie Blevins. She owns the vet clinic."

"Ah. This is about a woman. Should have known. Did she fall in lust at first sight over your charms and money?"

"We didn't exactly hit it off. There was a lot of yelling and her puppy pissed all over me. Nice to know you think highly of me."

Duggan laughed. "You're the only one I know who gets more action than I do. And anyway, I thought you liked it like that—quick, hot one-night stands with women you can buy off with fancy gifts."

"I've been re-evaluating my life."

Then Duggan howled with laughter. "Buddy, you do know you called me, not Dr. Phil, right? She yelled at you, her dog peed on you and now you're in love?"

"I did most of the yelling."

"Are you sure this is the same Jackson Kincaid I've been friends with for a decade? I know you have a temper, but I have never seen you yell at a woman. Even you with your one-night, no-strings-attached dates, you still seem to do it gallantly."

"Did you use the word 'gallantly'?"

"Fuck off."

Now it was Jackson's turn to laugh. "Right. Meet me tomorrow at the park. Ellie thinks she can change my mind about the condo development. I told her she could try to talk me out of it. I want you to meet her, seeing as you're my partner on this deal. And behave, Duggan."

"Please, I always behave around ladies."

"Hands off this one, Duggan. I'm serious."

Duggan was silent for a moment and Jackson said, "You there?"

"You've never ever acted territorial over a woman. This I have got to see."

"See you in the morning, Casanova. I'll text you where to meet."

"I'll be there."

Jackson hung up and walked upstairs to his bedroom. Duggan was right. He never yelled at women. He'd been a complete ass tonight. She thought he was a jerk and she wasn't wrong. One more reason why he didn't belong in her life. A cowardly past, a covered-in-filth present and a first-class jerk. Three strikes against him. Instead of wallowing in his mistakes, he imagined what it would feel like to run his hands through Ellie's hair.

Chapter Three

Like every morning, Ellie woke with the sun. She put on her yoga pants, her gray hoodie and running shoes, tied her curls up in a messy bun, grabbed Buffy's leash and headed over to the clinic to take the puppies out for a walk.

She found her vet tech Matt, who helped on the weekends and overnight, in the back surrounded by balls of fur.

"Hey, Matt."

"Ellie." He smiled. "Sweet! Puppies!"

"I know, pretty cute, huh. Abandoned at the front door last night."

"I called Rosie. She lost it. She can't wait to meet them."

Ellie smiled too. Rosie was Matt's girlfriend and her other tech. "How's our surgery patient?"

"Braveheart? Nice name by the way. He made it through the night. His stitches look good and he opened his eyes this morning."

"Good. He's a fighter. Thought he could use a fitting name. I'm gonna take the puppies out for a walk with Buffy before you leave."

"Righteous! Buffy'll show 'em how it's done."

"Hey, babies," she said, sitting on the floor. "This should be crazy. Wanna go to the park?" Chewie climbed in her lap and started gnawing on the edge of her sleeve.

The look on Jackson's face when Chewie had clung to the leg of his pants flashed in her mind. One good thing about being exhausted last night was that, after her sandwich and a shower, she had indeed face-planted into bed, and slept hard and deep.

Now, her problems slapped her in the face. He'd said, "Tomorrow," as though she was supposed to use clairvoyance to understand what he meant. Was he coming by? Going to call her? Since she couldn't decipher his code, she'd have to hope their next encounter went better than their first.

She got each of the puppies collared and leashed and was attempting to get them all out the door when Matt called, "Rosie said she'd love to pick up more hours once classes are done next month, Ellie."

One month. Ellie tried to keep the emotion out of her face. This wasn't just her problem — it affected everyone who lived and worked on this block. Matt and Rosie, the best employees she'd ever had, who loved learning from her, and she might have to crush their dreams too if she had to close her clinic.

"Sure, Matt," she said, leading the dogs away. "Let me check the schedule."

Other than the tiny black cloud hanging over her thoughts and emotions, the day promised perfection. Gorgeous blue sky, sunshine already warming everyone up. Ellie stood in the park half an hour later with all four pups sitting on their butts, gazing up at her and waiting almost patiently, aside from the barely controlled wiggles that ran through their bodies. Buffy relaxed on her belly right next to Ellie with her head up, but even lying down, Buffy towered over the pups. Ellie raised her hand with puppy treats. These four cuties would get adopted soon, but there was no harm in starting training now.

"Stay," she said. "Good dog." She bent down to pet the first pup, the only girl of the litter and the only blonde one, when Chewie yipped his puppy bark and tugged on his leash. Her calm, sitting puppies became a mess of barking and tangled leashes, all trying to get behind Ellie.

Ellie tried to turn, while Chewie pulled all their leashes loose from her hand to get at the something that had caught his attention. "Shit!" Not something, someone. Jackson Kincaid, but not angry, confusing, business-suit Jackson Kincaid from last night. Nope, this version wore an old baseball hat, a long-sleeved navy T-shirt, faded blue jeans and flip-flops on his bare feet. *Oh my!* He didn't seem angry, and he did not hide his perusal of her. *Shit! Shit! Shit!* She was certain last night that she could not have looked worse, but she'd been wrong.

Right now would be the definition of worse with her bed-head riot of curls piled on top of her head and her yoga pants that did not do her body any favors. Not to mention her ankles were splattered with mud from the dogs and the leashes wound around her, caging her in. Chewie escaped and raced around Jackson's feet, barking and playing with the frayed hem of his jeans. The other three puppies rolled around to free themselves from the tangle.

"Ellie," he said. "Morning."

"Um, hi? What are you doing here?"

"Told you I'd see you tomorrow." God, his voice was even sexier when he wasn't yelling.

She reached down to untangle her body *and* her thoughts. She wasn't supposed to be lusting after the man, merely convincing him to do the right thing and not destroy this beautiful neighborhood.

"Brought you a coffee."

"You? Thank you. I…" She studied the tangled mess at her feet.

"Here," he said, handing her both coffees and kneeling down to unhook the leashes from the pups' collars. "I think it might be easier this way." He unwrapped them from around her body.

"Right," she whispered. He stood in her space, unwinding the material from around her. He put his hand on her hip to steady her. But even once she was steady, he left it there while he studied her. And, like waking from a great dream, he smiled slow and beautiful. And she nearly did fall over.

"You're not yelling at me," she said.

"Left my inner jerk at home this morning."

"Kincaid!" Ellie and Jackson both looked toward the shout.

"Well, well, well," the man said, walking up to them. Full of muscles which even his gray sweatshirt and work cargos couldn't hide. His huge smile lit up tawny brown eyes. Even his crow's feet were handsome. *Have I stumbled into a dream where every human is perfect and gorgeous?*

"You said this meeting was important. Now I understand why." He glanced back and forth between Ellie and Jackson, grinning.

"Duggan," Jackson said, stepping away from Ellie with his coffee in his hand. His voice held a warning.

Salvaging Love

The heat from his strong hand still warmed her side where he'd steadied her. What had she been she thinking wearing these tight, ugly pants? Her mother's sharp voice forced its way into her thoughts. *Those pants do nothing except force people to come face to face with your disgusting curves.*

"Kincaid."

The men shook hands and she wished like hell the strawberry splotches of embarrassment would disappear from her face and neck.

"Duggan, this is Ellie Blevins. Ellie, this is my friend Con—"

Right then the girl pup ran straight into Duggan's legs, tripped over herself and scrabbled back up to try to climb up him. *Jeesh, even the puppies are entranced.*

Duggan reached down with his free hand to pick her up. "Hey, pretty girl."

"She's your type," Jackson said. "Willing. Blonde. Throwing herself at you."

Ellie glared at Jackson. "You don't have a high opinion of blondes, do you? That's the second insulting comment you've made about them in less than twenty-four hours." There went her foggy brain from the heat of his hands on her hips. He was worse than rude. How could she ever have thought he was gorgeous? She hadn't been stupid enough to be lured by someone's good looks in a long time.

"I was talking about the dog, Ellie, teasing Connor. He lost his dog, Beauty, last year. She was a blonde Lab."

"Oh." Embarrassment flooded her cheeks again.

Duggan roared with laughter. "Connor Duggan. Excuse this jackass. I, on the other hand, know how to talk to women without insulting them."

27

The pup in his hand stretched up to his face and poured sweet, slobbery puppy kisses all over his beard.

"Sweet talk is more like it," Jackson said.

"Is there any other way to talk to a pretty lady?"

"Who are you people?" Ellie said in disbelief.

"Connor's my partner. He owns Duggan Construction."

Dammit! When Jackson had showed up casual and sexy, almost smiling at her, she'd gotten her hopes up that maybe he really did want to hear what she had to say about this place, why he shouldn't tear it down. "I see," she said. "Changed your mind about the one-month thing already? To be honest I couldn't figure out why you made that deal. Save the old and charming or make billions of dollars with a brand-new development. It's not a hard decision for most. A girl can hope, though," she said, quieter. "Listen, I have to get back to the clinic."

Jackson put his hand out on her arm to stop her. "Ellie, Connor came to have a closer look to see if anything about this block is salvageable. It's not only me you have to convince."

"Everything's worth saving, Mr. Kincaid. Everything deserves a second chance."

"I disagree."

"This place is worth it," she said. They stared at each other. Wow, those eyes of his. This was going to be a lot harder than she thought if she kept getting distracted by those deep green-blue depths, because when she did, all her words, all her arguments flew out of her head. It was more than the intense, unique color. His eyes showed his emotions. The strange thing was she felt like he searched into her depths as she did his. It felt frightening and exhilarating at the same time.

Chapter Four

"How 'bout this, kids." Duggan cut into the tension. "Let's walk for a few minutes. Ellie, you can give us a general idea about what you think is worth saving. I have to be at my job site in half an hour, and you have your hands full." He indicated the three puppies on the ground who were trying to wrestle with Buffy. The blonde pup snuggled tight in Duggan's arm.

"It's all worth saving." She reached down to put the leashes back on the dogs and they all headed out of the park. It didn't seem to bother her that the uncoordinated puppies constantly tripped over and tangled up in one another. Buffy powered through the chaos and kept the lead. Kincaid swore the older dog rolled her eyes a time or two. "This park is amazing. Everything's built around it. It's a great place for people to gather and kids to play. People hold weddings here. At the other end is a playground and I know the playground equipment is falling apart, but that can be replaced. The gazebo—"

"Is about to crumble," he said.

"True, but imagine what it used to be — a jazz band up there, couples sitting on picnic blankets or dancing to the music in the late afternoon light... The community has organized music in the park on Sunday afternoons again and it brings everyone together. You two should come back for that on a Sunday."

"The band better be careful the gazebo doesn't fall apart around them." *Jesus, she's a complete romantic.*

"It's not that bad. It needs a new coat of paint."

"Princess," Duggan chimed in. "No offense, but it needs to be put out of its misery."

"Then build a new one. But don't bulldoze the entire park so people can stare out of their tenth-floor condo windows at their million- or billion-dollar river view."

"A perfect, pristine, brand-new view sounds good to me," Jackson said.

"Don't you already have a million-dollar view, Mr. Kincaid?"

She vibrated with frustration and Jackson found he liked it when she got frustrated with him. Her eyes heated up and her cheeks flushed again. He wanted to see her hair down. He'd bet she was a stunning mermaid rising from the sea.

"People live here and work here. It's their community. Oh, shit!" She stopped walking. "I forgot George. Hold these. I'll be right back." She shoved the leashes in Jackson's hand and ran into the bakery. The line was long, but people waited, chatted with friends, sat outside on the benches, read their papers. *Content.* Ellie bypassed the line and went right behind the counter.

She came back with another coffee and three small bags. "Here," she said, holding out bags to him and

Duggan. "Marie's cinnamon rolls might help convince you."

He tossed his empty coffee cup into the trash and took one of the bags from her.

"These smell like heaven," Duggan said as they continued walking.

"Needed more caffeine?" he asked Ellie.

"What?" She tried to take the leashes back from him.

"I've got them. You got another coffee?"

"This is for my friend, George. There he is." Sitting down in between two of the buildings was an older white-haired black man, who looked homeless.

"Hey, George," Ellie said softly.

"Sweetheart, gorgeous day, isn't it?" the man said.

Ellie sat right down next to him on the ground and handed him the coffee and pastry. "It is. We might have a nice spring after all. George, these are my...um..." Ellie motioned toward Jackson and Duggan.

"Friends. Jackson Kincaid and Connor Duggan," he finished for her.

"George Franklin. Nice to meet any friends of my precious Ellie," George said. "Looks like you have new responsibility today, Ms. Buffy." Buffy sat at George's feet and he scrubbed the fur behind her ears. "When did you get more puppies, Ellie?"

"They were left at the clinic door, and I couldn't *not* take care of them."

"Of course not, that's not your way. Our Ellie rescues everyone and everything."

"I do not," Ellie said. Her blush, highlighted in the sun, made her even more beautiful. "George, I'm running a bit late today." Before she got up, George stood and helped her.

"Sure thing, honey. Thanks for the breakfast."

She patted him on the back. "You have a good day. Stay out of the sun and come into the clinic if you need anything, okay?"

"Sure thing, sure thing," he said, sitting back down to sip his coffee.

"I know what you're thinking," Ellie said. "That homeless people aren't going to convince you this is a neighborhood worth saving. But homeless people are everywhere and it's not always their fault. At least there are a lot of people here with compassion. The whole neighborhood helps George out."

Now she was more than frustrated — she was impassioned. And the gold flecks heated up in her eyes. *What a sight.* Fired up, dressed in her tight yoga pants, which did more for the eye than that stupid apron she'd had on last night. He'd sat in his office imagining what was under that apron and he was not disappointed at all this morning to see she had curves. Curves he wanted to get his hands and his mouth on.

Cooling his desire, he focused. "The development plans are for condos and retail. People can do what you're saying they do now, but in much nicer, newer, *safer* surroundings. It doesn't take a construction god like Duggan to see these buildings are in serious disrepair. The roofs haven't been replaced in years. Irresponsible painters did a crap job too many years ago to count and I can see down to the bare wood in several places. The windows look original, which means they let more heat out onto the street than they keep inside. And I don't see any gutters on several of the buildings, which means water damage is affecting more than the roofs. God knows what Duggan would find behind the walls, and by that, I mean old knob and tube wiring, poor plumbing and mold."

"Wow, you're more than a pretty face," Duggan joked.

"Stuff it," Jackson said.

"You two think this is funny, don't you?" Ellie snapped.

She wasn't impassioned anymore—she was pissed. He was hard at the thought of all that passion under him in his bed. *Fuck, that's the last thing I need to think about — Dr. Ellie Blevins, naked, all warm, lush curves.*

"You knock all this down, build up your condo-retail development and the people that live and work here now won't be able to stay. You'll ruin a community. My friend Ruby, after her mom died of breast cancer, she picked herself up from all that grief, started her salon, all with her own money. Across the street, Carl and his daughter, Molly, who has Down's syndrome, run the hardware store owned by Carl's father before him. Lachlan's pub is packed most nights with live Irish music that people come from all over to hear. You" — she pointed to Duggan—"didn't even take any notes. I can see this isn't serious to you at all."

"My apologies, Ellie. You have my attention." Duggan quit joking. "And, to be fair, I take notes in my mind. And I've been taking notes on this place for the past year. Jackson's right. What he didn't say is that there's no question the roofs are leaking, which means there is massive damage in the walls, mold and decaying wood beams and supports, which is a serious hazard. Water causes more damage than people ever realize. At least three of these buildings need heavy foundation repair. I can only guess what disasters I'll find inside, but I do take notes, and I do take you seriously."

"I get emotional about this place." They stopped walking in front of her clinic. "It's important to me," Ellie said.

"I think we both get that," Jackson said, studying her. "Can you save it?"

Although he enjoyed watching her range of emotions, the defeat she wore on her face now was much less fun for him to witness.

Duggan sighed. "I'll need to get a better assessment of the insides and write up repair cost estimates. Then Jackson and I will talk about what we think," he said.

"Okay," she said, and breathed a sigh. "I have my first patient at nine. Here." She held out her hand for the puppy in Duggan's arms.

"If she needs a home, I think I'll keep her," Duggan said.

"Just what you need, a puppy to train, with your work schedule," Jackson said.

"Katie and the girls won't mind." He turned to Ellie. "My sister and nieces live with me and they are going to love this baby."

"Well, she seems smitten with you," Ellie said.

"The ladies usually are," Jackson said dryly.

"I'll bring you a crate, bowls and a little puppy food to get you started. She's had her shots."

"I have stuff at home already. I'll see you again later this week to take more notes," Duggan teased her.

"Why the pencil behind the ear and the clipboard if you don't write anything down?" Ellie asked.

"In case I need to get a pretty lady's phone number." Jackson shoved his friend on the shoulder.

"You working by yourself today?" Jackson asked her.

"Matt's here for another hour, then another assistant and my receptionist will be here."

"Right. Lock your doors when you're alone," he insisted, holding the door to the clinic open for her.

"Things are only a bit run-down. That doesn't mean it's an unsafe neighborhood, Mr. Kincaid," she said, giving him her attitude.

He leaned in close. Damn, he wanted to kiss her. "Lock. Your. Doors."

"I wondered where Mr. Bossy went," she said.

"Trust me," he replied, "I'm familiar with crime. And there's no sense inviting it." She searched his face, as if trying to understand him. "Please," he said.

"Okay," she whispered.

"Good, Ellie. See you tomorrow."

"Tomorrow, again?"

"Music in the park. Now that I own it, I might as well make sure no one injures themselves on that wreck you call a gazebo. You still have lots of convincing to do."

"I will convince you," she vowed.

"Looking forward to it."

Her cheeks blushed rosy again, and she walked her motley crew into the clinic.

"I had no idea how much fun this morning was going to be," Duggan said.

"Shut up."

"However, aside from watching you two together, this was a waste of time since there's no way I could get a full assessment this morning. And I'm sure you knew she had to work. What's this all about, Caid?"

Duggan studied him.

"Fuck, you've already changed your mind. I can kiss our fancy condo development goodbye," Duggan said, chuckling. "Well, she is a million times prettier than most of your women. And it takes one heck of a brain to be a veterinarian. Plus, it's almost like she enjoys sparring with you."

He glared at his friend.

"I'm not going to make a move on your woman, Caid. It was harmless flirting. You know me."

"She's not mine. Not yet. And I want the month."

"The month?"

"Told her I'd give her a month to try to convince me not to tear the block down. Said she could spend time with me and talk me out of making billions."

"You're playing with her?" Duggan snarled at him. "Jesus, Caid, she's not that kind of girl. You can see kind and innocent written all over her."

"I'm not playing." Jackson was insulted. "It's not a game. Not to me. Maybe after a month of spending time with me, she won't want to run away."

Duggan relaxed his angry stance. "Maybe I'm the one who needs to have his head examined. Did you, legendary player, admit you met a woman who might take you out of the game forever?"

"Thought you had to get to work, jackass," Jackson said, and rounded the hood of his SUV to climb in.

"You're a good man, Caid," Duggan said, serious now. "It's time you let a good woman know that about you." And with a puppy in one arm and his clipboard in the other, he walked away.

She called this clinic her dream. Her entire face lit up when she spoke about this neighborhood, about her career. For a year, he and Duggan had been working with an architect to design the new development here, but dreams? Jackson Kincaid sure as fuck didn't have any dreams. His had died the day he was separated from everyone he loved. His father dead, his mother in jail and his sister put in a separate foster home. But he wanted. Fuck! He wanted Ellie. He wanted to be surrounded by her light and dreams. Could he ever belong with someone like her, someone who believed in dreams? Could she see her way to sharing her dreams with him?

Chapter Five

Aside from all his hovering, gorgeous, sexy amazingness, unbelievable eyes, a voice that when it went deep might have her agreeing to anything, Jackson Kincaid was all kinds of irritating.

Noon on Sunday and all Ellie knew was that he'd said he'd see her tomorrow, *again*. He hadn't said when or where. They didn't even have each other's phone number. Not that she'd be brave enough to call him anyway.

And she hadn't slept well. Ellie loved sleep—she excelled at sleep. But last night all she'd been able to think of was his face when he'd smiled at her with that sexy *I-want-to-devour-you* smile. *Yes, please*, she wanted to say, *devour me*. When she had dozed off, he'd been there in her dreams.

Then there was the locksmith he'd sent over yesterday afternoon to put new heavy-duty locks on the clinic's doors. The man had been grumpy and had said no more than three words when she'd tried to talk to him, and pay him, and those three words had been, "It's paid for." He'd left without any explanation. So she didn't know Jackson had done it, but she suspected.

Now she strolled through the farmers' market stalls at the end of the park, wondering if he was going to appear out of thin air like he had a habit of doing.

"Thought you were closed today?"

Startled, Ellie glanced up to see Jackson standing there. He had the most confusing way of starting conversations. "I am? I mean I am." He was leaning up against a tree studying her, looking delicious again in faded jeans and a black long-sleeved shirt. *Is delicious an appropriate word to describe men?*

"Do you wear scrubs for fun?"

"No." She suddenly felt self-conscious and crossed her arms. "The clinic is closed, but I still had to check on the animals this morning. And later."

He walked closer. "Ellie, I was teasing you."

"Teasing me?"

"Christ, you do know what that is?"

"You know, Mr. Kincaid, we could have a conversation without you angry-swearing at me, *again.*"

He closed his eyes for a minute and when he opened them said, "I'm not angry at you. I'm mad because I don't understand how a gorgeous, successful, intelligent woman like you doesn't understand teasing."

She jerked her head at his words. *Gorgeous, successful, intelligent.* He thought she was all of those?

"Jesus, Ellie," he said. He reached out and put his hands on her shoulders to steady her. "I apologize. I don't mean to sound like a complete jerk."

"It's okay," she said, and almost walked away right then from humiliation, except his warm hands were on her again, soothing her soul. She *didn't* know what it was like to be teased. No one had treated her like that. Especially not while she was growing up. Taunted was more like it. She was comfortable in her scrubs and yoga pants even though they weren't flattering. Shopping gave her the hives. Memories of clothes shopping with her mother made her nauseated. He made little circles on her shoulders with his thumbs and studied her.

"Let's start over. I'll keep my mouth shut, and you can tell me more about this community you love while we listen to the music," Jackson said.

"Why?" She'd been daydreaming about his eyes again. Green, today. They were dark like a forest. Like they changed colors based on what he was wearing.

"Why?" he asked. "We have a deal. I thought you wanted the chance to convince me."

"I get the feeling nothing I'm going to say will change your mind."

"I want you to try." He moved an inch closer and stilled his hands, but the warmth remained.

He sounded sincere, but he was so many things she didn't understand, male, hot, bossy, confusing as heck.

"Yesterday you said that everything and everyone was worth saving. Make me believe that."

Ellie sensed a hidden depth to his words. Did he really care to hear about the neighborhood? Standing close to his warmth, she wanted him to. Initially, he'd come across rough, but bringing her coffee, being pissed about her unlocked clinic door at night? No one in her life had ever been concerned enough about her safety to get pissed.

He dropped his hands and she wanted to lean into him to get his warmth back. The tiny hairs on her skin were tingling from being so close to him.

"I promise not to be a jerk for the next hour, Ellie."

He used that quiet, deep voice again and gave her that killer grin.

"Are you sure you can handle an entire hour without being a jerk?" she asked and tipped her face up to grin back.

For a second she thought she'd pissed him off, but then he threw back his head and laughed. *I love that gorgeous sound.*

"Are you teasing me, Dr. Blevins?"

"I'm a quick study, Mr. Kincaid."

"Good to know," he said. His voice had grown deeper and his smile was downright seductive. "And it's Jackson."

Holy cow! His voice felt like a caress down her whole body.

"Shall we?" He gestured to the people gathering by the jazz band in the park.

"Okay," she breathed, barely able to get that word out.

As they walked the park and enjoyed the music, Ellie started with a history of the neighborhood. How it had begun with German immigrants who'd built the park and the buildings around it. How, during WWII, the people living here had built gardens in the park to grow their own food. She pointed out the Nakamura family's small grocery store at one end of the park and explained how, during the war, the neighbors had kept it open for the family till they'd returned from the labor camp.

"You had no idea what you were getting into when you asked me to talk about this place, Mr....I mean, Jackson." His eyes got a shade darker when she said his name. *Oh, my.* "I don't want to bore you."

"I'm not bored. I'm listening."

"Okay," she said again. He was difficult to figure out. She didn't know which was better, the Jackson who worried over her unlocked door, or quiet Jackson, who let her expound on a topic she loved, who asked good questions, who told her she wasn't boring him.

"Then again," he said, "no one's ever tried to bore me into changing my mind. Maybe that tactic will work for you."

Ellie grinned. "Were you teasing me again?"

He winked at her.

Did he just — ? That tingly feeling shivered through her again. She didn't know what to do with that, especially since he was here so she could sell him on the idea of restoration.

Ellie was so caught up in Jackson lust she almost missed his phone ringing.

"Kincaid here," Jackson said into his cell phone.

Ellie studied his profile. Strong, intense. She wanted to study him forever, to lean closer and put her fingers on his jaw, his cheek. Make her way around to those lips of his.

"I have to go."

"What?" Ellie shook the fog from her brain, pulled from a great daydream to realize none of those wonderful thoughts and sensations were real. *Hmm,* she might need to hide that phone of his.

"Emergency, babe. Gotta head to my office." He gave her hand a squeeze. She brought her gaze from their

hands to his face in a daze because she was stuck on
babe.

He dropped her hand and walked backward away
from her. "I'll talk to you later."

*What in the heck is happening here? That seems to be my
question of the week.* She sat before she fell over. *Babe?*
She couldn't decide if it was the way he'd said it, or that
hot, bossy Jackson Kincaid had called *her*, plain and
simple Ellie Blevins, 'babe' that made her blush. Ellie
sat in the warm sunshine and enjoyed the sensations of
his flirtation. She didn't even care how red her cheeks
were from blushing.

Eventually her blush faded. She imagined how many
women in his life he called 'babe'. *Silly*, she chided
herself. It was ridiculous to get caught up in his
handsomeness and the sparks he shot through her. He
could have any gorgeous woman he wanted, and she
was certain it wouldn't be her. No one had ever wanted
her.

Shocked back to reality, Ellie found, for the first time
in a long time, those thoughts hurt, and she rubbed at
her chest. She headed for her clinic, deep in thought at
the way her emotions had hovered right near the
surface ever since Jackson Kincaid had stormed into her
clinic. She wondered what he did that called him into
his office on a Sunday afternoon.

Not that she was one to talk. She worked all the time,
but her clinic was her life — taking care of animals,
saving injured ones, rescuing litters, finding homes for
ones who were abandoned. After all, animals never
insulted her or shamed her for not being good enough
or beautiful enough.

She shouldn't be wondering about him at all, except for how to convince him not to destroy this community she loved.

Chapter Six

After nine on Monday night, Ellie curled up on her red velvet sofa to read about the history and importance of the Corvallis neighborhood. To convince Jackson not to tear all these beautiful buildings down, she wanted to sound like an expert. There was history about the Italianate and Queen Anne-style buildings and more current articles about new urban living with business, retail and homeowners all coexisting together to form strong communities. Everything she already knew and felt in her heart was here on paper for Jackson to see. He seemed like a man who needed absolute proof, hard facts, success stories. And Ellie planned to give them to him.

But she was having trouble concentrating and organizing her thoughts. *Do men randomly call a woman 'babe'? Is that a casual word?* It didn't feel casual. It stunned her. It made her face flush and it started those tingles up in her body again. She wanted to call Nat or Ruby and ask them, but she had no clue how to chat with girlfriends about men. And if she told them who he was, she'd have to explain about the buildings being sold, which she didn't want to do yet. When her phone rang, she answered it without looking at the caller ID.

"Hey."

"Babe." Before Ellie could come out of her shock, he said, "You always answer the phone like that?"

"Jackson?" she whispered.

"Yeah, who else did you think it was?" He sounded angry and she was super puzzled.

"No one. I assumed maybe Matt was calling because he needed my help with an animal at the clinic or maybe Nat. How did you get my number?"

"Your cell is on your business card, Ellie."

"Oh, right," she said. "Are you mad?"

"It felt intimate, friendly, the way you answered."

What? Am I losing my mind? "Well, that's how I talk to my friends, Jackson." She spoke slowly now, not sure who was more confused, herself or Jackson.

"Right," he clipped.

"You're mad?"

"I'm not."

"Well, you say that, but you *sound* mad."

"I like the way it sounded when you said, 'Hey.'" His voice was grumbly, but intent, serious.

She could not keep up with this man.

"Okaaaay," she said. She was a tiny bit freaked out because Jackson Kincaid had just told her how much he liked the way she'd answered the phone, and she didn't know what that meant. His silence freaked her out too, because she couldn't tell if he was still there or not, and she wanted him to still be there.

"Jackson?"

"I want to be the only one who gets that soft, intimate 'Hey' from you."

What? "I'm confused," she said quietly.

"I'm not," he said. "I like the way you look, your gorgeous skin, that cute break in your nose, although I doubt I'd like the way you broke it."

No, he absolutely would not, she thought, sucking in a breath.

"I like the way you talk to your dogs, the way when you say 'Hi' to people you make every single one of them feel special. I fucking love the way your hazel eyes get darker when you're fighting with me, the confusion in your face when I catch you off guard. You've got a fucking fantastic body, and that's only from seeing you in your scrubs and your sexy yoga pants and I bet I'd like what's hidden underneath. I like the way your soft voice hits me, the way you smile at everything, except when you're pissed, which I might like even more. I don't want the month to learn why a bunch of buildings are worth saving, I want to spend the month getting to know you. Still confused?"

Stunned was more like it. He liked her in her yoga pants? Her nose that was so far from model perfect she could not even go there?

"Ellie? Are you still confused?"

"No?" she squeaked out, but it was definitely a question, because, hell yes, she was still confused. Was he high? Or blind? Maybe both?

He laughed. "We'll get there. How was the rest of your day?"

We'll get where? He'd shattered her world, in a good way and he wanted to hear about her afternoon? "Um…" *Pull yourself together, Ellie.* "Good. I vaccinated a new patient, changed the dressings on the surgery

patient I had the other day and had an old greyhound
in for ultrasounds. Not too busy."

"Most people would call that busy, Ellie."

"Um, sometimes things come up and I try to fit
people in. How was your day, Jackson?"

"Not worth talking about."

"That doesn't sound good."

"Nope, but now I've got your sweet voice on the
phone. Talk to me, Ellie."

"Talk?" God, she cringed and knocked her head
against her knees. She was such a loser.

"Yeah, babe, tell me what you're doing now, or if
Buffy got enough naps today."

He certainly paid attention. Buffy liked nothing more
than napping, aside from French fries.

"I just finished dinner."

"Another peanut butter sandwich?"

"Well…" *Yes.* She debated which would make her
appear more stupid — admitting that to someone like
Jackson Kincaid, or staying silent, thereby giving him
the impression that she couldn't hold a simple
conversation. "I had stuff to catch up on tonight. And I
haven't gone grocery shopping in a few days."

"What does a vet catch up on during evenings by
herself in her apartment?"

"Research on historic neighborhoods, urban
planning, benefits of tight-knit communities."

"Babe," he said. His deep voice softened as though he
was smiling while he said it. He could call her that all
day. It moved deep into her, the sweetest song she'd
ever heard written for her. She set her papers aside and
snuggled down into the couch with her throw blanket.

"I don't want you to think all my reasons about this
neighborhood are purely emotional. I want to prove to

you that this neighborhood could be even more beautiful and amazing than it already is. It's been here since the late 1800s. Many of the buildings are original. There's history here."

"Not all history's good."

"This one is. It's full of generations of families, historic architecture, love and loyalty. People take care of each other here. It's a beautiful thing. Jackson? You still there?"

"Right here, Ellie."

Even over the phone she sensed the atmosphere had changed with the tenseness in his voice. Was he angry again?

"I'm sorry, I'm running on again. I can't help but get carried away. You frustrate me. I don't know how to make you see things my way."

"Again, don't apologize, Ellie."

"Um, okay," she started. She might as well say it to him, maybe then she wouldn't be flustered in every one of their conversations. "I have a hard time reading you, Jackson. I'm...um, not very good at this, whatever *this* is. And I sensed you might be mad again or at least not happy." *Jesus, could I sound more stupid?*

"You spent your night, after working hard taking care of animals, and I suspect, the people around you, doing research to convince me?"

"It's important to me." He'd told her—in a pretty fantastic way—that he liked her. This was her being herself.

"I get that. But you're also doing it for me."

"Well, I suppose, yes," she said. "You are the one I have to convince to change his mind out of a billion-dollar development."

"Got one good friend in this world, Ellie. You met him, Connor. Aside from him, I spend my day surrounded by people who take from me, not people who stay up late after a long hard day at work to try to show me a beautiful and worthwhile project."

"There's so much there, in your words, I don't know where to begin. I can't imagine you letting anyone take from you?" What she didn't ask out loud was what kind of person, as obviously powerful, gorgeous and smart as Jackson Kincaid, only had one single friend in the world? Even she had more than that.

"Let's have that conversation later, El. It's too much for tonight. It's late, babe. I've got an early meeting. Gonna let you get some sleep. Call you tomorrow evening and you can elaborate on urban community development to me."

"You're teasing me again, aren't you?"

"Yep. Only thing better than seeing your smile when you understand I'm teasing you in person is hearing your voice soften when I've got you on the phone. It's debatable which one's cuter. Thursday night, I'm taking you out. Get some sleep."

"Okay, Jackson. Goodnight."

"Night, El," he said, right before he hung up.

Chapter Seven

Jackson's early meeting blackened the glow he'd had from hearing Ellie's sweet voice over the weekend. A week ago, his client, Lucciano, had claimed an old enemy had beaten his wife, that Lucciano was innocent. Yesterday Jackson's investigator had discovered the faulty alibi. Hence the current meeting with the bastard.

Smug and slimy, the fucker, Lucciano, walked right into the meeting and said, "Who cares if my alibi's fake? He'll do a good job on the stand." Then, in his snake-like voice, "Does it matter who beat the bitch?"

Tossing his chair back, fury running through him, Jackson nearly leapt across the table at Lucciano. His partner, Mark, grabbed him and tossed him out of the conference room.

Fuck him! Fuck him! Jackson might work with the lowest of the low, but one thing he never did — he never took domestic violence cases. His partners were fine with it. There were enough other criminals to defend.

Lucciano had been Jackson's client for years, and now Lucciano would only work with him. The sick fuck *liked* Jackson for some reason.

"He's fired!" Jackson yelled.

"We can't fire him—he's our client. He fires us. You know how this works. What the hell is wrong with you?" Mark asked, following Jackson into his office.

"His alibi is a joke. He lied," Jackson said to his partner. He could barely get those words out in unrestrained fury. He grabbed his basketball and bounced it hard against the wall in his office. He wanted to throw the goddammed thing out through the window.

Mark laughed. "They all lie. Our clients are all guilty, which doesn't fucking matter, because it's our job to get them off so they can pay us, and we can enjoy the lifestyle we're all accustomed to. That's it. You signed up for this gig when we started this firm, and when you accepted Lucciano as a client years ago."

Disgust filled Jackson, disgust at himself, at his one-time friend. Or maybe they'd never really been friends. The full weight of what they'd become, lawyers without ethics, was that it? One asshole boosting another up at the expense of people's lives? Both made him want to vomit. But it was more this time. It was Jackson's past coming back to spew all over him.

"I never signed up for this. Defending innocent people in our messed-up justice system was always my goal, not this bullshit. I'm out. Not taking this case."

"What the hell is wrong with you?"

"He tried to beat his wife to death!" Jackson yelled.

"And?" Mark scrolled through his phone.

"Are you out of your fucking mind? I don't know what the fuck happened to ethics around here, but I'm out. I'm done with this partnership, this career—this everything."

"You're going to throw it all away, everything we've built?" Now Mark was incredulous. A man putting his wife in the hospital so bruised and broken she didn't even resemble a woman anymore couldn't draw him away from his phone notifications. But Jackson handing over their firm pissed him off.

"What have we built?" Jackson seethed.

"An empire—"

"Of greed and filth. I can't even wash the stench off me anymore. I do not defend pieces of shit who beat their wives. Ever."

"I know, I know." Marc tried to pacify him. "But you know Lucciano. You do not want to make that man angry. You will handle this the way you handle every other case, which is to say, you kick the prosecution's asses. And unless you have a reason a judge would believe, or want to face the wrath of Lucciano, you don't have a choice."

Fuck. Mark was right. "After this case, I'm done."

"I can't afford to buy you out." Now Mark was pissed.

"Take however long you need. I don't care. I'm done. Now get the fuck out of my office."

"We have to finish the meeting."

"You finish it. I need to cool down. You do *not* want me in that room right now." The last was said more to appease Mark. Jackson didn't want to cool down. He wanted to beat the shit out of Anthony Lucciano, like Lucciano had done to his wife.

"Fine, but you're not dropping this case. There's too much at stake." Mark stalked out of Jackson's office.

Too much at stake? Crashing from the adrenaline rush, Jackson sat in his office chair and set the basketball down. The only thing at stake was the amount of money Anthony Lucciano brought to this firm. And Jackson had fostered that over the years — more money, more high-paying clients. *Always more.* Anything to keep his memories and the fact that his life had become an empty pit.

He sat in his office for hours past dark, thinking about what he could do. Like it or not, Lucciano was their client. No longer could Jackson draw the line between a criminal like Lucciano and himself, because every time he defended the slime, Jackson might as well have done the crime himself. And this was a crime he couldn't stomach.

He wanted to walk away now, but when Lucciano didn't get what he wanted, the man was evil. Just because Jackson usually dealt with Lucciano's business affairs didn't mean he was unaware of the dark mafia underworld in town. How had Jackson become this man? Taking on clients he wouldn't invite into his home.

Lucciano would uncover Jackson's weak spots and slice them open. Jackson only had a few. *Connor. Connor's sister, Katie, and Katie's girls.* Somewhere in the world he believed *he* still had a sister.

And now Ellie, a woman he wanted in his life more than he wanted to breathe. Meeting Ellie had burst his cold, dead heart wide open. He'd been feeling stirrings of change in his life, wanting to be a better man, but a few moments in her presence, all the longing in the world to be a better man flooded his insides.

But, sitting in his office twenty floors above the city, he was plagued by how Ellie would feel when she found out what kind of a man Jackson Kincaid was. Even scarier, what his connections to people like Lucciano could do to her. He had no right to keep Ellie in his life when it wasn't safe for her to be connected to him. She filled the world with her pure beauty and goodness and he was the exact opposite.

Chapter Eight

Very carefully, Ellie closed the last stitch on the cat's paw she'd sewn up. The cut was long, but clean. She'd had to sew closed two layers. Underneath she used the absorbable sutures, then sealed the outer layer with glue. This crazy cat, Granger, had been in before, always curious, always getting into trouble. He'd have to wear the collar for a few days and he'd be a beast to get in and out of his cage, hissing at her, crying out all his complaints. "You'll live, buddy," she said to the sleeping form. "It's a small wound. It'll heal. They always do."

Almost, but not always. Some wounds remained forever. And no matter how far down they were buried, they could fester and hurt all over again.

She should have been able to handle disappointment better. It was how she'd grown up. Holding on to expectations and having them shattered, until she'd built that shell around herself at age thirteen and stopped having any expectations. She'd only opened herself up once more, when she was seventeen and dating Andy, which had almost shattered her. After that debacle, as soon as she was able, she'd left New York for good.

Ellie was at her clinic early this morning. The animals were the only thing that could make her feel better. She'd already taken all the dogs and puppies out for a quick walk. Now she took notes on a few patients to keep her mind busy. Unfortunately, she failed. *Why did he even go to all the trouble of saying nice things to me, to tease me, to flirt with me?*

Over the years she'd lived in her apartment over the bakery in this Corvallis neighborhood, she'd developed a few friendships. And she should have been fine with that. She should never have gotten greedy, or allowed herself to want Jackson's attention, the heat from his touch, the way his eyes seemed to see more in her than anyone ever had. She should never, *ever* have let his words warm a place deep inside her that had been locked up for years.

But in three days, no less, she was hooked on Jackson Kincaid being sweet to her. She'd wanted his attention once he gave it to her, and she'd enjoyed it. She'd almost felt like they were drawn together. *Stupid girl.* She'd let herself believe and hope in a stranger.

Now she hurt. Worse than that, she felt ugly and worthless like she had when she was growing up.

When he'd called late last night, and she'd answered the phone with the "Hey" he'd said he wanted for him alone, she'd known almost immediately something was wrong.

'*Jackson?*' she'd said into the silence.

'*I can't do this,*' he'd said. His tone had been harsh.

'*Can't do —* '

'*This getting to know each other. Whole deal's off.*' And before she'd been able to say anything, not that she would have been able to, he'd hung up. She'd sat with the phone cradled to her ear for a long time in the silence, so confused, so hurt, so stunned. It had been her own damn fault. For a few precious days she'd let herself believe that maybe she was, in fact, beautiful. At least beautiful to him.

Once again, she'd focus on what was important, taking care of animals. Only now she had to pretend that everything was all right because she hadn't told anyone about him to begin with. Nat and Ruby were her friends, but Ellie felt ashamed of getting caught up in the feelings Jackson had stirred in her. Because, before she'd even had a day or two to appreciate them, he'd snatched them away. After years of being strong, she'd let herself be bullied again. She could barely stomach that thought, and she didn't know how to explain any of that mess to her friends.

When Jackson had said, '*Whole deal's off,*' she'd guessed he also meant the month she'd got to persuade him to salvage Corvallis Street. What his condo project meant for her and those she cared about made her sick. She told herself she was trying to come up with the best way to tell them all. Maybe she was waiting till she could get the words out without crying. It was time to build her shell back again and be Dr. Blevins, veterinarian, nothing more. She'd find a new location and start over when this place was torn down. She was no stranger to starting over.

* * * *

On his way to the office Friday morning, Jackson detoured back to Corvallis Street. Images of her had plagued his sleep while the sound of her voice seduced his waking hours. He hadn't been able to quit thinking about Ellie, about being close to her, dreaming of a journey with her in it, her warmth making him a better man. How could it have only been a few days since she'd come into his life? When he turned onto the block, he saw her exit the bakery. An older woman followed, an apron around her waist, thick white hair tucked up in a bun on top of her head. She kissed Ellie on the cheek and waved her away. He parked his SUV and watched. Ellie wore pale green scrubs. Bright pink sneakers snuck out from the bottoms of her pants. She had a backpack draped over one shoulder, and carried two coffees and a bakery bag. *Fuck!* He wanted her to be buying that coffee for him, because from the first minute she'd blinked those fiery eyes at him in her clinic last Friday night, eyes surrounded by sexy, black lashes, he'd thought, *Mine*.

Unlike that first night, her hair was down, and the long, wild curls played in the morning breeze and caught the sunlight as she walked. He was right about her looking like a mermaid goddess.

She stopped to chat with a pretty woman who was sweeping and picking up litter in front of the hair salon. They stood close to each other, both women smiling and intent, connected. When she was close to her clinic she visited with George, handed him a bag from the bakery and the second coffee she'd been carrying. They spoke for a few moments, again close, tight friends.

Whatever George said made her laugh. Then she patted him on his arm, waved goodbye and made it to her clinic. Even if the sun hadn't been shining, her presence would have lit up the entire block. She opened the door to walk in, hesitated and glanced around the neighborhood. *Does she sense me watching her?* When she walked inside, taking her light with her, he nearly choked on the promise of his empty future. *Fuck that!* He decided right then and there to quit being a coward to prove to Ellie and himself that he was worthy of her. He'd have to find a way to protect her. The one task that scared him more than anything, protecting the ones he loved. No more hiding behind his job and his excuses and his fear. It was time to step up to the plate and be the man his mother would be proud of, a man *he* could be proud of, the kind of man Ellie made him want to be.

It was not yet seven when he got to his law firm, images of Ellie's smile flooding his head. He stepped off the elevator and ran right into Clare, the woman who did the flowers for the firm.

"Clare, *Jesus*. I'm sorry. Didn't mean to run you over." Jackson knelt to help her pick up the flowers she'd dropped.

"No worries. You're distracted. Everything all right? Don't think I've ever seen you anything less than one-hundred-percent focused, like a silver bullet targeting the bull's-eye. Trouble in your kingdom?"

She came in every week to bring fresh flowers. Quiet and respectful of all the lawyers, she'd always shown a fondness for him, asking about his life as if they were close relatives. No one asked Jackson about his life. Most people were intimidated by him. Unless they wanted something from him or were forced to deal with him, most people left him alone.

Clare often joked about his 'kingdom' and his 'love life' as she called them, because he'd used her shop often over the years to send roses after he took a woman out. Big, expensive, showy roses. She might have used the words 'love life' but she knew as well as Jackson did that he didn't love any of those women. It was rare for him to see them more than once. The roses were often much more of a goodbye. A player in a game, he used his money and power, and most women used him right back. Then when he'd gotten what he wanted, he moved on.

What Clare didn't know was that he bought the biggest, showiest bouquets *not* to woo the women or show off his money, but because Clare was one of the kindest people he'd met. A widow who supported herself with her flower shop. They'd spoken over the years, when she'd been arranging flowers throughout his offices and talking about life, and she'd often suggested to him that he stop playing around and find himself a queen. She was a romantic. And she didn't approve of his many women over the years. *'Find a gem. Find someone who can see the real you,'* she'd said. But Jackson didn't believe in soul mates and happily ever afters, so he humored her. And because he liked her, he spent a fuck of a lot of money on her flowers.

"What are these?" he asked, touching the petals of the white flowers laced throughout with hints of pink, wisps of color fading into the white. The blooms were large, softball-like on thick green stems with unruly leaves, a bit wild, free.

"Peonies. Blush peonies to be exact."

Blush peonies. Almost the color of Ellie's cheeks when she blushed. *Fuck.* It might be too late. She'd likely never speak to him again. But Jackson Kincaid, the one he used to know and like, did not give up. In Ellie's presence he felt alive. Her beauty and the way she treated people stunned him. He wanted that, he wanted to surround himself with her. What good was being a stubborn hardass if he couldn't prove himself worthy of the first woman to crash through his walls? Now, what should be the first step in his apology? "Hmm." He fingered the petals of one. "How many of these do you have in your shop today?"

"Another date, have ya?"

"More than that." *Hopefully.*

"Well, that's different now, dear, isn't it? Been waiting for you to find someone special."

"She's too good for me."

Clare sighed. "You're old enough and smart enough to know any woman should be allowed to make up her own mind whether or not she wants to be with you. Please tell me you didn't decide this for her?"

Jackson blinked back his shock. Not many people lectured or chastised him. "Clare," he began.

She held up her hand. "Answer me this, do you like this woman?"

"I do."

"Then let her make her own decisions. Now, I've got several dozen in the cooler, and a light work day. Want me to deliver them?"

They stared at each other for a moment and Jackson smiled his first smile in days. *Hell yes!* he thought. Clare might be delusional about her happy endings, but for once he was going to listen to her. He took out a business card and wrote the address to Ellie's clinic and a short note on the back. "Thought you had a delivery man, Clare?" he inquired.

"It's his day off. Your firm is my only client today and you know I always deliver and arrange the flowers here. But for you, young man, for someone different, which I'm certain she is," she said with a wink, "I'd be thrilled to deliver them myself."

"Don't get any matchmaker ideas," Jackson said. "I may have screwed up bigger than even I can fix."

"Jackson Kincaid, you must not know me very well after all these years of friendship. Romance novel addict, met and married the love of my life, make my living on hoping the right people connect." She patted his arm. "You may not believe you're special, that you deserve someone precious to make you see that special, but I know better. And if there's even a slim chance that" — she paused to read the note he'd written — "Ellie makes you unfocused and uncertain and interested in peonies, then you bet I'm going to check her out." She put the card in her apron pocket. "I'll save the matchmaking for after I meet her. Good day to ya."

Years of friendship, he thought, watching the elevators close on her. He could use all the friends he could get.

Chapter Nine

"Uh, Ellie!" Nat called from her receptionist's desk out front. "There's someone here to see you."

Ellie stood up from her crouch where she'd been inspecting the stitches of a dog she'd operated on. She stretched her back, not sure which exhausted her more, the actual work or the stress and worry over the animals. Honestly, the worry nearly flattened her at times.

"Ellie," Nat said, walking to the back. "You need to get out here, pronto."

"Prepare me. Is it an overbearing, intimidating, gorgeous man in a suit that cost more than a car, with a huge chip on his shoulder and the most amazing blue-green eyes you've ever seen, who happens to be a complete asshole?"

Nat stared at her like she'd grown a second head. "What?"

"Sorry. Never mind, I'll take care of him myself."

"*Him?*" Natalie asked.

"What the heck?" Ellie stopped, and Nat stumbled into her back. In the waiting room stood a woman with two huge bouquets of the most beautiful peonies Ellie had ever seen. Tall stems with huge blooms, many of which were still waiting to open. More bouquets in large vases lined the counter.

The lady holding the flowers smiled huge at Ellie. "You must be Ellie. Perfect," she ended on a near whisper.

"What…are these?"

"If you're Ellie, then I have a delivery for you from Mr. Kincaid. There's a card here in my pocket for you, honey. Let me set these vases down."

Ellie closed her eyes and shook her head. "No," she whispered because she'd already been down that path of hope, which he'd crushed.

"Ah, it seems like there's a story here. A good one from the looks of it."

"Not a good one," Ellie said, trying like crazy to ignore Nat's eyes bugging out of her head.

"Hmm," the woman said and her face grew tight with concern. "Well, I don't know any part of the story that comes before, which puts me at a disadvantage, but I do know everyone deserves another chance. And every great story has moments that make our hearts hurt. Maybe your heart got bruised. But if we never hurt, then when love comes in, it wouldn't feel quite so exquisite. Isn't that right? A kind, generous man, who doesn't have much beauty in his life, sent all these gorgeous flowers to you, honey. If that doesn't say 'Give me another chance,' I don't know what does. I've known Jackson for years and he's never done something like this before."

Still afraid and uncertain, she swallowed and breathed in the scent from the flowers, all five or six dozen of them. "Like what?" Ellie asked, letting herself hope a tiny bit.

"Veered off the normal path."

"What do you mean?"

"Always red roses with his initials on the card. No more."

"Oh." Ellie's face fell again. "He sends a lot of those?"

"Too many he doesn't even think about it anymore. And never to the same woman twice. Never have I seen him gobsmacked like I did this morning. It's about time something happened to shake that boy up. Or should I say some*one*."

There was too much to take in with everything the woman said. Instead, Ellie closed it up inside her. "You know Mr. Kincaid?"

"Yes. I do the flowers for his office. Here you go." She handed Ellie a card with the name of her flower shop, *Luscious Garden,* on it and one of Jackson's cards with a handwritten message from him.

"Have fun tonight," the woman said before she walked out of the door.

"There is so much going on I don't even know where to begin or what questions to ask," Natalie said. "You." She pointed to Ellie. "Start talking."

Ellie read the message on the card.

I'm a jerk, Ellie. I'm sorry. There were reasons I tried to shut this down. Give me another chance, please. I'll pick you up at 6:30. Dress up. I'm taking you to one of my favorite restaurants. We'll be enjoying something much better than

peanut butter and jelly sandwiches. These flowers reminded me of you.
Jackson.

Um, what? She reread the card. Even from the beginning when he'd been both bossy annoying and nice, he'd confused the heck out of her. Then he'd gone from exposing how much he liked her, calling her "babe," and asking her out, to being a complete jerk on the phone Tuesday night to this? *Reasons he tried to shut this down.* What the heck did that mean? It might be stupid and her heart might end up more damaged, but she wanted to know why he'd acted interested in her, then had frozen her out without any explanation.

"Ellie." Natalie interrupted her thoughts.

"Well, it, um... I guess I'm going out with Jackson Kincaid tonight."

"You guess?" Natalie screeched. "Talk, now."

"Jeesh, suddenly everyone's so bossy."

"Bossy?" Natalie yelled. "First of all, there are more than seven dozen expensive peonies out here for you from Mr. Jackson Kincaid, who you have a date with. A date! Should I remind you that since I've known you, for the past four years, you've never *ever* had a date? And do you even know who he is?!"

"Yes, Nat. I'm aware I haven't had a date *ever*. You don't need to rub it in." Ellie's voice was tight. It wasn't like her complete lack of dating history felt good to her. No woman, even someone like her, who didn't have much in the looks department, wanted to be reminded that she was essentially undatable.

"Ellie! The reason you haven't had a date is because you work *all the time,* and when you aren't at work or with people you feel safe with, which is me, Ruby, the

Heelys, Molly or George, you keep yourself closed up and tuned out to the world around you. And even with us, it took you years to open yourself."

"There's nothing wrong with being careful who you trust," Ellie said defensively.

"There is when you lock yourself up in a safe where no one can touch you. If you ever did anything besides work, say, like, made eye contact with cute men, and shined your light on them the way you do to people you care about, you would see that they would be racing to the finish line to win all that is you." Natalie finished by waving her hand up and down Ellie's body.

"What?" Ellie whispered.

"You don't have a clue, do you, honey?" Natalie said. "I'd love to know what hell you lived through to make you feel that way, but I know you won't tell me that either."

She would never tell anyone about her past. And, duh, obviously she didn't have a clue, but a friend shouting that at her did not make her feel good about herself. She'd taken her father's insults and her mother's abuse until she'd escaped, and she would not take it from anyone else.

"Maybe you can enlighten me, Nat." Ellie was good and pissed off now. "About what am I clueless?"

"How amazing and beautiful you are inside and out," Natalie said, walking closer to grab Ellie's hands.

"What?" Ellie sucked in a breath, shocked by Natalie's words. Her face burned with emotion. "I'm not," she whispered, shaking her head.

"You are. I hope someday you believe me. Apparently," Nat said, pointing toward the flowers, "Mr. Kincaid thinks so too."

"He doesn't," Ellie said, pulling away. He'd called her gorgeous and intelligent, been kind, even flirted with her. God, he'd teased her. Then he'd taken it all away because she wasn't worth it.

"Okay, then tell me why he spent hundreds of dollars on stunning peonies for you and is taking you out tonight. On. A. Date? And how in the hell did you meet him anyway? I mean I'm thrilled you have a date, but I might have picked someone a bit less, uh — "

"Less what? And it's not a date. It's not what you think. He — " *Shit!* She couldn't tell Nat that Ellie was only going to go out with him to try to convince him not to tear down their block of buildings. And there was no way in hell she could explain why *he* was going out with Ellie, because she had no clue.

"Not a date? Jesus help me," Natalie said, threw up her hands and went to arrange vases of flowers from her seat at reception. "Even when it's a date, she doesn't know it's a date. I mean *everyone* knows if a man asks you out to dinner and buys you flowers, it's a date! But not our straight-A student, magna cum laude, Veterinarian Dr. Ellie Blevins."

"Nat!" Ellie yelled. "I'm still here and it's not a date. Trust me."

Natalie shook her head. "Fine, what are you going to wear on your not-date? Scrubs? Pink ones or blue ones, or maybe the gray — those turn you invisible. Yes, go with the gray, then you can go on your not-date, and be not-seen. That should be loads of fun, Ellie," Natalie snapped.

"Now you're being mean," Ellie said, her hackles up again. Jackson had teased her about her scrubs too. He'd been gentle and flirtatious, she'd thought.

She stormed back to her office, but before she could slam her door, she heard Natalie shout, "Not mean, sarcastic, Ellie! Maybe you need a dictionary, Dr. Blevins!"

* * * *

At five o'clock Matt showed up. "Hey, Ellie."

She grabbed her backpack, shut off her office light and went out to meet him. "Hey. Not much going on tonight. Braveheart's doing much better, but he hasn't eaten much. Keep an eye on him. I think he needs love. Poor guy."

"Got it," Matt said. "He'll pull through."

"Yeah. I'll be back later tonight to grab Buffy."

"Rock on. Have a good night," Matt said.

Against the warning in her scared heart she took two of the vases of peonies and walked out.

An hour and a half, Ellie thought, walking home. The good news, it was plenty of time for her to get ready. The bad news, it was plenty of time because she had nothing to wear to go out with Jackson Kincaid as per his instructions of 'Dress up.' And even though she did not consider this a date, she still wanted to look her best when she blasted him with information about why he should not tear down this block. Because that was what she intended to do, not get lost in his eyes, or hope he'd touch her again or use that voice of his that felt like the caress from a gentle ocean wave.

Focus, Ellie. What to wear to look professional and dressed up? Ironic that she was using a lesson her mother had tried to drill into her—that a great outfit could be a form of armor.

Problem was Ellie's armor was in the form of scrubs. "I don't have any dress-up clothes," she said, letting herself in to her apartment, where she put the flowers on her coffee table. "Why? Because I'm not a normal girl. I'm a freak of nature." She fell onto her bed. "Shit! How in the hell did I get myself in this predicament?"

She pulled out her phone and dialed Ruby's number, but it went straight to voicemail. Ruby, the owner of Spa La La and Ellie's first real friend, was a fashion goddess and would have helped Ellie in a heartbeat.

Ever since Natalie had asked her what she was going to wear, she'd been freaking out, but the day had gotten super busy, and Ellie had never had a chance to ask Nat to help her. Correction, she hadn't made the effort to put aside her stubbornness and anger. She didn't really know if tonight was a date or not. One awesome phone call. One so painful she didn't want to remember it. Everything was all twisted up in her mind.

Ruby didn't answer, and Nat was mad at her. But desperation took over. She picked up the phone and dialed.

Nat answered. "I'm still annoyed at you, but I love you."

"I don't know what to wear," Ellie said quietly.

"Ellie, honey." Nat's voice was full of concern now. "What about the blue dress you bought for your graduation from veterinary school when Gage and the girls and I took you out?"

"Yeah, I... That's the one dress-up item I own, but, Nat..."

"Yeah, honey. I'm right here."

"He's gorgeous. I mean he's sexy professor meets hot football player meets surfer dude gorgeous all rolled into one."

"So?"

"I can't go out with someone that beautiful! I'm not even close to his magnificence. What is he thinking being seen with me? He could send anyone flowers — apparently, he has. He could take anyone out to dinner."

There was silence for a moment and a muffled choke. "Nat? Are you crying?"

"Honey," Nat whispered, and Ellie heard Nat breathe in through her tears. "You have it all wrong. It doesn't matter what you wear, because you are a priceless, beautiful soul. It breaks my heart that you think you are not in the same ballpark, when, honey, you are so far out of it you are the stars in the sky."

Ellie sucked in a breath. "I'm not—"

"He didn't send *anyone* flowers. He sent them to you. A lot of beautiful, unique flowers. He's not taking anyone out to dinner on a date. He's taking you. I don't know what else to say to make you believe me. Maybe it'll have to be someone else breaking through that shell. I don't know. Wear that dress. Leave your hair down. Put on a little makeup. Have fun and go out for a nice dinner with a hot man. Now, I need to hang up, so I can attempt to put the pieces of my shattered heart that is breaking for you back together. Love you, honey. I hope you believe that. I'll see you in the morning, all right?" She hung up.

Ellie sat on her bed against the pillows with the phone to her ear while her own tears streamed down her face. "All right," she whispered back to no one.

Chapter Ten

Jackson pulled up outside the bakery at exactly six-thirty p.m. He would have been there an hour earlier if he hadn't thought it would freak her out. He'd been a complete asshole and he had to make it right. He got out and scanned his surroundings out of habit. The street needed new streetlights. One was blown out, the others were few and far between and the sidewalks were a hazard. The shops were all closed, aside from the pub. A dark night did this crumbling mess of a neighborhood no favors.

There were two doors to the bakery, the main one leading into the shop and one to the side that must lead upstairs to Ellie's place. He was searching for her bell when she came down to meet him. One look and his chest tightened. Not just because of her beauty, but because she wouldn't make eye contact with him.

"Um, hi," she said briefly, while she locked her door.

Fuck! Two words in that uncertain breathy tone stoked his desire. And her dress, *fuck me*. A shade of dark blue or purple in a flowy fabric. Sleeveless, it showed off her shoulders. The top was fitted, but from her waist it flowed out below her knees. Simple, plain, not-very-high black heels. No jewelry, light makeup. Although she'd taken his breath away wearing that stupid rubber apron with water dripping off her, holding a shivering puppy to her chest, tonight she stunned him.

She'd wrapped her hair in a knot at one side of her neck that left it tied back but not tight. A few curls fought to get free, and behind one ear she'd tucked in one of the peonies he'd sent. He smiled. He'd been a jerk, but she wore one of his flowers in her hair.

"Um, should we go?"

"What?" He snapped his head back up to her eyes. "Right." Fuck, he'd lost his ease with her. Jackson couldn't remember the last time he'd been nervous about anything. He took her hand and led her to the car.

"What is this?" She didn't hide the awe in her voice.

"A car," he said, grinning. *There it is, her cuteness.*

"I mean, it's… I've never seen a car like… Can you even fit in that?" She looked at him as if he was crazy, like he was the one standing in the spring night stuttering instead of climbing into the car.

"It's a Scorpion."

"A who?"

Cute. Jesus. Innocent. Or maybe he'd become so much of a snob over the years he couldn't relate to people anymore. "Ellie, get in," he said, getting closer. He took her elbow to guide her down into her seat.

"All right," she said quietly, and he shut the door. Damn, he had work to do. She was trying hard to be standoffish. He'd break through that shield.

74

When he took off into the night, after a few moments of silence, she said, "It's beautiful. Your car." He doubted she knew how sexy her soft voice sounded.

"It's just a car, Ellie." His black Scorpion was a beauty, but nothing compared to the stunning woman sitting next to him.

"Right." She studied the city from her window.

"What I meant, Ellie, was my car's a thing. You, on the other hand, are breathtaking."

"Me? Right."

Jesus, the shock in her voice.

"I don't," she began. "I mean I don't often have occasion to dress up very much, or at all. I know this dress is simple, and I have no idea where we're going, but if it's anywhere close to as amazing as this car, I will absolutely not fit in."

"What in the hell makes you say that?" How could she not have a clue about her fucking phenomenal beauty, her light?

"Why are you mad again?" she asked, her voice laced with hurt and confusion.

Calm down or you're going to fuck this up. "Who filled your head with that bullshit?"

"What bullshit?"

"Everything you spewed about not fitting in. Fuck me, you were shocked when I called you beautiful."

"Listen." She raised her voice at him. "I'm pretty sure you swearing at me isn't helping whatever the heck this situation is. And anyway, why do *you* care?" She was angry again and rightfully so.

Jesus. He couldn't get a handle on his emotions around her. He gripped the steering wheel and tried to rein in his temper that was not intended for her. "The fact you don't have a clue about your own beauty says to me someone filled your head with crap instead of telling you every day how amazing you are." He reached over, took her hand and squeezed it gently. And he didn't let go. She started and studied their joined hands resting on her thigh.

"What's going on, Jackson? You don't have to lie to me anymore. I get it. You acted sweet. I believed it for a few hours. Then you were way more than a jerk. You hurt me. And I realized you didn't mean anything nice you'd said to me at all. Why do you care?" Her voice, hushed, questioning, surprised him. "Whatever this is, tonight is so I can talk to you about your development. This isn't a real date. You don't have to bullshit me anymore."

Jackson pulled the car over to the curb, put it in park, unbuckled his seatbelt and leaned in. "I'm sorry, Ellie. Should have apologized immediately, but I took one look at you under the light and my brain emptied of all rational thought at how stunning you are. I'm angry at whoever made you not see your worth. You are the light and fire in my dark world. I don't deserve you or your forgiveness, but I want both. You told me everything deserves a second chance. I want mine."

He studied her eyes, widening this time with surprise. Her guard started to crumble and the warmth came back. "Now, I'm gonna kiss you. You okay with that?"

She tilted her head and blinked and, without hesitation, she nodded.

And without another word he took her head in his hands and crushed his lips to hers. Jesus Christ, her lips were so fucking soft, and full. She tentatively put her hands on his chest. If she pushed him away, he'd stop, but she didn't. And when her mouth opened on a sigh, he dove his tongue in and tasted. *Sweet, honey, fresh.*

When he knew he had to stop or lose control, he raised up, kept his hands on her head, rubbing his thumbs along her temples, and searched her face. Her small hands gripped his jacket. He kept her gaze pinned with his and said, "I meant every nice thing I said to you, Ellie. I was a jerk on the phone, and in not calling all week, because I got scared. But this is a date, the realest fucking date I've had in a long time, maybe ever. I fucked up, thinking I was protecting you. But this morning I got my head back together. We made a deal. You spend time with me for a month. The flowers, tonight—this is me apologizing and hoping you'll give me another chance. You can try to convince me not to tear down that disaster of a block, but I'd like this to be a date regardless. You and me."

Her eyes were wide open and stunned, and that sparkle flickered. "Um…" Then she surprised him. She reached one hand up and touched his lips. Her gaze followed the path of her hand and Jesus if that wasn't the most exquisite thing he'd ever seen. Total fucking beauty and joy in her eyes.

"Ellie, you got me?"

"This morning?" Her voice was quiet, but not defeated like before. Fuck, he'd take it.

"Yeah, came by on my way to work. Watched you walk down the street after you got your coffee, laughing and connecting with everyone along the way. Had a chat with Clare, decided trying to convince you to like me may be the stupidest thing I've ever done in my life, but I don't care. I want to be close to your light. You want to make this about our deal, fine. I'll take what I can get. For now. But I'd like it to be more. Especially after that kiss."

Still dazed, her eyes found his. "Um, that…kiss was really nice," she whispered.

He smiled. "You got me." He grinned and got back to driving.

"What did you mean by stupidest thing you've ever done?" she asked. He held her hand while he drove, not wanting to lose contact with her now that he'd broken through the hurt and wariness he'd caused.

"You know who I am." He glanced at her.

"What?"

"Babe, you know who I am."

"I know your name, Jackson. I know you have a car that's pretty enough it should be on display where no harm can ever come to it. I know you dress nicely, even when you're in jeans and flip-flops. I know your eyes remind me of a lake in Switzerland I saw as a child. I know you're bossy and you swear a lot. But that's pretty much it."

A lake in Switzerland. Jesus, thank fuck her guard was down again. He didn't realize how scared he'd been that she wouldn't give him another chance. "Kincaid, Turner & Hotchkiss," Jackson said.

"Which is?" she asked.

"It's the biggest law firm in the city."

"Oh."

"Babe," he said. Her hand clenched his at the word, which made him smile.

"I haven't ever had a need for a high-profile lawyer in my life."

"Right, but you pay attention to the world around you." Did she really not have a clue who he was? It was surprising and kind of nice that she didn't. Everyone in the city knew him, or wanted to, or wanted to take from him. And that wasn't his ego speaking.

"Right," she echoed, still uncertain. "But in case it's escaped your notice, we don't run in the same circles."

Jackson pulled the car up to the valet and went around to open her door. He took her hand and kept it when they left the cool night breeze behind and entered the high-rise. As the elevator doors closed around them, he leaned against the wall and pulled her to him with his hands around her waist.

It was now or never. "I'm partner and equal owner of the biggest criminal defense law firm in the city." He had to expose it all, so she would know what she was getting into.

She stared at him, all that beauty gazing into him. He gently dug his fingers into her hips and leaned close. "I defend people, Ellie. A lot of them have committed crimes, and I'm not talking about stealing candy from a store."

She put her hands on his chest the way she'd done in the car, and, again, he was grateful when she didn't push him away.

"Okay," she said. The way she studied him, like she could read his entire life's story, like she *wanted* to. For the first time in his life, he wanted someone to know him, horrible past and all. "I'm not sure how that explains the stupidest thing you've ever done."

They arrived at the top-floor restaurant and secluded jazz club overlooking the city. He'd wanted to take her here to one of his favorite places he shared with no one, but at that moment, he resented the interruption of the elevator. He sighed and led her into the dimly lit club. The hostess walked them to a curved corner booth at the back of the restaurant against the wall. To their right, a window gave them a glimpse of the city spread out below them, lit up in the night's darkness. There were a few other tables and booths. At the other end stood a small stage where instruments waited for their musicians.

Jackson guided her into the booth, then sat down next to her, close, touching. He didn't want to lose her warmth.

"Jackson?" She wasn't going to let it go. She might have been innocent on some levels, but she was also intelligent and bold in a way he liked.

"I'm surrounded by criminals, Ellie. I defend them. I'm good at it. I get them off. Me bringing that into your life equals stupid." *Or complete insanity.*

"Are any innocent?" she asked.

Of course she'd want to believe the best. "Very few. My job connects me to nasty people. This week I was faced with that in a way that made me think the smart thing to do would be to cut you loose and end anything we'd begun, because you're the opposite of that. You spread light and goodness all around you. And I don't want to be responsible for hurting your brilliance."

She sucked in a breath and he couldn't decide if he liked the astonishment on her because he'd put it there, or if he found it frustrating that she'd spent a long time being told the opposite in life. Instead of dragging her onto his lap and kissing that look off her face, he was honest with her. "I want to get to know you. I want a lot more than that. But I'll leave it up to you, Ellie, if you don't want to get tangled up in my shit."

He watched her thinking, that serious look that was sexy as hell. Then she glanced back down at his lips and he knew right then and there he'd made the right decision to pursue this. When she met his eyes again, she smiled huge at him. "You do believe things can be saved."

"What?" Now he was the confused one.

"You defend people. You believe people deserve a second chance. You do believe people can be saved. It's your job, who you are. You told me the other day you didn't believe everything could be saved. That you wanted me to convince you. You don't need convincing. you already believe it."

He closed his eyes and rested his forehead on hers. He did believe that, or he had a long time ago, when he'd started out. How did she see through all his layers of bullshit to his core, a core he thought he'd lost?

"You have no idea how much I want to take you out of here right now and worship that body of yours with my hands, my mouth, my tongue," he whispered to her.

"What?"

He pulled back and grinned at that breathy tone, at the curiosity and shock on her face. He chuckled. "Don't worry, we'll take it slow."

Chapter Eleven

This night's unreal, Ellie thought, trying her hardest not to freak out moment to moment. Their food arrived, which was good, because it gave her the chance to collect her thoughts or her heartbeat or both. She'd never, *ever* had a date, relationship — did one call what she and Jackson had been doing the last week, sparring, uncommunicating, connecting, disconnecting then connecting again, a relationship? She'd never felt like her emotions wanted to pour out of her, like her skin was warm and alive and humming.

She had prepared herself to be businesslike this evening, to talk about Corvallis Street. But he'd kissed the bejeezus out of her and said all those crazy things, like he was sorry that he was a jerk and he really liked her. When he put his head on her forehead and told her what he wanted to do to her body. *Check, please,* she wanted to yell, so he could take her away and do those things. But she'd only just met him. Nerves and excitement fluttered through her at the same time.

"What's going on in that head of yours? You got quiet." Jackson put his hand on the side of her head. She leaned into his warm touch without thinking and watched him smile.

"God, you have a nice smile," she blurted.

His hand clenched slightly, and his smile got heated.

"I'm a little overwhelmed, I think," she said.

"Me too."

"You don't seem like the overwhelmed type, Jackson."

He moved his hand away, and her heart skipped a beat at the loss. God, but his touch felt nice. But then he put a bite of his ribeye on his fork and held it to her mouth. "Never met you before," he said, as if that explained everything. She needed an entire book on how to decipher him.

She pulled the bite into her mouth. He stared so intently into her eyes she had to look away or she'd forget to chew or breathe or both. His essence surrounded her, made her dizzy with want.

"Good?"

"Delicious," she said.

"How's your pasta?" he asked. "Better than peanut butter and jelly, I hope."

"It's one of the best things I've ever tasted. Would you like a bite?" *Am I really enjoying an amazing meal in a secluded, beautiful restaurant with all that is Jackson Kincaid?*

She held her fork out. *Gah!* She felt such a dork. Part of her wanted to meld into him, his touch, his words, his eyes. The rest of her felt as though she'd walked into a movie and didn't know any of her lines. But every time she felt awkward, he was there to rescue her. He brought her hand to his mouth and focused on her the entire time he bit the linguini di mare off her fork.

"You're nervous too," he said.

She let out a sigh. "It's that easy to tell? I'm sorry."

"Hey." He lifted her chin. She wanted to reach up and run her hands over the planes of his face, to memorize every line, every curve to hold on to it forever. "You do not ever have to apologize to me for being honest. I don't want you to be nervous if it's uncomfortable or scary for you. But you nervous, like you are right now, is not anything to be ashamed of. It's another layer of you I'm enjoying getting to know."

"Who are you? You say these things and I get all fluttery inside. Then I blurt out whatever's on my mind too," she admitted with a small grin.

He laughed and took her hand. "I like how you say whatever's on your mind. Let's dance."

"Wait, what? I'm not a dancer — Jackson, wait."

But he'd guided her to the tiny dance floor in front of the jazz band that played a seductive and bluesy tune. He settled his hands on her lower back, bringing them flush against each other, and started moving slowly with her in his arms.

It feels so nice, being pressed up against him. Okay, maybe she could do this. Ellie wanted to sink right into him or climb his beautiful body. Never in her life had she felt that. She bit her lip and glanced around to try to squash her desires. This place was like a dream. She took in the dark wood, gleaming, old-style chandeliers, tall windows with dark red velvet curtains, intimate tables and curved booths. All the men in the band wore tuxes. The lights of the city spread out below like diamonds sparkling on a black cloth.

"I've never seen anything like this," she whispered. The place, the moment called for whispers.

"Like what?" He bent his head and leaned it against hers. She felt his quiet deep voice near her forehead, at the same time she heard it. The vibration shot down through her entire body. How strange—she felt relaxed, yet excited all at once.

"This place, swanky, charming, hidden, beautiful."

"Like you," he said.

"What?"

"Don't you ever look in the mirror?"

"I don't…" She shook her head. "I don't understand."

"You, Ellie, you're all that, but every time I give you a compliment, the disbelief is all over your face."

"It's not disbelief if it's the truth." As soon as the words left her mouth, he pulled her closer.

"Who the fuck told you that?" The quiet whisper was still there, but his words were intense.

Everyone in my past. What could she tell him? What did someone like her, whose father had left when Ellie was conceived, a father who'd made appearances over the years to fuck her mother, but who'd barely spoken to Ellie unless it was with disdain? How did Ellie begin to explain that her famous fashion model mother blamed Ellie for the destruction of her marriage and never let her forget it? A mother who… Certain things were too painful to remember. What should Ellie share with Jackson Kincaid, a man who could easily fit into that same world with his model looks, his charm and his wealth?

"Jackson, I—"

"Who, Ellie?"

85

At his words and his touch, both possessive and comforting, she said, "You're not going to quit asking, are you?"

"You got me," he said, this time practically burning her with the force of his gaze. "I know it might take you a while to trust me, but I promise you can. I'm going to work hard to prove it to you."

She went with the lesser of two evils. "My father."

"What did he say?"

"I don't want to tell you," she whispered. "It's too embarrassing, too painful."

"Babe."

Whoosh. One word and she melted closer into him. Her mouth curled up at the way he called her that, with reverence.

"Tell me, Ellie. It's not you who should be embarrassed. It's the jackasses who told you anything besides how precious and amazing and beautiful you are." He rubbed his hands over her back. "Someone poisoned you and I can help you dig it out. I *want* to help dig it out."

"Why is it easy to believe anything you say when you look at me like that and hold me close?"

He smiled that dark, seductive smile again. "Because I will never lie to you, ever. Maybe I should feed you more steak—will more steak get you to talk?"

"Jackson!"

"I'm teasing you, honey. Trying to bust the fear out of your eyes. I won't hurt you, El, I promise, not again. I know me being a jerk on the phone on Tuesday didn't feel good. If I could I take it back… I have never in my life felt a connection to anyone the way I feel with you. Now that I have my head out of my ass, I'm going to take care of that connection. I won't hurt you again."

The darkness, the music, the warmth of their bodies close together... In his arms she was precious, held tight in a cocoon, but safe. She reached up and ran her hand over his cheek. "He didn't want me. My father," she began. "I'm not sure if he blamed me or my mother for getting pregnant, or both, but he left before I was born. He came back around into our lives once in a while, like he couldn't stay away from my mother, or maybe he felt entitled to her, but he always left again, and he never wanted me.

"I kept thinking I could change his mind, that if I did everything perfect, got good grades, kept quiet, tried to look pretty, he might grow to love me. Mostly he ignored me, which was almost worse than his insults. I remember when I was ten. I came home from school one day and he was there waiting for my mom. I'd gotten my report card. They invited me to be in a gifted class. I showed him. And he...he sneered at me, laughed and said, 'It's a good thing you're smart, 'cause you'll never be anything in the looks department.'"

"Jesus, El." His grip on her tightened a fraction.

"There were other comments over the years, things about my frizzy hair. How my freckles marred my skin. That I needed to lose weight. And worse, but you get the idea." She avoided his eyes.

"I'd like to beat the shit out of him. What about your mother, did she protect you?"

No. My mother did not protect me. I don't think she even cared about me. Even after all these years, the scars were still there, and they still hurt.

"I take it by your silence that she didn't?"

Ellie shook her head. Jackson moved one of his hands from around her and she felt the loss like an ache, but he brought his hand to her face.

"There is not a damn thing wrong with your skin. It's sheer beauty. The freckles are my favorite part." He played with a curl of her hair that had come loose. "I can't decide if I like your hair down with all your curls floating around like a goddess or pulled back like it is now so I can do this." He leaned down and placed a featherlight kiss where her neck met her shoulder.

She felt naked and hot all over yet cherished at the same time. "Jackson," she whispered. She reached up around his neck to hold on, but once she encountered his hair, she closed her eyes and toyed with the ends, wanting to memorize every moment of this night.

"And, babe, your body is phenomenal, sexy, gorgeous, perfect." He roamed his hand lower to knead her back, above her ass, hinting at even lower. "I need to get you out of here, so I can show you what I mean," he said into her ear. "But I sense your need for me to go slow and I want to give you everything. I want to prove myself to you. I want you to trust me."

"Okay," she breathed. He chuckled, which also felt nice in her ear. She wanted more of that, more of this closeness, this heat, this tingling sensation while he seduced her with his words and his laugh, so close she could feel her heart beating against his.

"You're easy," he said with a smile in his voice.

"What?" *No!* She reared back, but he had a tight hold around her. Those same words rushed at her from a decade ago. The panic set in and the breath whooshed out of her. "I'm not." Ellie shook her head and tried to pull away. "I'm not easy. I'm not like that." Pain stabbed her chest from not being able to get a breath. Oh, God! She had to get out of here. She couldn't let him believe that of her. Not him. *Please don't let me be wrong about him like I was about Adam.*

The memories flooded back. Age seventeen. She'd finally given her boyfriend of a few months her virginity one night while her mother was out of town. When Adam was finished, he'd left with his parting words, *'Didn't realize you'd be that easy.'* She hadn't cried at first, too stunned and sore to realize what had happened, but later in the shower when the hot water hit her body, she'd sunk down to the tiles and sobbed. Once more, a person close to her, a person she'd thought loved her, had proven her wrong.

"Ellie, calm down." Jackson held her with both arms. "Ellie, look at me."

"I need to go." She tried to run and gasp for breath at the same time.

"Shhh, honey. Calm down," he said. He kneaded her back, deep into her spine. "Look at me. I'll let you go if that's what you really want but talk to me, honey. I'm sorry. I didn't mean whatever caused that reaction. I know you're not easy, that way."

She focused on the concern and worry on his face, and she took deep breaths. *Okay, calm down. Okay. You're okay.* After a few moments, she relaxed a bit into him while the oxygen moved through her and the motion of his hands rubbing up and down her spine helped to calm her.

"I'm so—" she tried to say, but it came out raw as if she'd just finished a marathon. She was too mortified to make eye contact now that she was breathing again, and her thoughts cleared. She'd had a full-blown panic attack in his arms, in public, at this beautiful club. It was a good thing he held her, or she'd be flattened on the dance floor.

"*I'm* sorry," he said, lifting her chin and probing her gaze again. "Ellie, listen to me. I like the way you melt into me when I give you compliments. I like it when you say, 'Okay,' in that breathy, gorgeous voice of yours. I like you open and honest and yourself. You make me want more than I've ever allowed myself to want, Ellie, but by no means do I think you're easy in the sense that you're cheap."

He rubbed the back of her neck and she relaxed more.

"I'm sensing I have more than one demon to slay for you," he murmured.

She didn't know what to say to that. She'd thought she'd put all her demons behind her when she'd left New York at eighteen. She wasn't feeling confident about that at the moment. And the look on his face said he *wanted* to slay her demons. No one had ever wanted to do that for her before. Ever. Instead of saying anything at all, she let her head drop forward into his chest.

"Ellie, I want you to give me the chance to prove that you can trust me with who you really are, okay? Whatever you need."

Nat had said she locked herself up, closed herself off from the world. And she did, because she was afraid of what would happen if she opened up to someone. God, how she wanted to trust Jackson. He made her feel things either that had been dead inside her or that she'd never felt in her life. She wanted all those feelings and more. Was she brave enough to try?

"All right," she said and smiled a tiny smile.

He let out a breath and relaxed into her. "You want dessert, or do you want me to take you home, babe?"

"I love dessert," she said into his chest and he laughed softly again. His laugh rumbled through his body while her head was right there to feel it.

Chapter Twelve

"I don't want this night to be over," she said when they walked up the steps to her apartment. They'd stopped off at the clinic and found Chewie flopped over Buffy's neck, snoring gentle puppy snores. When Ellie had reached down to wake them, Chewie had gone nuts, yipping and jumping all over Jackson's legs, as if he were saying, "Hi! I'm yours, take me home. I'm your dog, can't you tell?" They'd leashed him and brought both dogs back with her. Now they stopped at the top of the steps and she leaned against her door. She was tired and tipsy, but not drunk. She hadn't had a ton to drink. Maybe she was tipsy on Jackson. Could one get drunk off a man?

He took her key and unlocked her door. Buffy walked in and the puppy tripped and rolled in, but Jackson didn't come in. She turned back to him and he pulled her into him.

"Can I kiss you goodnight, Ellie?"

"Yes," she whispered when she saw the scorching intensity in his eyes. It had her melting. He took her face in his hands and started slow, brushing his lips over her cheeks, first one, then the other, like a feather. His lips seared a path toward her ear and lower on her neck all while he caressed her head. It was a long, slow burn and she craved more. "Jackson."

Without any words, he made her feel precious. The way he touched her with his hands and lips, with reverence. Then he took her lips again. God, the man was killing her. But he nipped her bottom lip and her need became a moan. In a heartbeat, his slow seduction changed. He slanted her head and dove in, colliding his tongue with hers and sliding one hand low till he pulled her hips tight against his body. She couldn't get enough. Wanting to touch all of him, she pressed deeper into him, running her hands through his hair. His hands were down the back of her dress, roaming over her panties.

"Fuck." He pulled away from the kiss. "You have no idea what you do to me."

She'd never done anything to any man. But with Jackson, she felt the desire racing through him. Desire for her. For the first time in her life a gorgeous, sexy man wanted her. "Want to come inside?" She could barely find her voice after that kiss.

"Can't, El," he said, his voice still rough.

"Oh," she said, biting back the disappointment. She tried to pull out of his arms.

"I want to, but I promised you I'd go slow. And if I come inside right now, there is no way in hell I'll be able to go slow. You make me lose control with one kiss."

"I've never been kissed like that," she whispered in his ear. She rested her forehead in his neck, knowing her face must be rosy from her embarrassed flush.

"Me neither, babe." He set her away from him but kept one hand in his. "I promise we'll do more of that, all right?"

"Okay," she answered.

His hooded gaze roamed her face, her body, and back up, but when he made eye contact again, the darkness had taken on another aspect, almost like guilt or fear.

"You okay?" she asked. She was still trying to figure out how to read all his emotions, the ones he admitted to and the ones he tried to mask.

He sighed and rubbed her hand. "There's a lot about me, Ellie, a lot of baggage in my past and my present. I've never had anyone in my life before who mattered enough for all that baggage to feel like a threat."

He could have been talking about her life. "I think we all have baggage. Don't we? I had a full-blown panic attack while dancing with you over things I thought were long buried." Did she really matter that much to him? And why did he sound tortured when he admitted it? She wanted to know everything about him. "You helped me talk through it, Jackson. I could do the same for you?"

He briefly closed his eyes, as if denying one of his own demons.

After such a wonderful night, she didn't want anything to break the spell of wonder and warmth wrapped around her, yet in that moment she felt him pulling back, and there was nothing she could do.

He gave her one more gentle kiss, maybe to soften the brush-off, and she wanted to melt into that kiss, but now he had her worried and uncertain again. She couldn't keep up.

"I work late tomorrow," he said.

"Me too." She searched his eyes for more information.

"I'll call you when I'm done."

"Okay," she said again and smiled, because maybe all she could do at this moment was leave him with a smile.

He kissed her hand and let her go. "Night, Ellie."

"Night, Jackson." And before she could jump him or beg for him to come inside and *not* go slow, she shut the door, locked it and leaned against it. Part of her body felt like smiling as big as Texas, but another part of her could still see the fear and vulnerability in him. *Is this what real relationships are like?*

Staying behind her shell had kept her heart safe, but it hadn't helped her learn how to navigate someone so tough and locked up, yet warm and amazing as Jackson Kincaid. Or how to deal with all the confusing emotions the man stirred inside her.

Chapter Thirteen

She was busy the next morning with one surgery, several follow-up appointments, and she spent way too long catching up on paperwork, but Ellie's smile never left her face. Could a person ache from over-grinning? Her pal sleep had deserted her. Last night when her head had hit the pillow she'd replayed all the different Jacksons. The one who'd flat-out told her how attracted he was to her, who'd apologized for being a jerk. The one who'd kissed her like she was the most beautiful woman on the planet. The one who'd reined in his temper when she'd told him about her dad and calmed her down from a panic attack. And the one who, she could tell, was holding a huge part of himself back.

But then, when she'd gotten up this morning, there'd been a text from him waiting on her phone.

Have a good day, beautiful. Talk later.

And her worry had whooshed out of her. Still the tiniest bit leery of him changing his mind about her again, she was trying to be brave, to give him a second chance. Maybe he didn't know how to trust either. She had to show him she wouldn't do anything to hurt him.

She kept remembering the way he'd kissed her. And every time she did, she practically melted into a puddle of lust on the floor. She was in one of those puddles when Nat came in at ten and found Ellie daydreaming out of the window. Nat took one look at Ellie and screamed.

"Nat? Uh, you okay?"

"Oh, honey." Nat pulled her in for a huge hug. "You are sparkling on cloud nine. You had a good time last night?"

Ellie hugged her tight. "Yeah."

Nat threw back her head. "Hallefuckingluja!"

"Nat!" Ellie screeched. "Hush!" But they were both giggling.

"I want every single sexy detail. Now."

Ellie blushed and grinned again. "He likes me. God, I feel like a goofy teenager, but Jackson Kincaid likes me."

"Duh, honey. Told you. Did he kiss you?"

"Uh, like I've never been kissed before. Well, I guess I haven't been kissed all that much."

"Mmm-hmm, I can see by the blush all the way up your gorgeous cheekbones. Did you get laid?"

"Nat!" Ellie screeched again and smacked her on the arm.

"What? I wouldn't be a good girlfriend if I didn't ask about your welfare. And that includes your sex life."

Ellie laughed. "You are the best friend a girl could have. Thank you, Nat."

"For what, honey?"

"For caring about me and being honest with me."

"Goes both ways, honey. Now, tomorrow, at noon, Matt, Rosie and Jefferson are working for you because I am taking you shopping."

"What? No, Nat—"

But before she could get the words out, Nat punched numbers on her cell. "Ruby? Guess who had a date last night!" Ellie heard more screaming through the phone. "Yes, a real live date with a hot badass. Now she has stars in her eyes, and I'm taking her tomorrow for an emergency girlfriend shopping intervention. I know, we should have done it a long time ago. Are you free? Good. We'll meet you at Nordstrom at noon. Will do, love you."

"Nat! I can't go shopping. I don't do shopping."

"I know, honey, it's all part of your shield to keep your heart locked up. But now you need the right clothes for that cute, amazing body of yours to go out on more dates with your sexy hottie so when you do get laid, you're not wearing scrubs. Well, hopefully you won't be wearing anything, but you know what I mean, before getting laid when he takes you out on dates. We are busting your shield wide open."

"Nat, I mean it, shopping and I are not a good combination. I suck at it. I get... I panic. I...I'm getting one right now just thinking about it."

A stunned look clouded Nat's face. "You're serious."

Ellie nodded.

"Do you want to tell me why?" Nat asked.

It would take way too long and way more courage than Ellie had at that precise moment to tell Nat all the reasons she hated clothes shopping. "Maybe later." And she wondered if this was how Jackson felt when she asked him about his past, that sometimes it was too much to face, let alone share.

"Okay, honey. Well, I'm guessing one reason you think you hate it is because you haven't done it with girlfriends who are looking out for you and who are hilarious and wonderful. Please, let Ruby and me help you. I promise it'll be fun, and if it's not, we can leave. Sound good?"

Ellie studied her friend, a true friend. Someone who listened, who supported her, a friend she trusted deeply. "Okay," she whispered.

Natalie squeezed Ellie's hands. "Awesome! By the way, Ruby says she forgives you for not telling her about the date. And she can't wait to hear all the sexy details." Then Natalie strutted back to her desk out front.

"Holy shit! Dates, amazing kisses and shopping all in the same week. Holy shit, shit, shit!"

* * * *

"Hey, Jackson." Ellie's soft voice floated through the phone and while the right thing to do was take this slow, damn, he wished he was knocking on her door and not sitting on his back deck talking to her on the phone. When he'd said, "Goodbye,'" to her last night, a sharp pain had nailed his gut when memories of his past had surged up. Eventually he'd have to tell her, if he wanted a real chance with her.

"Babe." He stretched his legs and breathed in the warm spring air. He smiled at the way she answered the phone to him. He'd never had that intimate warmth from a woman before and it worked its way inside and soothed him.

"Did you have a good day?" she asked.

And his day had been shit again, gathering witnesses for the Lucciano case and seeing the photographs of Lucciano's wife all black and blue. Her face covered in stitches and sutures. One eye swollen shut. He'd had to hold back his vomit. But now, Ellie's voice washed it all away.

"I mean, uh, I guess defending unsavory citizens who maybe do or do not deserve a second chance doesn't make for a good day, but you can still tell me about it."

He imagined her as she'd been in his arms on the dance floor, her entire body pressed against his, while he listened to her siren words, tempting without even knowing she was tempting. Even without attorney–client privilege, he'd never tell her any specifics about his day. But he liked the way she'd asked, even if she sensed what he had to talk about wouldn't be good.

"Jackson?"

"I'm here, El. Taking in your sweet voice." *And letting it soothe away the scum of my day.*

"Oh," she said in that seductive, breathy way, and he really wished he was at her door.

"Chewie, no! Chewie!" The goofy puppy barked up a storm and, in between that and Ellie trying to calm the dog, he heard her giggling. *Jesus. Fuck. Take it slow?* What the fuck was he thinking? She should be here in his bed, under him, right fucking now.

"Woof!" One loud bark from Buffy silenced Chewie. Well, if he couldn't have her here, at least he could be entertained. And he let out a laugh.

"What in the hell's going on over there, babe?"

"Well, Chewie was asleep on my chest, but when he heard your voice, he, well, you know, he did what he always does around you. He lost his cool and he proceeded in complete puppy-riot to profess his loyalty and love to you, his one true pal."

"El," he said, through a grin.

"But it's late, and you know sleep is vitally important to my girl Buffy. With one bark, she got Chewie under control."

He sipped his beer and scanned his empty yard. A yard meant for a dog. "His one true pal?"

"Yes, honey." She sounded hesitant.

"Babe?"

"Okay." She let out a breath. "He bonded with you that first night. And every time he's seen you since, he goes crazy over you. Dogs don't hide their love, Jackson."

He was quiet for a second, but he didn't want to make her worried or nervous. "Never had a dog, El."

"Never?" she said, sounding like a child who'd been told Santa Clause was a dressed-up drunk trying to cheat shoppers out of their money.

"Always wanted one," he said, hoping to take her out of her sad shock and back into her happy, breathy voice.

"You have?" Right there, the way her voice spelled out all her emotions too. Beautiful, hopeful, warmth that he wanted for himself for the rest of his life.

"When I bought this house, I imagined dogs in this yard. Haven't thought about it again until last week, after I met you at your clinic, and Chewie, as you say, 'didn't hide his love for me' by peeing all over me."

"Really?" she asked. And he enjoyed her light, beautiful laughter. "Maybe it's time for you to get your dog, Jackson."

"I'm not sure, with my schedule, now would be the right time, Ellie. I'll be out of town next weekend, and work's pretty hectic." But, damn, he liked the thought of getting his dog, *and* the girl.

"I could help," she said with that open kindness she gave when she wasn't holding back or putting up her flimsy shield.

"Any man who wants a dog would be a fool not to want Chewie, and especially if he comes with you. And I'm a lot of things, Ellie, but a fool isn't one of them."

"Okaaay," she said, and he could hear the slight hesitation in her voice. And he didn't want her hesitation anymore, not when it came to how he felt about her.

"Guess we should find a time to introduce Chewie to his new yard."

She let out a breath and he realized he still had to work on gaining her trust. She didn't give it easily, due to nasty demons in her past, demons which he sensed he'd barely uncovered on their date. Well, good thing he liked a challenge. And the challenge of earning and gaining Ellie's trust was the first challenge in a very long time he looked forward to.

"That is a great idea, honey," she said. He took in the sweet sound of her voice calling him 'honey' that once again soothed an ache he'd long since tried to bury.

"You working tomorrow?" he asked, even though he knew her answer. She worked more than he did.

"Actually, I'm going out on a girls' date with Natalie and Ruby. We, uh, after we do girls' stuff, we're going to Lachlan's pub for dinner. Do you…? Would you like to meet us there later?"

"Absolutely," he said without hesitation.

"Good." He liked hearing the smile in her voice.

"I'm gonna let you get to sleep. Night, Ellie."

"Night, Jackson."

Chapter Fourteen

"Oh, my God!" Ruby's shriek caused everyone in the café to stop and stare at the three of them as Nat and Ellie slid into the booth with her.

"What's wrong?" Ellie asked. Ruby put both hands on Ellie's shoulders and studied her face with shock. Ellie glanced at Natalie and saw her huge grin.

"I know, right!" Nat chimed in.

"Praying, I've been praying, which says a lot, because I'm more of a fake Catholic than anything." Ruby leaned back a little.

"You've been praying. I've been wondering what in the heck is wrong with the men in this world," Nat said.

"Seriously," Ruby agreed.

"What?" Ellie asked again. "Will you both stop acting strange and talking in code?"

"We're not acting strange," Ruby began. "We're happy. Because our Ellie has stars in her eyes. I might cry."

"I already did," Natalie said. "Happy tears for once, I might add."

Ellie relaxed and couldn't help her smile because she felt as if she'd been in a dream after the last two days with Jackson back in her life and everything they'd talked about. And his kisses. Mmm, the man could kiss. Her smile grew at how her body felt when he kissed her. Which was good, because she needed a boatload of amazing thoughts to get her through this day of shopping.

"I want every single detail, Ellie. Let's eat before we get you a new wardrobe. After food, you are going to spill every detail. First of all, how'd you meet him?"

Ellie's smile faded. She hadn't told them about the sale of their beloved neighborhood. "Oh, shit," she whispered. "He bought all the buildings on Corvallis Street, I mean he and his friend Connor bought them together, to tear them down and build a new sleek condo development and make tons of money."

The silence might have been more disturbing than Ruby's scream when they'd walked in if the waitress hadn't shown up at that exact moment. "Iced tea or coffee for anyone?" she asked.

"We need wine immediately," Ruby said. "A bottle of white, whatever you have, hurry."

"What did you just say?" Natalie said, looking calm, but sounding livid.

"It's okay," Ellie began and put a hand each on Natalie's and Ruby's. "I don't think they intend to bulldoze it anymore. They've agreed to investigate and see if the buildings are worth saving."

"Wait, this is how you *met* him? How could you not tell us this, El?"

"Please don't be mad. I... The whole week, since I met Jackson has been insane, and confusing. In fact, I don't know how any of it happened. He sort of sprang the whole he's-the-new-owner-thing on me Friday night right before one of the puppies peed all over him. He yelled at me because the clinic's door was unlocked. The next day he was super nice. Then switched off the nice and hurt me, which he apologized for with a gazillion peonies, and explained why after he kissed me. And I've never met someone like him, ever, like *ever*, ever. I didn't know how to tell you both. Then you organized this terrifying idea of a shopping day on me and I, well, Nat, I can't stand it when you're mad at me."

"Good Lord!" Ruby exclaimed. "I'm not sure where to begin, but first of all, the words *terrifying* and *shopping* should never be uttered in the same sentence."

Ellie ignored that and pressed Nat. "Please don't be mad."

"I'm not mad. Maybe a little hurt that you kept it from us, but I'm not mad, honey."

"Did you say he kissed you?" Ruby interrupted. "Sooo, is he a good kisser? Wait, I can pretty much tell that he is from those stars." She pointed at Ellie's eyes.

Ellie blushed, but Ruby wasn't wrong. "He is," she whispered and covered her face in embarrassment.

Ruby put her arm around her and squeezed her tight. "It's about damn time!"

The waitress brought their wine. They put in their food orders and, after a minute of silence, Nat asked, "Did Chewie really pee all over him?"

Ellie nodded and grinned and they all burst out laughing.

After unloading her burdens into the hands of her two best friends, who, if it was possible, became even better friends daily, Ellie felt awesome. It was freeing to explain Jackson's involvement in Corvallis Street and her life. And it was fun to talk about a hot guy who made her feel special and smart yet wanted to help fight her demons at the same time. They listened and laughed and supported. And Ellie bubbled over with emotions.

Lunch had been delicious, the wine had relaxed her and now she stood in a dressing room with Ruby and Nat taking turns finding things for her to wear. Another thing she'd missed out on while growing up — girlfriends who made her feel good about herself, and pretty clothes that fit her body. Still, it was a bonus the girlfriends and pretty clothes came as a pair today, because she still had no idea how to put together an outfit.

She'd been trying on clothes for two hours and for every item she thought she liked, there were at least four or five that were hideous on her. But, at the same time, over those two hours, with Nat's and Ruby's help, she'd started to realize that the hideous had nothing to do with her, but with the fact that not every piece of clothing was made for her body. What a revelation.

Now she faced the mirror in shock. Dressed in a glamorous tight-fitting dress that came to her knees, had a boat neck and long sleeves, dipped way low in the back and was made of a sequin-like material in shades of pale gold, silver and rose-gold woven together to shimmer, Ellie felt almost sexy.

"El, come on, honey, show us the dress. Does it fit? Do you need a different size?"

"Uhm, no," she answered quietly.

"No, what?" Nat asked. "Ellie?"

Ellie took a deep breath and opened the door. She stepped out to see her friends' faces exploding into pure delight.

"Holy freaking cow! You are a goddess, Ellie!" Ruby jumped up and down and shrieked.

"Ruby!" Ellie hushed her.

"She's right. You are," a lady walking into the dressing rooms said.

Nat moved her in front of the large mirror. "Did you look at yourself in the mirror?"

"Yes." She tried to blink back her tears. She squeezed Nat's hand.

"Then why the tears, sweet girl?"

"I…I feel…pretty."

Chapter Fifteen

Lachlan's pub was packed, but Jackson wasn't surprised when he walked in. Friday night and the music gave the feel of a tiny village pub on the west coast of Ireland. Impressive, the moody, dark wood tones, leather booths and intimate tables invited one in to sit awhile. The awesome copper bar top and antique artwork hinted at style and substance. Whoever designed this place had known what he was doing.

"What can I get ya?" the bartender asked.

"Jackson Kincaid. I'm looking for Ellie and her friends." After another shit day of being mired in scum, it was all he could do not to hunt her down, haul her over his shoulder and carry her away to a hidden, magical island where he never had to see Anthony Lucciano again. Never had to defend the piece of shit. Now that he had Ellie's light to look forward to, his days at the office were becoming unbearable. Work had always been his drive, the thing that filled him. He'd been fucking ignorant and frozen.

"Ah. Lachlan MacGregory. Prepare yourself, my friend," Lachlan said and nodded toward the back booth. "The girls are tipsy."

Jackson saw them, in the last small booth near the wall, Ellie and her friends laughing hysterically. "You're Jackson Kincaid?" a huge bald biker-clothes-clad guy with a trim silver goatee, sitting on one of the stools, asked Jackson. "Gage Kovacs. Nat's husband. Lachlan's right, they're hammered. Should be a fun night. Time to get my girl. My babies are all spending the weekend at Grandma's house." He tossed a few bills on the bar and clapped his hand on Jackson's shoulder. "I know who you are, man. Gonna give you the benefit of the doubt and say I hope there's more to you than a hotshot lawyer who defends pieces of shit, but nonetheless, I'd say this to any man interested in Ellie—take care, or I'll have to rearrange your face."

Jackson's body locked. *Pissed off* didn't begin to express his feelings.

Gage smiled at Jackson's reaction. "No offense. She's our Ellie. You may already know how special she is, but what you don't know is that there's something heavy inside her. Heavy, deep shit she's never told Nat or Ruby and those girls are the closest thing she has to family. So be pissed at me but be mindful."

Jackson studied the man. He knew Ellie's dad was a piece of shit, but from what she'd told him, her dad wasn't the *heavy* or the *deep* shit, and yet there were hints that what Gage said was true. He could get angry or he could respect the man for looking out for her. "I've got her."

Gage slapped him again, this time with a smile. "Let's go get our ladies then." Lachlan followed them over to the booth.

"Is *that* your hottie?" Ellie's friend gasped when they approached. Ellie giggled. He liked seeing her with her friends, letting loose. That was until her friend's demeanor changed when she pointed at him. "You! I'm mad at you. Don't think you can buy all these buildings and tear them down. I won't let you."

"Heard there was a new owner," Lachlan said and crossed his arms. "Figured a hotshot would swoop in and morph this neighborhood from classic to snazzy, wiping out all the old charm. Is that your plan, Kincaid?"

"We'll see," Jackson said, studying MacGregory. He didn't feel like discussing his business at the moment, but he could see it was important to these people. "My partner and I are also considering restoration. Either way, it shouldn't affect your business much. From what I've read, your success is enviable. A huge, loyal following. Diner's Choice Award five years in a row for Best Casual Spot and Best Cocktails *and* Best Live Music. Bands on a waiting list to play here. Your pub should be fine, whichever way we decide."

"I see you've done your homework."

"Always," Jackson returned.

"But first and always, this is a neighborhood pub. And the neighborhood matters very much to me."

"Understood."

"If you gentlemen are going to fight, can we get another cocktail?"

"Ruby," Ellie admonished. "We don't want them to fight."

"We don't?" Ruby gazed at Lachlan. "I don't know, I heard Lachlan's a pretty good fighter."

"Ladies," Lachlan said, "I'm cutting you off. Time to go home."

"I don't wanna go home." Ruby pouted up at Lachlan.

"I, um...don't know if I want to go home," Ellie said, giving Jackson her wide, beautiful smile. It was almost more of a question. She was even cute when she was drunk.

"Natalie, babe, you ready?" Kovacs asked.

"*I* wanna go home." Nat smiled huge at Gage. "If I go home," she whispered loudly to the girls as if the men couldn't hear her, as if the entire bar couldn't hear her, "then Gage can get to home base." The other girls burst out laughing again. Natalie spilled out of the booth, but Gage caught her.

"Come on, baby. The girls are at your mom's for the whole weekend. It's you and me and a suite at the Westin downtown for two nights."

Nat reached up to put her hand on her husband's cheek. "You planned that for me?"

"You buy any new lingerie for me while you were out shopping with your girls?" He leaned in close and walked her away from the others to the exit.

Nat peeked around Gage's huge body, waved to the girls and gave air kisses.

Jackson watched Ellie's stunned eyes come back to him. Then she sucked back the rest of her cocktail and reached out her hand for his. He took it, said goodnight to Ruby and Lachlan and headed out.

"How many have you had?" he asked as he walked a stumbling Ellie home. He couldn't hide his grin. It was obvious she was ready for nothing but sleep. She leaned against him when he unlocked her door.

"Oh, four, or maybe five. I remember number four. I think. I don't drink very much, Jackson Kincaid."

"Think I got that, Ellie," he said, walking her into her apartment. Chewie was out cold. Buffy started to get up and he said, "I'll be back for you guys."

"But the girls thought I needed a little few drinks. They had important, estrmeemely interesting things to tell me about..." She started giggling.

Ellie giggling again. Fuck him. "About what?" He got her into her bedroom and angled her over the bed before she collapsed.

"You know," she whispered. "S. E. X."

He didn't know whether to shake with laughter or shock. No way in hell she didn't know about sex.

"You do know what that is, don't you, Ellie?"

She started laughing again and he enjoyed the view. It made her expression light up and sparkle and it spread into him. "Of course I do, hot, growly Jackson." She patted his chest, and that was damn cute too.

He was relieved, although strangely upset too at the thought that he wouldn't get to be her only. "Right," he said, moving down her body to get her boots off.

"Can you imagine?" She kept giggling. "A veterinarian who doesn't know about the birds and the birds. I mean bees, the birds and the bees. Jeesh," she said. He tugged one of her cowgirl boots off. "You're so cute. Hot and cute. A man can be hot and cute. Do you know how cute you are? But you're also moody. A girl could have a hard time figuring out you. I'm a girl and even though you kiss really, really, *really* well, and you're hot, I'm still a little tiny confused. I mean...but I didn't know there were *so many*, you know?" She threw out her hand and when he looked up she was blushing again.

He couldn't follow her. "So many what, Ellie?"

"I'm sure you know." Her eyes bugged out of her head again as if she could say what she wanted to say with her shiny blues alone.

He got her other boot off and leaned back next to her on the bed. "Enlighten me. What do I know, Ellie?"

She studied him, and her smile tipped lopsided before she closed her eyes and whispered, "Positions, Jackson. S. E. X. So many, many, many different positions for it."

He put his head down on her shoulder. *Kill me. Please, God. Kill me right now.* He had to change the subject or leave because he wanted to do every position with her, but not while she was drunk. Drunk *and* confused by him. He couldn't blame her. Last night he'd left her a bit unsettled. Jesus! He didn't know how to talk about his past. He especially didn't know how to explain his upcoming trip.

"How was shopping?" He changed the subject back to neutral territory.

"What?" Confusion took over her face and made her do that slow blink.

"Shopping with your girls?"

"Oh! That!" She grabbed his shirt and pulled him closer. "It was fun!" she said like she'd won a million dollars. "I never knew it could be fun."

"I thought that was part of the sisterhood for girls growing up, to love shopping," he said, peeling her arms out of her jacket. He was surprised she hadn't passed out yet. Her body was limp and floppy.

"I'm not most girls," she whispered. Her voice went straight from whimsy to sad.

"Ellie? You look like I kicked you in the gut." Dark ghosts washed over her face.

"She said it didn't matter what I wore. It wouldn't ever change things. I would never be beautiful. I never did it right, never did anything right."

"She who? Who are you talking about, babe? What do you mean never did anything right?"

"Shhhhhh." She closed her eyes and felt for his lips. "Don't wanna talk about it." She'd let something slip, an important tidbit he didn't want to let go, but now wasn't a good time to pursue it.

"Jackson." Her eyes were still closed, but she'd lost the sadness.

"Yeah, honey?"

"Are you gonna kiss me again like you did in the car and when you brought me home, that way that made me feel all melty and tingly inside? That way I never wanted you to stop kissing me, *that* kind of kiss?"

Jesus, how in the hell did he end up with such pure and honest goodness in his arms? He drank in her beauty. The flush on her porcelain skin, the freckles on her cheeks, the cute, small crookedness of her nose. The liquor won. Softly her hand fell away from his lips and she was out.

"Yeah, babe, I'm gonna kiss you again like that. But not now when you're drunk." He touched his lips to hers and leaned back up to get her jeans off and tuck her in. He almost lost it when he saw what she had on underneath, teal blue lacy undies. This had to be punishment for all the shitty things he'd done in life. Pure torture. He burned the sight into his brain while he tucked her legs under the covers.

"Jackson," she said, startling him. He'd thought she'd passed out.

"Yeah."

"That was the best date I've ever had. And the dancing…"

"Me too, babe. You need sleep now."

"But I'm worried about you. I want to slay your demons too. Are you going to tell me about them?"

Pure beauty. How in the hell could he mar her with his life, not only everything that happened to him when he was a child, but all the filth he'd been swimming in for the past decade? "You gonna rescue me too?" he asked. Her face lit up in a lazy smile.

"You can trust me," she said. "We can go, we can have another best date ever with all the kissing too." Then she was out for good.

Best date she'd ever had? Fuck him again. He hadn't been lying when he'd agreed with her, because every moment spent with her had been the best. She was beautiful and kind and her warmth put life into everything around her. But for her to say that was the best date ever, when he'd demanded that it was a date, stirred up a past so painful it showed in every pore of her skin, and denied her his own story, well, he had a lot to make up for.

He smiled, tore himself away from her sleeping form and went to see to the dogs.

Chapter Sixteen

Ellie peeled her eyes open and wondered if she'd somehow glued them shut the night before, because moving her lids was seriously difficult work.

"Ouch!" she shrieked when the morning light from the windows splintered into her brain.

Maybe she'd stay in bed in the dark until this serious pain throbbing in her head ended. She must be in a nightmare right now. Except, she had to pee. Ellie pulled her body upright and crawled across the bed, trying not to send blow after blow of pain through her. She got to the edge, put her feet on the floor and half-walked, half-dragged her body to the bathroom.

"This has to be a nightmare. Feeling this badly can't be real. Oh, my God!" Ellie sucked in her breath when she saw herself in the mirror. Her curly hair had been electrocuted. She still wore the makeup the cosmetic artist had applied to her face at the mall yesterday. However, now it decorated her face like war paint. It hadn't held up well in battle. She washed her face, the pain in her head taking on a more powerful beat, then flipped the bathroom light off and opened the door. "Definitely a nightmare," she whispered. "A living nightmare."

"Mornin'."

"Shit!" Ellie screamed at Jackson standing in the doorway to her bedroom. She leaned against the wall, slid her body down and buried her head in her knees. "Wake up, Ellie, wake up. My head has never throbbed like this. I have clown makeup, Medusa hair, and Jackson Kincaid is standing there in all his gorgeousness witnessing my mortification. And I'm only wearing my shirt and underwear. What is going on?"

She felt him sit down next to her on the floor and peeked up at him. Holy freaking crap! And she'd said all that out loud. She buried her head in her knees again. "Go away," she said into her knees and he laughed at her. "This isn't funny. What are you doing here?"

"I got you home from Lachlan's, put you to bed and spent the night on your couch. I'm pretty sure that headache of yours is what most of us would call a hangover, but nightmare works too, depending on how bad the hangover is."

"Last night I was… I've never been hungover before. I'm so embarrassed."

"Nothing to be embarrassed about," Jackson said, handing her ibuprofen and a cup of coffee. "Here."

"Are you insane?" she whispered because it hurt to talk. She glanced at him and took the pills he offered. "Nothing to be— You… Look at you. You're perfect, gorgeous, hot." *You like me*, she wanted to say, because she was beginning to believe it and now he'd probably never want to see her again.

"And?" he asked.

"And I look like the Wicked Witch of the West got into a catfight with her flying monkeys."

"Babe." He chuckled, then turned her face to him and left his hand there, caressing. "You are beautiful. When you walk down the street bringing coffee to George. In your sexy yoga pants. When you're drunk and giggling in your bed and telling me what you and your girls talked about while you threw back too many cocktails. Beautiful when you're angry. Beautiful now. I can see by the shock on your face that you don't believe me, which means I'm going to have to show you. But now I have to get to work."

Ellie stared at him. She listened and leaned into the warmth of his hand. *No!* She remembered the girls, the bar, the conversation. "Oh. My. God," she whispered and buried her head in his chest. "I can never face you again."

He laughed and this time she felt it. Boy, did she like hearing and *feeling* his laugh. And his chest radiated warmth, like a furnace. That was it, she'd stay here, face-planted on his body, warm and happy and safe.

"Had a good time with your girls?"

"Yes," she said into his chest. Her head shot up. "You and Lachlan almost got into a fight?"

"Babe, we didn't."

"What was Ruby talking about? Oh, lordy! My memory is foggy and my brain hurts. I do remember you and Lachlan talking about his pub and how your plans won't affect him. What does that mean?"

"Lachlan MacGregory owns that building on the end. His business and the entire structure. It wasn't part of the deal Duggan and I got."

"Wow." Ellie rubbed her head. "That's why his building is in awesome shape. I think he restored the whole thing himself."

"Yep. Did a good job too, from what I can tell. That bar is phenomenal."

"Maybe he can give you and Duggan pointers." She gifted him with a small smile.

"That is not a bad idea," Jackson said.

"Are you beginning to see things my way, Mr. I-Only-Want-Brand-New-Condos Kincaid?"

"Love it when you tease me, babe." He stood and helped Ellie up. "I called the clinic. Matt is there and he can stay until ten. Go back to sleep for a few hours. It won't cure the hangover, but it will help."

She was too blown over by his words, in too much pain to argue and mortified, so she climbed back under the covers and dragged them over her head.

* * * *

Jackson stood at the window to the hospital room and watched the woman lying on the bed. Hell, she looked horrible. Unrecognizable. *One arm raised in a sling with a full cast. Her eye swollen or sewn shut.* He couldn't tell from this far away. The area around both eyes swollen black and blue. Heavy bandages covered one side of her head. He couldn't see the damage under the sheet, but he knew several ribs had been broken from where her attacker had kicked her with boots on. The doctors were still waiting to see how the internal damage healed itself.

Victoria Lucciano had been at St. Mary's Hospital for almost two weeks now. This was the first time he'd seen her, aside from the crime scene pictures. The nurses seemed surprised to see him. He wasn't allowed in to see her—he'd known that ahead of time. Something had compelled him to come here, however. How could a man do this to his wife? Even faced with the knowledge that this kind of thing happened over and over again, Jackson still couldn't believe it.

He couldn't seem to get the photos of her out of his mind. Especially since he suspected Lucciano himself had been the one to do this unspeakable damage. Ellie had unlocked his humanity, his heart, and now he questioned every single step he took. Seeing Victoria Lucciano took him right back to memories of his mother's cuts and bruises, her beaten body at the hands of his own father. Memories he'd made a promise never to forget. That was why he'd come tonight, to remember.

After the last time his father had beaten her, she'd finally, fucking *finally* been able to get a restraining order, but his father had returned. That was when his mother had shot him, killed him to protect herself and her kids. She'd been sent to prison for manslaughter, of all the fucked-up verdicts in the world. Since then he'd been driven to defend people like his mother. Unfortunately, that road had taken him down the path of defending real, nasty criminals instead. People like his father. People like Lucciano.

Soon he'd have to question Mrs. Lucciano, which might feel like another attack on her, but not tonight. Tonight he'd come because he couldn't stay away, because of where he had to go this weekend. Even after all these years, he couldn't let go of the guilt.

He'd been trying for days to see a way of getting out of this case, but legally there wasn't one. And even with the amount of scum he'd defended over the years, he believed in the law, believed in every person's right to a trial. As a lawyer, he couldn't pick and choose when he wanted the law to work and when he didn't. But he didn't know how he would live with himself after defending Victoria Lucciano's husband.

Chapter Seventeen

The rain. *Ugh!* It had been raining all week. Rushing home with Buffy and Chewie, cleaning muddy paws, wet dog smell — Ellie was over it. And it was a cold rain. It made the days feel heavier and moodier. She hadn't seen Jackson since Monday, but he'd called her every night and texted her a sweet message each morning, which got her through a crazy week at the clinic with Matt and Rosie both out sick with the flu. Thankfully, everyone would be back to their normal schedule tonight. Even exhausted, Ellie couldn't help feeling giddy every time she thought of Jackson. Every text he sent her, she returned one with an interesting fact or story about the Corvallis neighborhood.

Jackson: *Morning, El. Have a good day.*

Ellie: *Hi, honey. Did you know the Corvallis neighborhood has ten of the oldest Italianate buildings in America?*

Jackson: *Babe.*

Or, Jackson: *Good morning. Sleep okay?*

Ellie: *I did. Studies show neighborhoods thrive when there's a strong community element.*

Jackson: *Good to know. Have a good day and give your pups scrubs from me.*

And, Jackson: *Beautiful morning, babe. Talk later.*

Ellie: *Hi, honey. Today I learned that the Corvallis farmers' market is over fifty years old. Think of how many people it supports. And the music center offers free music lessons and instrument rentals to low-income kids. Kids learning music! Yay!*

She hoped he was chuckling through the texts.

After she got the dogs dried off, she changed into a new pair of skinny jeans. Dark, cute skinny jeans that felt amazing on her body, her body full of curves. She paired them with a long-sleeved gray T-shirt with sparkly detail along the neck and fun black rainboots with tulips on them. A new simple outfit that she loved. She was drying her hair with a towel when she heard a knock and Jackson's voice. "Ellie? You home? It's me."

"Hey," she said, opening the door.

"Hey, beautiful." His rough voice wrapped around her before his arms did. He pulled her close. *This.* This warmth, this strength, this was what she'd been missing, craving. She loved the way their bodies fit pressed up close together, how it comforted and excited her at the same time. And she sensed he enjoyed it too.

She felt tipsy all over again. "Hey," she said again, quieter, and watched him smile and take in her entire body.

"You look cute." God, but the way he said it didn't say 'cute' at all. It said he wanted to rip her outfit off and take her right there in the doorway. She swayed into him, nearly losing her ability to stand up. But before he could kiss her, Chewie went into high-speed puppy yipping, then ran headfirst into Jackson's leg, his tail wagging like crazy.

"Buddy," Jackson said, kneeling. He scrubbed Chewie's head and the pup sat his butt on the ground, his tongue flopping around while he tried to paw Jackson's hand. "First rule of being a man, never get in the way of a guy and his beautiful girl when he's about to kiss her."

Chewie climbed up Jackson's lap and assaulted his face with puppy kisses. Ellie couldn't control the laugh bursting out of her. "He's confused. He thinks he's your 'beautiful girl'." And she doubled over with laughter now.

He stood up with Chewie in his arms and grabbed Ellie around the waist, pulling her into him. "You think this is funny?" He trailed his mouth over her ear and down her neck. His hand around her waist started tickling her and her senses sparked with a combination of desire from his mouth and being crazy ticklish.

"Jackson," she screamed, and tried to wiggle her way out of his grip.

"Love your laugh, babe," he said, stopping tickling her. Chewie let out a bark before he assaulted them with puppy licks.

"Okay, pal. Enough." Jackson put the pup down. "You," he said, taking Ellie's hand, "come grab a bite

with me at Lachlan's? I haven't eaten since this
morning and I want to take my beautiful girl out to
dinner before I won't see her again for a couple of
days."

Beautiful girl. Gah! "Okay," she said, getting lost in his
deep-sea eyes.

"Do you know what I'm thinking, babe?"

She shook her head but kept her gaze on his.

"I'm thinking," he began, "that I can't wait till I can
take my time with you."

* * * *

It might have been packed at Lachlan's. It might have
been empty. Jackson didn't notice. Everything around
him was a dark, warm hum. He sat close to Ellie at the
bar and the mire from his day disappeared. She'd
angled her body into him, fitting her legs between his.
They'd feasted on double cheeseburgers and fries, and
now he sipped his beer, while Ellie drank tea.

"No cocktails for you tonight?" he teased.

Ellie shivered. "Please. I may never have another
cocktail again. That hangover has been haunting me all
week. I might strangle Nat and Ruby. I'd heard people
complain about hangovers before and I used to be a
little jealous, but not anymore. No. Way." She took a sip
of her tea that she'd loaded with honey and lemon.
"Plus, I love tea when it rains. I can never seem to get
my feet warm in these chilly rains and tea always
helps."

Even in the dim bar he could see she was tired, but
she exuded happiness, and her smile made her even
more beautiful. God, he liked sleepy El too. "Tough
week with all your help being sick?"

"My gosh, yes," she said. A huge yawn came over her and he laughed. "I'm embarrassed, Jackson." She scooted a bit closer and put her hand on his thigh. Her warm hand was all it took to make him hard, knowing he'd never felt anything better than her touch. If forcing himself to visit Mrs. Lucciano in the hospital was his penance, then Ellie was his salvation. And whether he deserved it or not, he was going to take every ounce of goodness he could get. He put his hand over hers.

"I'm always yawning at the most embarrassing moments," she whispered. "I'm so cozy and comfortable." She tried to hide her next yawn but started giggling instead. He took her hands and stood her up.

"Let's get you home." He tossed cash on top of their bill and walked her out. He could have sat there forever, looking at her, talking with her. He hadn't been cozy and comfortable at all. He was hard and needy. She obviously had no idea what she did to him when she touched him and flirted.

One of these nights he wasn't going to be tucking her into bed and leaving either. Once he got through this horrible weekend that crept up on him every year. A weekend he wished he could erase from his memory forever. But because he couldn't, because it haunted him, he'd decided long ago to go where the memories lived and face them down, alone. It was his own ritual. Most would call it self-torture, but it was the only way he could deal. They headed into the downpour and ran across the street to Ellie's apartment.

Two loud, hysterical barks assaulted them before they even got the downstairs door unlocked. By the time they made it to her apartment door, the dogs were going crazy.

"What in the heck?" Ellie asked. "Holy crap!" she exclaimed at the destruction inside. Both dogs barked and jumped around them.

"Down!" Jackson said in a loud, firm voice, grabbing Buffy's and Chewie's collars. Both dogs sat immediately. "Stay," he commanded. Then he followed Ellie inside. Water dripped from several spots in the ceiling, poured through the living-room windowsill in its own handy fountain. One large spot rained over Ellie's red velvet couch.

"Oh, my God," she whispered. She'd made it to her bedroom where rainwater dripped from too many spots to count. Her bed was soaked and puddles littered the hardwood.

"Dammit! I knew this building wasn't safe. I should have gotten Duggan in here faster to check things out."

"What am I…? This is everything I own… I mean…"

Jackson realized he'd been yelling his own anger and disbelief when she probably needed comfort.

"El, I'm sorry, I—"

"You have got to be kidding me! Is this my life?" she started yelling as she walked around the room, rain dripping over her. "I mean first you bulldoze into my life, tell me I no longer have a business or a place to live, give me a month to convince you otherwise and decide you like me, then you don't. Now you do again, or you never stopped, but you had to act like a jerk in between. And I finally thought things were great and… Oh, my God! I cannot believe my life! What the hell?"

"Um, Ellie?"

"Yes, I know I'm acting crazy. This is what happens when a girl walks into her home, her beautiful, okay, a little bit small, but cozy home she put together all by herself—the first dream after vet school she'd allowed herself to dream — to find it *underwater!* I'm allowed to act crazy!"

His confusion changed into a grin. "You're right. I'm not scared of crazy, babe. I was worried I'd offended you with my yelling. I see your strength. I like this backbone you have. It's almost as cute as your vulnerable side. And I know your home is underwater, but you're going to be okay." He put his arms around her and pulled her close. "I've got you. We've got this. It's going to be okay.

"I might fall apart later," she whispered. The flush in her cheeks from her outburst gave her that vulnerable look that was damn cute. But now he could see the distress in her eyes, those eyes that didn't hide anything. "And I'm definitely a crier. Injured animals, survivor stories. I'm just saying, in case, well, I might, you know, cry later."

He full-out laughed then squeezed her to him. Wrapping his warmth around her, he spoke into her hair. "I can handle tears. Let's salvage your clothes. We'll take you and the dogs to my house tonight. I'll call Duggan and see how soon he can get an emergency crew over here."

"Your place?" she asked. "Are you sure? I thought you had to go away? I don't want to be a burden."

"You're not, El," he said, staring into her wide-open, trusting face. "And I have a feeling you'll like it. Trust me?" He hoped she understood he was talking about so much more than liking his home.

"I do," she said. Then she shocked the hell out of him when she stood on her tiptoes and placed her lips gently on his. She closed her eyes and kissed him. It was a few of the most spectacular seconds of Jackson's life.

Chapter Eighteen

For a minute, Ellie sat in her car in awe. This wasn't a house. *More like gigantic mountain ranch meets old-world chalet.* The huge front yard was lined with tons of trees, and she couldn't see how far back the property went in the darkness. Stunning, yes, but also lonely. Perhaps because it was night and no one was home to warm it up. She wondered if Jackson lived a lonely life here. She knew what it was like to grow up in luxury, to have things but feel empty and alone. Maybe she and Jackson were more alike than she'd thought.

Chewie's barks motivated her to get moving and she opened the car doors to let the dogs out. Jackson, looking hot and bothered, or maybe that was her, came walking back from his garage to help her. He knocked her breath out every time she saw him. She'd tried flirting with him in the bar, but instead of kissing her, he'd abruptly stood her up and walked her home. Maybe it had to do with her yawning. God, she kept making a fool of herself in front of him.

After wiping off the dogs, Ellie stood and gasped. She followed him into a kitchen which opened up to the most beautiful, vaulted-ceilinged living room with a huge gas fireplace, already lit, and a humongous sectional sofa in a delicious charcoal fabric.

The enormous modern kitchen said beautiful and warm in a masculine way. It also said lots of friends and family gathered around laughing, eating and drinking, and from what she knew of Jackson, she wondered if this gorgeous space ever got to enjoy lots of people.

"This place is amazing." She turned to see him watching her intently. "Excuse me while I drool over your kitchen. And this living room... Did I walk into a dream? Don't tell my little red velvet, but your couch is divine."

"It's even comfier than it looks," he said and grinned. "Want to try it out?" His words were light, the smile casual. She thought he must be trying to make her feel comfortable after the night they'd had, but his eyes burned. She marveled at how he kept that desire leashed.

"Only if you'll join me," she said, wrapping her arms around him. Maybe if she made the move, she could set that desire free.

"That's the plan. Beer?" He kneaded the muscles in her back. It felt so good she puffed out a breath.

"Sure, why not," she said. "My home is a disaster, I'm not sure what my insurance is going to cover, and I saddled you with two rambunctious dogs who might not take quite as good care of your place as I promise to."

"Rambunctious, huh?" He turned her toward the pile of dogs on the rug by the sliding doors, Buffy already asleep and dreaming. Her paws chased imaginary squirrels and Chewie curled up in a tight ball between Buffy's neck and chest. "I think this place could use a little more of the 'lived-in' look. Make yourself at home and I'll grab drinks."

"Okay," she said, not letting go of his hands wrapped around her waist. She loved feeling him pressed up against her back, his warmth against her body. His scent surrounded her, a woodsy cologne mixed with the rain. She wanted to feel his warm, bare skin. Before he could pull away, she turned back around and pulled the shirt from his jeans, desperation taking over.

"Ellie?" he whispered as if he sensed her mood.

"I don't want a beer, Jackson." She roamed her hands over his back, warming her skin with his. She settled them at the waist of his jeans, itching to move them down. Her want was so great it made her dizzy. She stared into those hazy eyes of his. "I want you."

Jackson didn't speak, yet it seemed she was in tune with everything, the intake of his breath, the pounding of his heart, the way hers beat through her skin, the rain falling outside. Right before she thought she'd made a mistake, he tightened his arms around her and crushed her mouth to his. He didn't hesitate and she witnessed his desire unleash itself.

Jackson pulled her up against him, holding her so her feet were dangling, and walked her to the couch. As if he couldn't get to her fast enough, he dragged her sweater up over her head. She felt the fine fibers on every sensitive part of her, like the hum of a heat lightning storm pulsing through her body. With her sweater off, he kissed her neck and slid the straps of her bra down, so, so slowly it felt like torture.

His fingertips on her shoulders and chest for the first time were such beautiful agony. He trailed his tongue down her chest and made her moan with need. Her entire body arched toward him while she tried to drag his shirt off. "Please, Jackson. Please let me touch you."

He tossed his shirt off, brought his chest back to hers and kissed her like his life hung on this one kiss. She touched his lips with her tongue and he devoured her. God, she could spend her whole life kissing him like this, their bodies pressed together, but then he nipped her bottom lip and her need became greater. She wanted more. Before she begged, he braced himself up on one arm and danced the other over her skin, on her cheeks, her neck. Torturously he trailed his fingers down until he found her nipple that ached for his touch. Both nipples hardened with need. An overwhelming ache, such a beautiful ache. "Jackson, I..."

He changed from a caress to... *Oh! what a sweet pain*, when he took one nipple in his mouth, tugging and sucking until she nearly came from that sensation alone.

"Jesus Christ, Ellie." Jackson's voice was harsh as though he'd been holding in his desires for eternity. Using his tongue, he teased her other nipple, while he skimmed his fingers down her belly. She shivered and didn't know if she was that ticklish, or his touch made every inch of her super sensitive.

He stilled and met her gaze. "El?"

"I'm good," she rasped out. "Please don't stop. I'm so sensitive from your touch. I didn't know I could feel like this, like my entire body is electrified." A dark, predatory and needy expression took over his face. And it was all for her.

He roamed his hand up and down her body, alternating between gentle and almost rough. "You sure, El? Say the word and I'll stop." It was slight, but his hand shook when he touched her, holding himself back by the thinnest of restraints. And he kept that contact with her, reassuring her with his touch, that touch that was like a furnace.

"Don't stop." She smiled. "I want to have all of you, and I want you to have all of me."

"Ellie, Ellie, Ellie," he spoke into her skin, caressing her with his words. "What you do to me. Your skin, your scent, the way you blush for me." He dragged her jeans and panties down her body so quickly she squealed at the change. Here was the Jackson she'd been trying to free. And her insides lit up again at the heady knowledge that this man wanted her.

"Come here," she said, her voice a whisper. She wanted his warmth back. She wanted the fire.

"Let me look at you for a moment. I planned this, in my head — the first time I'd have you was to be a slow seduction," he rasped. "But now, seeing you naked and lit up by the light of the fire, I'm not sorry. All I see is a goddess rising from the flames, and I wonder what I ever did in my life to deserve you."

"Jackson." He was going to make her cry. She met his gaze, the intensity in his fierce and loving at the same time. He tore his pants and boxers off, grabbed a condom from his wallet and dragged it over his hard, throbbing cock. Instantly her tears dried, replaced by want, by pure need at how gorgeous and huge he was. *Jesus.* She swallowed. *He's going to make me come without even touching me.* "I need you," she said and offered her hand to him, inviting him down to her.

As he covered her body with his, he took her head in his hands. "I need you too. I just don't know if I should be allowed to have you."

"Jackson." Even in the darkness she could sense the demons, the pain he tried hard to hide. "I want to be near you. You make me feel like I'm flying and on fire and deliriously happy." She leaned up and kissed him, putting all her passion into it. If he couldn't hear her words, she would use the language of her touch.

He kissed her back. And when he seemed to have sipped his fill of her lips, he tasted her body, dragging his tongue and hands down, whispering words she both didn't want him to say but wanted to understand.

"I should stop this now." He placed a kiss between her breasts. Even his words on her skin aroused her. "I should take you back, anywhere away from me." Jackson caressed her hips and darted his tongue lower, seducing that most private place that burned for him. He pushed her thighs apart and nipped at her sensitive skin. She was shaking in expectation. Her pulse jumped, and she arched her body closer to him.

"Jackson, Jackson."

"But I can't let you go, Ellie. I'm going to make you mine, even if it destroys us both." He stroked her pussy with his tongue, bringing her to a delirious high, her mind full of nothing but sensations. Then he dragged himself up and in one dark, dangerous, powerful thrust pushed into her, sending her crashing over the falls and exploding in orgasm. She clawed at him, dragged him closer, moved with him so he could rock in deeper. His mouth took hers and she felt feral. She thrust her tongue in and tangled it with his, dragged her nails down his back till she found his ass and begged him closer with her own limbs until he lost all control.

Even after he came, she wanted more, wanted him never to leave. She arched her body up, keeping them connected. His breath on her neck felt like feathers caressing her. He trailed his tongue up her neck, kissed her eyelids and nuzzled her neck as though he couldn't get enough of her. When he pulled out, she gripped his back, feeling the loss of him like a sharp pain in her ribs.

"Be right back, El," he whispered. He dragged the throw blanket over her and she nestled under the knitted feel of it. He came back with a warm washcloth, which he used to clean her. Then he lifted her and carried her up to his bedroom and, tucking her in tight to his side, he tangled their legs together, pulled the blankets up around them and threw his arm around her waist. "Sleep."

She was about to say, "No." She thought she wanted to talk and cuddle, making this night last forever. But the warmth of him wrapped around her and the sex were like drugs to her delightfully happy body. And feeling full of life and safer than she'd ever been, she let the dreams take her away.

Chapter Nineteen

Jackson watched Ellie sleeping on her stomach in the early morning light, naked and tangled in the sheet with one leg drawn up. It was a battle for him not to climb back in with her. She smiled in her dreams and he wondered if she always did, or if he'd been the one to put that happiness there. He needed to leave before she woke up or he'd never go, and he had to, to be back by Monday.

Without touching her, he strode from the room, let the dogs outside to do their business, wrote Ellie a note, climbed into his SUV and left.

Never before had it been this difficult to go home on this anniversary and honor his past. He'd been returning to his small hometown since he graduated from high school twelve years ago. It had never been easy, but it had been necessary. At first it had been out of grief and respect and guilt. Always guilt. As he'd grown and raced through law school, it had been his reminder of the path he pursued, a part of the debt he owed them. But today he was torn. For the first time ever, he had other things on his mind, namely Ellie.

He shouldn't have left her like that. In his bed. Alone. But he didn't know how to explain a past that left him feeling damaged and unworthy. He wanted her too damn much. If she knew the truth, she might never stay. She might never want to be near him. *You never should have taken her like that last night. She's not yours to have.* Or was she? Because every time he was around her, she reached into his soul and healed a part of him. She wanted to connect to him in the most intimate way. Would she when she discovered that he hadn't been able to protect and save his mom or his sister?

* * * *

"Jackson?" Ellie had never slept so deeply. "I want to stay in your bed forever. It's a million times better than mine. Jackson?" she called again. Ellie reached over to his side of the bed. It felt cold, like he hadn't been next to her all night. She pulled her cell phone close. "Holy shit! I need to get to work!" *Where is he and why didn't he wake me up?*

"Hey, Rosie, I'm going to be a little late this morning. Okay, thanks, girl. I owe you." Ellie hung up the phone and fell back on the bed. Wow! Last night... She couldn't help the grin. It felt like she'd slept and dreamt with a grin. Heck, her cheeks still felt flushed. From his touch, from his tongue on every inch of her, from the most fantastic orgasm.

She threw the covers off and called out again. "Jackson?" She'd gone from perma-grin to hot and bothered to confused. Where was the man who'd given her that orgasm, who'd treated her like he'd die if he couldn't have her, who'd worshiped her entire body?

"Hi, babies," she gushed. Chewie ran into her legs and Buffy strolled in behind her. She threw on her jeans, grabbed Jackson's shirt and made her way downstairs to the kitchen. There was no smell of coffee brewing, no breakfast cooking, no noise from someone else moving in the house. Silence. *I don't understand,* she thought when she saw the note. Even though the words were kind, her happy thoughts fled quicker than they'd arrived.

"Oh, Jackson," she whispered. She glanced at the living room, more memories of last night rushing through her. *The man needs love.* Where had that thought come from? Ellie had never had love growing up, not from her parents or her closed-off self. Could one recognize a thing one had never had? Or see the need in another? Over the years with her mother, she'd given up and realized some people, like her, weren't meant to be loved. She'd learned, in order to protect herself from pain, not to expect anything. And she was okay with that. She'd moved on from those childish dreams. Hadn't she?

Now the bright morning light poured in through the windows. The rains were gone, their remains sparkling on the bright green lawn that stretched away from Jackson's house. It was going to be a beautiful day. But Ellie was struck with the same thought she'd had when she'd arrived the night before. *How lonely this house seems.* The kind of lonely that felt raw and empty.

* * * *

"Wait, he left you a *note?*" screeched Natalie.

"It's not a bad note, Nat, calm down."

"My girl finally lets her guard down to get her taste of beautiful and that jerk leaves you a note?"

"Nat. He's not a jerk," Ellie whispered. She sat on the bench in the laundry room. It had hurt, more than she realized, seeing the note instead of Jackson the morning after they'd...what? She didn't even know what to call what had happened last night. Although she'd only had sex once before and it had been horrible, she thought what had happened with Jackson was way more than sex. It had been amazing, wonderful, new, exciting...

At the same time, something had felt off. She'd been pretty in tune with Jackson since they'd met. Even when he'd been confusing the hell out of her with his words and actions, his eyes had let her in, from the very beginning. And last night hadn't been supposed to happen. She'd known he had to go out of town. She was never supposed to be at his place at all.

"I'm sorry. What? He takes you to his place, takes advantage of you then leaves you there with a *note*?"

"He didn't take advantage, Nat." Was she trying to convince herself or Nat? No, she shook that thought away before it could eat at her. Since his apology with the flowers and amazing words, he'd been nothing but wonderful. Troubled but wonderful to her. "We've been, you know, working up to it. Here. Read the note. He's coming back. I knew he had to go out of town. Last night wasn't planned, but after my place flooded, he insisted the dogs and I go to his house and it...happened, Nat."

"Your place flooded? Why didn't you tell us about this sooner? You used to be a good communicator." She grabbed the note out of Ellie's hand.

Ellie, beautiful. I had to go. I'll be back no later than Monday morning. Please stay. Jackson.

"That's it? Jesus, for a schmoozy-ass lawyer he sure left a lot out, like *words*, for example. An apology? An explanation?"

"I think something's wrong and he couldn't or wouldn't tell me," Ellie said quietly.

"Well, that is not your job to figure out. You deserve better." Nat sat next to her. "I thought maybe *he* was the better."

"I think he is, Nat." Ellie squeezed her friend's hand. "The times he mentioned he had to be gone this weekend his eyes got haunted. And when he, when we—" Heat crept up her cheeks. "He made me feel more beautiful and powerful and amazing than I've ever felt."

"Oh, Ellie." Natalie sighed.

"Don't 'Oh, Ellie' me. I know you think I'm naive and ignorant, but I feel amazing when I'm with him, when I hear his voice, when he touches me, when his eyes search mine. And even though I wish he'd at least woken me to say goodbye, I want to be with him when he gets back."

"No. That's not what I meant, honey. I want for you what you said he made you feel, because you *are* those things, and you deserve to feel them. I wish he hadn't left you alone in his bed. Ugh!" Natalie rubbed her temples. "I want the fairy tale for you, Ellie, but there's no such thing. And I don't think you're naive about people at all. You know me. I'm all hot-headed. Then I calm down. I don't want you to get hurt, but I think you're being mature and if he's good enough for you, then he's the luckiest man alive to have you on his side."

"Thanks, Nat," Ellie whispered.

"But if he hurts you, Gage will make him feel pain like never before." She crossed her arms with a huff and Ellie burst out laughing.

"I love you, Nat." The words were out before she'd realized them. She did have love in her life. And that thought made her smile. Maybe love, in all its forms, was more complicated than Ellie would ever understand. Nat had been her friend for years, almost since the day she'd moved here. She'd helped Ellie when she needed it, laughed with her, treated her with respect, wanted the best for her, showered her with goodness. And Ellie treated Nat the same way. That was love.

"Love you back, girl. Always. What are you going to do? And what the heck happened to your apartment?"

"Talk about Gage making someone feel pain—could he get on that with our former landlord who let these beautiful buildings go to hell? I had dinner with Jackson and he brought me home to find water pouring in in the bedroom. And living room. Down the walls. All over my couch. He called his partner, and I called my insurance company. Connor's there now assessing the damage. I wouldn't be surprised if mine wasn't the only place with flooding. He said the roofs and gutters should have been replaced decades ago. The bakery seems fine with just a bit of damage from my floor to theirs. Connor's got a crew checking all the buildings for damage and safety, but I won't know until I see him when or if I can move back in or anything."

"Oh, Ellie! Well, I sense you want to stay at Jackson's since he asked you so nicely and all."

"Cut it out!" Ellie smacked her on the shoulder. "I do want to stay there. I mean, to be honest, it frightens me a bit. I have all these strong feelings for him that I've never had for anyone before. I'm not sure what they all mean. But I want to be there for him. I want to make him see all the good he keeps hidden inside, smash his demons the way he wants to smash mine. I want to make him feel the way he makes me feel, alive and amazing and safe all at the same time. At least I want the chance to try."

"Well, girl, he couldn't have found a more loving person to help him shed his demons and all that broody, dangerous aura he walks around with." Nat waved her hands in the air.

Ellie giggled. "Broody, dangerous aura? You make him sound like a tortured duke from the nineteenth century. Although, he is kind of broody, isn't he?"

"Definitely. However, as a badass defense attorney, it works for him."

Ellie settled beside Nat, serious again. "You really think I'm loving, Nat? Don't look at me like that. I've been thinking a lot about that word, love. I didn't have much love during my childhood, and I learned or, rather, talked myself into believing I didn't deserve it."

Never, she'd *never* had love growing up. And she'd never said one word about that to Nat. Out of shame and because she believed she'd buried it all. But she was learning love had many forms.

"Honey, I'm not going to tackle any of that right now, because there is so much behind your words, and we need wine or brownies or both for that conversation. And it breaks my heart that you had a loveless upbringing. But, regardless, you bloomed into the most beautiful flower who showers love all around her. I can't wait for you to see it in yourself. No one without love could be such a wonderful and compassionate doctor like you are. No one without love could be such a caring friend and boss. No one without love could count one of her best friends a homeless man whom she feeds and takes care of and makes sure he has a warm place to sleep at night. Everyone in this neighborhood adores you, because you are wonderful to them."

Natalie wrapped her in a warm hug, then headed to her desk, leaving Ellie swirled up with emotions again. This time they were mostly beautiful ones. She rubbed a hand over her aching heart. And she wiped her tears—even the beautiful emotions could bring tears. And maybe that wasn't a bad thing at all.

Chapter Twenty

"Wow!" Ellie took deep breaths, awed by the destruction in her apartment, which no longer resembled her apartment at all. Men were everywhere. Hard hats and jeans and work boots flitted throughout her vision, but center stage was the mess. Soaked, rolled-up area rugs, buckled wood floor. Her precious couch, destroyed. All her living room and bedroom furniture had been pushed into the middle of the rooms. Walls had been ripped open. The ceiling was half gone. One guy tossed soggy pieces of wall, trim and ceiling out of the window to the dumpster below. She didn't even recognize her kitchen. The crew had taken it over as a command center.

"It looks bad, but chin up, Ellie." Duggan rose from crouching behind a dismantled radiator when he noticed her.

"Ah, it *looks* bad?" she said with a hint of sarcasm.

A small grin replaced the worry and concern on Duggan's face. "I see she still has her sense of humor. That's good. You're going to need it."

"I'm not sure this is my sense of humor you're noticing, but rather my attempt not to lose my shit." She covered her mouth with her hand. "Sorry."

Duggan laughed. "Did you apologize for saying shit?"

"Uhm, yes?"

"You are fucking perfect for him," he said, and she thought her eyes might bug out of her head.

Duggan's tone changed to kindness. "You have nothing to be afraid of. Jackson's the one who should be scared. Bet he has no idea what's hit him." And he raked his gaze over Ellie, smiling the entire time. "This is going to be a blast to watch," he added.

Ellie tried to follow Duggan's words. She was afraid of all that encompassed Jackson. Not afraid *of* him. But what the heck did Duggan mean, *scared*, *hit him* and *fun*? "Well, you appear capable of reading my mind? But I have no idea what you're talking about. Maybe we could move on to the disaster of my apartment?" she asked to avoid any further analysis of her and Jackson. *Shit!* And shit again, she couldn't believe there was a her and Jackson.

"Right. Well, Dr. Blevins," he said in a serious tone, but one with a hint of tease to it. She appreciated that. He gestured through the apartment as he spoke. "The roof is shot. Same with the gutters. We tore out the damaged walls, because we needed to see what's inside them anyway. And most of your stuff is unsalvageable. The bakery will close for a few weeks while we clean and see how affected the walls, wiring and plumbing are, but they should be able to open back up in less than a month."

"Tear out walls a good thing? Unsalvageable? The French Connection has to close? Stop sounding downright giddy or I might swear at you again." And this time Duggan burst out laughing. "Yeah. You are the ray of sunshine that man needs in his life."

Ellie beamed at him, but then she thought about this morning. "You two have been friends for a while, haven't you?"

"He's like a brother to me, like a favorite brother."

She debated for a second because she honestly had no idea what she was doing in this relationship, but as she'd told Natalie, with Jackson she wanted to try.

"He, ah... I'm staying at his house," she started. The blush rose up her neck and covered her cheeks.

"He told me last night when he called. I'm glad," Duggan said. He crossed his arms and smiled at her. Two simple words, *I'm glad*, delivered an entire story full of background and secrets that should come to light and warmth.

"He was gone this morning when I woke up. Left me a note," she said quietly.

"What the..." Duggan's smile faded while his face hardened, then understanding dawned on his face. "Shit. This is the weekend." He scrubbed his hands over his face and sighed. *Oh, yes, there are secrets.* "He didn't *leave you* leave you. I mean I'm pretty certain he'd never treat you like that, Ellie."

"No." She smiled to let him know she wasn't pissed off because she knew in her heart Jackson hadn't gone away to hurt her on purpose. "I know it's none of my business and I don't want you to break the friendship code or anything, but it seemed like he was upset about something significant."

"He is," Duggan said, and he seemed to be studying her and coming to a conclusion. "It's not mine to share, Ellie, or I would because he means the world to me. I can see how important you're becoming to him, and that man deserves happiness. All I can tell you is that today is his birthday."

"What?" she said, shocked. "His *birthday*? You say it like it's...horrible."

"To Jackson it is."

Ellie sucked in her breath. "What?" she whispered.

"Yeah." Duggan nodded, but didn't elaborate. "Maybe he'll talk to you about it, but it might take him a while. He doesn't trust easily. And, unfortunately, I think the person he trusts the least is himself. What I'm about to say is none of my business, but I'm going to risk it. He needs a gem like you, Ellie, someone kind, gorgeous from the inside out, and someone patient."

"I'm patient," she said, touching on the easiest compliment to handle. "Okay." She took another deep breath, as if they'd settled an agreement and signed a contract. "Well, I guess since my entire apartment and everything in it is headed for the dump and there are too many hot men walking around for me to concentrate, I should get back to work."

Duggan winked at her. "I'll let you know how the rest of the structure is once we get inside. And we'll see if salvaging all these buildings is in the cards. None of the others had leaks."

"Sounds good." She took a slow glance over her place one last time and offered Duggan a huge thanks to encompass all the aspects of her life he was helping with.

She had a full staff in today and often that meant more managerial skills and delegating and checking up on her employees, not because she didn't trust them, but because they were learning too. And when it came to the animals they treated, a second eye always helped. Today, however, most of their duties involved simple checkups, which left her with time to think. Her mind flew all over the place. Her apartment. Sex with Jackson. She couldn't even go there right now. Everyone would know her thoughts by looking at her face. Then there was Jackson himself and the note, and everything Connor had told her this morning.

He'd left without saying goodbye or waking her, and while she'd been hoping for his warmth this morning, she put aside her own feelings because there was something so much bigger going on here for Jackson. He'd left town on his birthday, *his birthday*, which Duggan claimed wasn't a good day for Jackson. Being with him felt better than any relationship she'd ever had with another human, and she wanted him to trust her too, to feel safe with her. She could take his burdens from him. If he'd let her.

A birthday. Ellie kept circling back to that. Maybe she could make this birthday not so horrible. From experience she didn't know many problems that couldn't be helped with a delicious cake. For the first time that day, she smiled because she knew exactly where to go for help.

Chapter Twenty-One

"Okay, you two, time to settle down. And no, you cannot have cake. Well, maybe a little lick of the spatula." Ellie nudged Chewie away from his attempt to climb her leg and he landed on Buffy. Her big dog was spread out on Jackson's kitchen floor, pawing Chewie and swatting him. Teasing him, but too tired to put in much effort. Chewie, however, didn't seem to mind Buffy's laziness at all. The little pup had enough energy for ten dogs and was jumping and darting and barking at Buffy's attempts, while simultaneously trying to climb Ellie's legs. She finished filling the last of the round pans with the yellow mixture that she'd infused with a tiny bit of passion fruit extract, and set them in the oven to bake. She had no idea what Jackson's tastes were when it came to cake, so she decided to be bold and if he didn't like it, she'd eat it.

The frosting had passion fruit in it too, with lemon zest for hints of color and a bit more tartness. Once the cakes were cooked and cooled, she could frost the layers and build the cake, hopefully after the dogs were asleep. "Let's go play ball, boys and girls. That should wear you out."

Eventually, Chewie did crash, draped over Buffy's front paws right by the larger dog's neck. But, boy, the crazies he expended before he dropped off to sleep, "If I had half your energy, cutie," Ellie said while she finished decorating the small two-tiered cake. Saturday night and the house was quiet. Dark except for the kitchen. She'd made herself pasta, and drunk a glass of wine. She enjoyed baking and cooking in Jackson's kitchen, but she'd prefer it if he came back.

And now that the cake was finished, the kitchen clean and the night settled in around her, she worried she'd made a mistake. What if he got angry with her? Dang, she hadn't thought of that. She'd been hell-bent on trying to make his birthday a happy thing, but she had no idea why it was awful to begin with.

It felt strange to be in his house, use his things, sleep in Jackson's bed without him, but after the last week of mental and physical exhaustion, she didn't spend much time worrying, especially once she climbed under the covers, and imagined his warm strong body wrapped around hers.

Wow! Ellie excelled at sleeping. And she'd always had good dreams. But she'd never had such an amazing-felt-absolutely-real dream as *this* before.

She was cozy-warm and...aroused. Maybe she should do this more often, tell herself what kind of a dream she wanted to have before she fell asleep, and boom, she'd have it. Like right now. She'd gone to bed hoping to be wrapped up in Jackson and right now it felt like his arms were touching her. One wrapped under her body as she slept on her side and the other one found its way under her tank top to caress her breasts.

"Mmm," she mumbled and stretched out against his hard body right behind hers. She loved his body, his muscles, his dark woodsy scent. She'd wanted more time the other night to explore him, to take in all that was Jackson Kincaid, but they'd practically devoured each other before they'd both fallen asleep.

"El," his luscious deep voice rumbled in her ear. *Best. Dream. Ever.* She rubbed her body up against the one behind her again.

"You stayed," the dream Jackson's voice said, one hand caressing her thigh. "Love this soft body. You smell like sugar and vanilla. Love coming home to you in my bed." His warm breath and his voice on her ear unraveled her. Then he reached under the hem of her sleep shorts and found her hot, wet, needy core. Gentle at first, he explored and teased at the same time.

"Best dream ever," she sighed when he pressed inside her and the hand under her reached around and cupped her breast.

"No dream," the voice said. He turned her and took her mouth in a hot kiss. He moved his head only to kiss her neck, her chest.

"Jackson?" Her eyes shot open at the realization that she wasn't dreaming. He was home. And *jeesh* he could kiss! And his hands on her body were better than a dream any day. "You're home?" She tried to convey a happy tone, but it felt way more like need. God, he made her crazy with want. Her whole body sizzled every time he touched her.

"Came back early," he said and kissed her again. She tasted him then, rich deep bourbon. A lot of it, she thought, coming more fully awake. "Missed you." He nuzzled into her neck. "Couldn't stop thinking of you, El. Don't go," he said, the last words out of his mouth before he fell asleep.

"Oh, my God!" she breathed out. A very drunk, naked Jackson was passed out, half on her, while her body still hummed from his touch.

"Uhm, Jackson?" She tried to wake him, but the weight of him settled over her. Yep, no question about it, he was out. "Where'd you go, honey?" Ellie asked, knowing he couldn't hear her. "You can tell me about it, you know. I wish you would. Maybe I could help ease your pain. Maybe someday." She couldn't have budged him even if she'd had a forklift. She wrapped her arms around him and tried to calm her heart and her body. Maybe her touch could seep into him while he slept and prove to him that he was home and he was safe.

* * * *

"What the fuck?" Jackson said. Something warm and wiggly draped over the back of his neck and licked under his chin. "Chewie!" The dog seemed half asleep, fluttering nearly closed eyes, his tiny pink tongue shooting out once in a while to give Jackson a kiss on his chin and cheek.

He turned his head and saw Ellie's neck and face right there under him sleeping, her face to the side and her golden ruby curls all over the pillow. *Fuck!* He'd come home last night, let the dogs out, proceeded to get wasted on bourbon in his office because he was trying to stay away from her, then, he vaguely remembered, his drunk ass had changed his mind and he'd wanted to crawl into bed with her. Which was what he'd done.

He called himself every name in the book while Chewie decided to fully wake up and start nipping at his fingers. He grabbed the pup, carefully climbed off Ellie, dragged on his jeans with one hand and ushered both dogs out of the bedroom and downstairs to let them out. Hopefully before this crazy puppy peed all over the place.

A pink hint of light sliced across the horizon at five-thirty in the morning while Jackson stood in his bare feet on the cold grass and tossed the ball for Chewie. Damn dog could hardly see the ball, which didn't prevent him from throwing his body through the air at Mach speed to retrieve it. If he'd been in the mood, he'd have laughed at the hilarity. The poor pup had so much growing to do that it was as if his hind legs ran faster than his front ones and tripped him up every single time.

Buffy rested against his legs while he scratched behind her ears. It was going to be a gorgeous day. His hell weekend was over. During this visit he'd realized he couldn't do it anymore. He didn't know what he should *do*, but visiting ghosts wasn't it. Sensing his feelings on the matter had to do with Ellie, he'd let his mind wander to her. He couldn't get back to her fast enough. Of course, on the drive home he'd talked himself into believing she wouldn't be there. He should have been relieved or happy when he'd pulled up and seen her SUV, but instead he'd felt fear. He'd sat in his study with a bottle of bourbon to chase those fears away. Fears over what he felt for her, fears over his past and figuring out how to deal with it, how to put it to rest so he could move the fuck on, fears of her leaving. Jesus Christ, he hadn't felt like a coward in a long time.

But she was here — she'd stayed. Maybe there was hope because damn! It had felt phenomenal to find her in his bed. "All right, you two. Enjoy the morning outside while I climb back in bed with your mama."

He left the dogs outside in the brightening sun, cleaned up the liquor he'd spilled in his office, that dark hole of a room. It was where he spent most of his time when he was in his house, one penance after another.

He'd had the living room, kitchen, dining room and bathrooms all redone when he'd moved in, but he hardly ever enjoyed those rooms he'd had designed for comfort, for family. Having El there the other night, seeing her in his house — he realized he wanted her to stay, to see her there all the time in every room. Regardless of how angry she might be with him, he was ready to talk.

Chapter Twenty-Two

The dogs and Jackson were gone when she woke again. *Okay, one of these times I'd like to wake up not alone in this huge bed,* she thought, going in search of her dogs and her man. *God, I hope he's not gone again.* But she needn't have worried because when she got downstairs and stepped into the dark hallway, she heard him.

"What the fuck?" he said in more of a growl than a question.

"Jackson?" The dangerous scowl on his face stopped her in her tracks. "Umm..."

"You made me a cake?"

Well, yes, duh was what she wanted to say, but the quiet intensity of his words made her pause. She nearly got distracted by his amazing naked chest that she still wanted to get to know better, but the silence and her nerves got the better of her.

"Connor told me about your birthday. I'm sorry if I... I thought... I wanted to do something nice for you, and I..." Yep, there she went babbling away in her nervousness when every sign coming off Jackson's body told her to Be. Quiet. Or more like Shut. The. Fuck. Up. Because well, he did like to swear.

Then it wasn't silent anymore as he stalked to her, lifted her and took her mouth like a savage taking his last drink. Hands, his warm hands held her up and his entire body pressed against hers and she couldn't keep up with his kiss, the way his tongue savored her mouth. He trailed his nose and lips up her neck and whispered, "You made me a cake."

Damn, she loved that, his lips on her neck, the sharp scrape of his stubble, but more, the way his words beat against her throat. She put her hand on his head to keep him there. "Yes, honey. Happy birthday." And his entire body went taut like a bow.

"Wrap your legs around me," he demanded. She didn't hesitate and was glad she didn't when he invaded her mouth with his tongue. She grabbed his shoulders and her mouth melted into his. He carried her over to the counter and sat her down, then used his fingers to grab a hunk of cake and feed it to her. She took the bite, still freaking way the heck out, but not in a bad way anymore with his pulsing body closing hers in and his gaze, which said he'd never seen anything more beautiful before.

Before she could finish the bite, he dragged her body to his ravaging her mouth again. "Jackson!" she cried, trying to pull away. "I have cake in my mouth."

"I know. Best fucking cake I've ever had. On you it tastes fucking phenomenal."

"Oh!" And she melted back into him. He lifted her around him again and carried her upstairs, drugging her with his kisses on her mouth, her chin, her neck. When his tongue sampled her neck, she arched forward, rocking him even closer to her.

He rested her on the bed, pulled his jeans off then prowled after her. In one second he had her tank top off and his scorching, powerful hands dragging up her skin had her on fire again. Before she could miss his touch, when he tossed her top away, his hands were back peeling her sleep shorts off while at the same time he kissed down her body. *Jesus!* The perfect feel of his lips on her skin mixed with the rough scrape of his whiskers while his fingers memorized her body. She lost all thoughts, all nervousness, all everything except feel and need.

"Jackson," she moaned. He rolled them over so she was on him. Her sensitive nipples rubbed on his chest. She felt his cock, insistent right where she needed it. He reached into his bedside table for a condom.

"Gonna take my time with you. I keep telling myself I'm gonna take my time with you, but, El, you make me lose control."

She didn't need him to take his time. She couldn't bear it. "I need you." He slid the condom down. He gripped her waist. She rubbed her core over him, teasing them both. Her head fell back at the sensation and he surged into her body, joining them. *Yes!* The feel of him… She arched her back and took him deeper as if she couldn't get enough.

Finally his chest was hers to explore and she roamed her hands over his muscles, relishing his taut body and smooth skin. He was one contrast after another. All the while he pulled her up and thrust her back down on him, pressing their centers together with each surge. And he watched them, where his cock disappeared in her with lust and desire. Every part of her body tuned in to his touch, like lightning and thunder, one racing after the other. An amazing rush.

Then he rocked her world even more. He lifted his head and gazed into her eyes. "Never had a cake before." He surged in, never breaking eye contact.

"Honey," she whispered, placing her hand to his cheek. He caressed her skin while he spoke, sending sparks all over her.

"Not since I was a kid. Too little and too much dark in between then and now to remember." He threaded his hand through her hair and pulled her down closer. His body kept up the delicious pace that was going to make her come any moment.

"Jackson." She couldn't bear it, his words, his trust, his body.

He nipped her ear and tightened his hold on her. "Never had such beauty, babe." And with that she shattered around him, her entire being exploding into wave after wave of exquisite tremors.

"Fucking so damn beautiful," he whispered. He quickened the pace, surging into her. "God, Ellie." And he came, taking her body on the ride of her life.

Ellie tried to control the tears, but there was no way. Jackson curled his body around her with his chest to her back, whispering his story into her ears, her soul. He'd brushed her tears away and kept her wrapped up in his embrace. But it appeared he'd had enough. "Babe," he called. "It's over. No one but Duggan, in my whole life, knows my story, and even he doesn't have all the details I told you, darlin'. Appreciate your tears 'cause I know they come from your heart, and I need you to know how much it means to me to feel safe sharing all that with you, but no more tears now."

"So." She grabbed his wrists that cradled her head. "You spent your childhood at the hands of an abusive father. Your brave mother got you away from him. He hunted you down. Your mom shot and killed him to protect you, which you witnessed, *on your birthday* at nine years old, after which you and your sister were separated and you've been searching for her since you were in college, with no luck? Your mom died in prison. You never got to say goodbye to her, and you go back every year on your birthday to visit her grave and *ask her forgiveness?* Punishing yourself even though you had no control over any of that? And you want me to simply stop crying?"

She wanted to rage and yell and hit someone. "I'm a crier, Jackson. I warned you. If that's not okay with you, maybe we should part ways now, because there will be more tears, especially when you tell me a story like that!" She felt the rumble of his laughter when he buried his face in her neck.

"Part ways?" he said, chuckling.

"Jackson!" she scolded. "It isn't funny."

"Babe, felt safe sharing my hell with you, in my bed, in my home, which I've never brought another woman to. Got your soft, luscious body tangled in mine. The taste of you still in my mouth, and you think we might 'part ways'?" He drew his nose along hers and kissed her long and slow and, as angry for him as she was, his kiss melted her immediately.

"Maybe I'll start swearing like you. Is that why you swear? Does it help? Does it help you deal with all the tragedies you've lived through and survived? I'm thinking it's part of your badass-ness." He smiled, that smile of his that warmed his entire face.

"I'm thinking you're already a badass without swearing, babe. Met you. Wanted you. You shared your warmth and beauty with me. I fucked it up, and thank God you let me back in. Then your stunning cake-making skills slayed every nightmare I've had."

"No one ever called me a badass before," she whispered, and her eyes filled with tears again.

Jackson leaned down and kissed next to each eye.

"No more tears now, babe."

"Happy tears, Jackson. Happy tears."

"Know something better than happy tears."

"Yeah?" she whispered. "What's that?"

"Cake for breakfast." He leaned down and nipped one of her nipples. Then he sprang up and left her lying there.

"Jackson!"

"Cake for breakfast. In bed!" he yelled. And he returned with a plate, one huge slice of cake and a fork.

"We can't eat that here. We'll get the bed all messy."

He sat, pulled her naked body onto his lap, picked up the cake and fed her a bite. Then he leaned in and licked her lips, like a feather teasing her most sensitive spots. "Gonna mess up the bed with you after we eat it anyway," he said before he held out another bite for her.

"Oh," she whispered when she could talk. And he did just that, he messed up the bed with her. And he took his time.

Chapter Twenty-Three

Hours later, after they'd slept, gotten up to play with the dogs and had lunch, after Ellie had checked in with her clinic and Jackson had caught up with a bit of work, they were getting dressed to run errands. Jackson smiled. He'd never run errands with anyone and he found he couldn't wait. *A fucking birthday cake.* Jesus, she had layers of beauty inside her that she openly shared with him. Aside from his mother, he'd never had anyone take care of him, and he found he fucking loved it. It broke him open inside and made him feel safe telling her about his childhood, about why he had to go away this weekend.

"I know you probably hate shopping, but I kind of need to stop at the mall since almost everything I own is drenched at the moment," she said, interrupting his thoughts when she came out of the bathroom.

Blinding, that's how beautiful she is. He stepped closer and dragged one hand over her collarbone. *Like priceless art.* He ran the other down her back and into her jeans, teasing the top of her panties with light touches. "You gonna get more of these sexy panties?"

Her gorgeous rosy flush bloomed across her cheeks.

"Yes," she said without hesitation and leaned into him. *Easy*, he thought, and he would treasure that *easy* for as long as she'd let him. His phone rang in his back pocket and he ignored it.

"We should get going then," he said, but made no move to step away. She leaned into his hand on her neck. He loved the way she did that every time he touched her, like a cat basking in sunlight.

"Okay," she breathed when his cell rang again.

"What?" he said into the phone, but he kept his hand on her ass and his eyes on hers. *Jesus Christ, those eyes.* "Right. No, I agree. Good. Yep, I'll tell her. Shut up, Duggan, we'll see you in a bit." He cut the call.

"Connor says even though the gutters and roofs are shot, the walls have moisture inside them and all the wiring and plumbing needs to be updated, the foundations on the bakery building, your clinic and the two empty buildings on the end are solid. Looks like you might have yourself a renovation project, Ellie Blevins."

Her smile grew wide, she sucked in a breath and her entire face broke out in happiness.

"What?" she screamed and launched herself into his arms.

"I think you heard me." He grabbed on and rocked back to steady them. She wrapped her legs around him.

"Say it again," she whispered, pulling his head closer.

"You bargained yourself into a renovation project of a historic district. Although," he teased, "I didn't get my full month of you trying to convince me. You still wanna hang out with me anyway, now that the convincing's over?"

The velvet touch of her hands on his neck worked its way into his heart.

"Are we hanging out, Jackson?" she asked in that serious, but sexy-as-fuck voice of hers. "Is that what you call this?"

"Nope," he said before taking her mouth in a hungry kiss and walking with her back to the bed. "It's a hell of a lot more than that."

"Jackson," she sighed, pulling her lips away from his but nuzzling his neck. "You sure?"

And he knew she wasn't asking about the renovation project. "Absolutely. You?"

"Mmm-hmm. But…I thought we had to get going?" She arched her body against his and he wondered who was needier.

He took his hand away from her hips, followed her down onto the bed and whipped her shirt off over her head and chucked it behind him.

"Change of plans," he said before he tugged her bra down and dragged his teeth over her nipple.

She moaned and he kissed down her belly. "You like to change plans on me."

He trailed his hands down her body, taking her jeans and panties with him, and as he slid back up, he removed her bra and she stretched her arms over her head, her skin flushed and waiting for him. "Think you like it when I do, Ellie."

"Uh-huh," she said and blinked that slow blink. It was debatable which was more gorgeous, the way she smiled or when she did that lazy, sexy blink.

He paused for a minute to take her in, roaming over every inch of her body with his eyes. "Remember last time how I took it nice and slow?"

She nodded, and her eyes lit with understanding.

"Now I'm going to take you fast. You ready?"

"Oh, yeah," she whispered, and he was on her.

* * * *

Ellie found Jackson in the pet store at the mall when she'd finished shopping for clothes. It hadn't taken her long—she still wasn't a confident shopper and after grabbing a few basics, she thought she should schedule another girls' shopping date. Her friends not only made it fun, but they'd helped her find outfits she liked on her body. She could admit, however, that she had had fun today picking out two short, sexy nighties with matching panties, one a deep red with black trim, the other a gorgeous, shimmery dark blue, like a mixture of the night sky and the ocean. Too bad one couldn't survive on nighties alone. *Hmm, Jackson might beg to differ.*

She stared at him. She couldn't believe that they were, well, whatever they were at the moment. *Is it too soon to label it?* Weeks ago, she might never even have noticed him, since she *had* been living inside her head unless she was at work, with her friends or her dogs. She smiled when she thought of the night he'd come crashing into her clinic, all pissed off and magnetic. How his face had battled between murderous and humorous the moment Chewie peed all over him. Now here he was buying out the entire pet store.

His cart overflowed. Two huge dog beds, dog food, puppy food, bowls, four kinds of treats, and he was tossing toys into the cart when he must have sensed her presence, because he caught her gaze and grinned. *Holy cow!* Jackson Kincaid smiling at her in the pet store while he shopped for stuff for their dogs. *Our dogs, holy cow!* She was going to hyperventilate. She couldn't move. She felt parched and her face was tight with anxiety.

The look on his face changed to worry as he came to her. "What's wrong, El?" He wrapped both arms around her and pulled her tight to him. "You're freaked out all of a sudden."

"I...you, me." She waved her hands around the store.

"El." He leaned in close. "Even without your words, I can see the panic on your face. Talk to me."

His warmth soothed her. She felt safe in his arms. Not much had made her panic the last few years because she made sure she was in complete control of her life, which meant, like Nat had said, Ellie kept herself closed off from anyone but the few people she trusted. It was all safe in a way. But this, here with Jackson, being held by him, ever since the first time he'd put his arms around her, had made her feel a buzz, but had also given her a sense of peace. Was this what real safety felt like? Healthy, put-her-heart-out-there-and-feel-love kind of safety? She didn't know anything, except her emotions had felt beehive crazy these past few weeks. Old memories, old scars and old insecurities taunted her.

"El," Jackson said, giving her a gentle squeeze. "You're freaking me out now. What the fuck, babe?"

"I like you." She wheezed out the words and stretched up on her tiptoes to be even closer to him.

He smiled and relaxed. "Think we established we like each other last night, this morning and again this morning," he half-teased.

"No." She leaned even closer. "I mean, I *like* you."

His face got serious then and she locked onto his gaze. "Good. I *like* you too. Like you in my bed, like you on my couch, in my kitchen, sitting next to me at the pub sipping tea, 'cause you're shy of drinking again. I like you describing the historical home registration process to me and explaining Chewie's devotion to me. Thought we covered all this, El." He studied her face. "Guess I need to up my game a bit and keep telling you, showing you. Love how passionate and smart you are. Crazy about that fucking cake. Really like your warm, curvy body wrapped around mine. Fucking love the way you laugh. We established this is more than us hanging out. Can't wait to see where this is going, because I've never *liked* anyone as much as you before, Ellie. Got it?"

It was all too much so she nodded and took a few deep breaths. "I freaked out," she whispered. "I don't usually freak out. I might weep at a story of a boy growing up without his family in foster care, but I'm not necessarily a freak-out kinda girl."

He chuckled. "Got that, babe. But it's safe to say I like why you did it. Now, you wanna help me pick out dog toys for our pups?"

Our pups. Maybe in Jackson's arms was exactly where she belonged. Maybe she needed to trust in him and in herself. Maybe this, whatever was between them that was risky, was also 'fucking phenomenal.' She peeked around him at the cart. "It appears you've got that covered, honey," she said and smiled up at him. Life was strange and hard some days and others it sparkled like the sun over the ocean.

Chapter Twenty-Four

They lay tangled together on the couch. Jackson's back was to the inside. Ellie faced him, and he was thoroughly enjoying kissing her. He loved how she softened in his arms every time he kissed her, how she relaxed into the connection they had. A connection he'd never had before, and one he did not plan on letting go.

He hadn't been lying when he'd told her that he wanted to see where this was going…but he hadn't been one hundred percent forthcoming either. As in, he already knew where he wanted this to go. Now he had to get her on the same page. He'd learned she still needed his reassurance. She wanted to trust him but part of her held back. He figured some of that had to do with how quickly they'd connected, and she, with all her openness and honesty, had given him so much. Then he'd been a dick and slammed the door on her trust. Thankfully, she'd given him a second chance.

He sensed her past also made her gun shy when it came to trust. Jackson had to handle her with care, but he wanted to know everything about her. And now he had to find the balance between making her his for good without freaking her out by going at warp speed. He was going to have fun finding the perfect balance.

"Like having you here," he said, pulling his mouth away from hers. She opened her eyes and blinked. Fuck, that sexy dazed look of hers, like she lost herself in their kiss. She nuzzled in closer to his body and *fuck*, but he liked that too. Once she felt comfortable, she was not shy at all. She was all in.

"So fucking sweet," he said. "Loved my cake. Where'd you learn to bake like that?"

"The Heelys taught me."

"The owners of the bakery?"

"Yeah, honey."

"Are they family?" He pulled one of her legs over his and rubbed her back.

Ellie was serious now. The haziness his kisses gave her had cleared. "Not blood family, but yeah. I didn't know anyone when I got here. I applied for a job and they helped me more than I helped them. I had just gotten into school and needed to find part-time work and a place to stay. During the interview they fed me all these delicious pastries, and I found myself telling them more than I'd planned and the next thing you know, they'd hired me, given me a place to stay and taught me how to make all the delicious things they sell." She kept her arms around him while she spoke, once in a while tracing her fingers on his neck. He wondered if she was aware of how much he liked it when she did that.

"They never felt like bosses. They were like the good kind of family, and I'd never had that. I grabbed on. You know?" Her voice had gotten softer. He touched her forehead with his, letting her know with his body that he understood.

"They lost a daughter years ago to cancer. She was eleven. I don't kid myself into thinking I replaced their daughter. I wouldn't even want to do that, but I think we filled a need for each other."

He could guess without even hearing the Heelys' side that El had brought light back into their lives.

"Glad you have them."

"Me too, honey."

"Best cake I've ever had, babe. Can't wait to taste what you make next," he said, lightening the mood a bit.

"I could make you dinner?"

"Nope," he said, rolling her under him and kissing her collarbone. She arched up to his touch and wrapped one leg around his.

"Nope?" she whispered, her breath catching.

"I'm cooking for you tonight."

She opened her eyes wide. "You are? You cook?"

"Yep," he answered and snaked his fingers up under her shirt. "Never had anyone to cook for, though. I'm bettin' I'm gonna enjoy it."

He kissed her belly and she let out an "Mmm-hmm." Then she was gone again, lost in their connection. Fuck, but he loved that.

"Hungry?" He moved down her body and started to peel her jeans off.

"Oh, yes," she breathed. She moved to help him get her clothes off when the doorbell rang.

Jackson stilled, glowered over the edge of the couch in the direction of the front door. "Fuck. Duggan," he said and rested his head on her. "Invited him, or rather he invited himself over for dinner tonight. Forgot all about it." He pulled her jeans back up and righted her shirt while she stared at him with the strangest expression on her face. Cute but strange. "El?"

"Wow!" She fell back onto the couch, covering her face with her hands. "That's twice now...from your touch I thought I might...and...no such luck."

"Darlin', you are cute as fuck, but I have no idea what you're talking about."

"You." She gestured to his body. "All of you touching me, talking to me in that sexy voice, getting me all worked up—"

"Twice?" He twisted his head and grinned at her.

"Last night when you first came home. My dream was amazing. It got even better when I realized it wasn't a dream, but you—"

"I passed out on you?" He leaned down close. "Forgot about that, babe. Was on my way to apologize for mauling you in my inebriated state when I found your cake and saw you standing in the hallway looking like the sexiest guardian angel I've ever seen. Then I got carried away."

The doorbell rang again, and they heard Duggan yell, "Jackass, I know you're home."

Jackson stood and pulled Ellie up with him. He propelled her in front of him to the front door. "I'll make it up to you," he whispered into her ear.

"Okay," she said, leaning against him.

* * * *

Wow! Jackson Kincaid and Connor Duggan playing ball in a huge yard with three dogs. One of the most beautiful things she'd ever seen. Even more gorgeous with the three dark-haired girls, Connor's nieces, running and laughing with them. Chewie and his sister, Connor's puppy, were still trying to get Buffy to play catch with them, and they were so fumbling awkward about it, jumping over her and tripping. Nipping at each other. In an instant they'd forget what they were doing and run off to chase one of the girls, ending up in a pile of fur, making the girls giggle and giggle.

Ellie wasn't sure which was cuter, the girls' laughter or the tiny puppy barks.

She sat on the back porch and watched them. Jackson had grilled a huge salmon and garlic bread and Connor had brought a salad, which his sister, Katie, had made for him because he'd spent all day, all *Sunday* at multiple job sites working and he'd almost forgotten about dinner.

Hmm. She smiled to herself. As much as she liked seeing Jackson with his good friend, relaxed and happy, she wished Connor had forgotten. Daydreaming about what he'd been doing to her on the couch earlier had her flustered and overheated. He'd turned her into a lust maniac. And he made her feel so amazing that she didn't even have the heart to be embarrassed by how she felt, by how much she wanted him. She couldn't stop smiling about it either.

"I cannot believe how amazing that cake was, Ellie," Katie said when she stepped onto the deck. "What was the flavor with the lemon?"

"Passion fruit," Ellie said, smiling at Connor's sister whom she'd just met tonight, but who was so kind and casual that Ellie had liked her immediately.

"Thank you for letting us crash dinner. When Connor told me about you, I let my curiosity get the better of me. I can see why you're the first woman Jackson Kincaid ever brought to his home."

Her smile was infectious and Ellie didn't mind Katie admitting to critiquing Ellie. She was glad Jackson had good people in his life.

"I do make a mean cake," Ellie joked.

"Honey, that's the best cake I've ever tasted in my life, but you..." She waved her hand over Ellie. "That man deserves special." She grasped Ellie's hand. "And you have 'special' written all over you. Inside and out. A lady can tell."

"Katie," Ellie said quietly as Katie blinked back her tears.

"He's got such a good heart, the best. Even if it's been battered to the point one could wonder if it had any spark left. He needs someone to take care of that heart, you know?"

"I do," Ellie said. "And I promise I will."

"Okay," Katie said. "Now tell me where you get your hair done, because, girl, those curls and layers are gorgeous. Your cut is fabulous."

Ellie laughed at Katie's enthusiasm. "Do you know Spa La La, down the street from my clinic on Corvallis?"

"No, but I can't wait to check it out now. I remember when we were kids, Connor and I and John, my late husband, we used to play in that park all the time. That neighborhood has gotten so run-down over the years, I'd nearly forgotten about it." Katie glanced back at the yard. "Being a single mom to three girls could have something to do with my brain fog too." She laughed, but Ellie noticed the change in her voice and the shadow that passed over her face. "My husband died of cancer almost five years ago."

"I'm sorry, Katie," Ellie said. "How do you recover from that?"

"At the time I didn't think I would. Kids force you to be present, whether you want to or not. I'm not sure which was harder, that one day he disappeared from our lives, or the entire year before when he suffered horribly through the disease, the surgeries, the treatments. CeCe was a baby. It shattered all of us. John and Connor were friends since birth. My grief has changed, but I wonder if Connor won't ever move on from it. His girlfriend at the time broke up with him and he's never been serious about anyone again, like he's afraid to love for fear of them leaving or dying." She smiled at Ellie. "Maybe now that Jackson's found you, Connor will let his own demons rest."

Ellie listened and thought about past wounds. "It's amazing that these big, strong, confident men have such tender hearts, isn't it?"

Katie grabbed her hand and squeezed it. "Yes."

"What about you, Katie? Do you want to find love again?"

Well, at least she'd said something to make Katie really laugh this time. She laughed so hard tears spilled down her cheeks. "Ellie, oh, I already love you to pieces. To answer your question, I do, but the kind of man who would want me has to also want those three beauties out there, which includes one brand-new diva teenager and two more divas-in-training and that, my friend, might be more difficult than asking the sky to change color."

"I don't know." Ellie smiled and took in the laughter and silliness in the yard, and her heart warmed. "I think whoever found you all would be one lucky man. To have all that instant joy and love."

Katie smiled. "Beautiful and wise. No wonder Jackson's all googly-eyed." Katie bugged her own eyes out in a silly face and she and Ellie collapsed into giggles.

"You know, Katie, my friend Ruby, who owns Spa La La, does do good hair, but you can also get manicures and pedicures. You should come with me one night and we could get all spruced up. Better yet, bring your girls and we'll have a princess party. My friend Nat brings her two girls. I bring baked goods. And we have a blast."

"You had me at baked goods, Ellie. That sounds wonderful. Can I say yes to both? A night without my little ones and a princess party with them?"

"Absolutely," Ellie said.

Chapter Twenty-Five

Jackson: *Morning, beautiful.*

Every morning, this man. Ellie sighed, put her phone down and wondered how fast a person could cause their own wrinkles from smiling too big. If so, those would be the best wrinkles ever.

"Bring 'em on," she said, and nuzzled the nose of one of the cats who were sprawled out on her chest purring. She was flat on her back in the kennel room of her clinic with two cats, Chewie and two of his litter mates using her as their jungle gym.

When she had to be in the clinic extra early or if Jackson left for work first and she was still asleep, he always texted or called her with a 'good morning.' Sometimes she called him first, but usually he beat her to it. And she loved getting his messages or his gruff voice every day. It almost made up for those days they didn't wake up together.

Ellie: *Did you know, the owner's investment in renovated buildings, such as the ones here on Corvallis Street, improves the area and boosts the real estate value?*

Jackson: *Babe.*

She couldn't help it, she giggled. She loved teasing him and picturing his smile while she did.

Jackson: *You do remember I already conceded and we are in fact renovating your beloved neighborhood.*

Ellie: *I do, honey. And do you know how happy that makes me?*

Jackson: *Yep. Can I make you dinner tonight?*

Ellie: *I wish. Matt and Rosie have finals, so this week is crazy again.*

Jackson: *Now that I convinced someone as amazing as you to fall for me, I need to figure out how to get us to spend more time together. We both work too damn much.*

Ellie: *Mmm-hmm. I agree.*

Ellie had never thought of it like that before, that she worked too much, but she'd never had an amazing person in her life she wanted to spend all her time with either.

Jackson: *Gotta go. Lock your door! I'll call you later.*

Ellie: *Okay, honey. Have a good day.*

She could sense his growly "Lock your door" through the text, but it didn't bother her anymore. If he liked knowing she was safe, she'd give that to him. He filled her life with goodness every day. "Your daddy is pretty good to us, Chewie." She hugged the pup who struggled to get out of her arms.

Morning, beautiful. She never got tired of hearing him say those words to her, not because he made her beautiful, but because the way he treated her made her feel beloved. Precious to Jackson Kincaid. It was more than his words. He held her hand and caressed hers when they walked the dogs. He tucked her in close at night, left little things around his house for her to find, like peanut butter and jelly—which had made her laugh out loud when she discovered them in the cupboard with bows tied around them—the most amazing rose-scented bath salts by the tub, a pink rhinestone collar for Buffy.

And he couldn't seem to keep his hands off her when they were at home. She was perfectly okay with that because she felt the same.

Ellie held her water bottle to her neck to cool herself off. For years, sex hadn't even been on her radar. She thought something was wrong with her, but Jackson Kincaid made her hot with one glance. Oh, the way his eyes had darkened into a swirling storm when he'd stalked her to bed last night, let loose that storm on her body and devoured her, all the while murmuring sweet words to her. Kissing her freckles. Giving her orgasm after orgasm before he let himself come.

She flopped her head down on her desk. She needed more days off so she could have more naked time with Jackson Kincaid. Too bad happiness couldn't get all her charts done, or the two surgeries she had today.

* * * *

"Ellie."

"Hi, honey. Everything okay?" She'd just spoken to him two hours ago when he got home.

"I'm out front."

She hung up her phone and smiled huge.

"Hi," she breathed, unlocking the door to let him in.

"Brought you dinner," he said, and leaned in to kiss her. "Took a chance with Thai. Hope that's okay? Brought treats for the dogs too. I can take Buffy and Chewie home with me after."

"You brought treats for the dogs?" She fumbled with the lock on the door, her heart speeding up. This man kept surprising her with his kind gestures. And his hotness, whew! He had on his sexy, worn jeans and an old, faded gray concert T-shirt. As magnificent as he looked in a suit all dressed up for work, when he dressed casually, she wanted to eat him up.

He set the takeout bags on the reception counter, wrapped his hands around her waist and tugged her tight to him. "Like taking care of you, babe." He brought one hand up to the back of her head and kissed her, and he did not go in slowly. Nope, he kissed her hard and deep. His warm body pressed up against hers and she couldn't get close enough. She snuck her hands up under his shirt to feel his skin and he walked her backward. Before she knew it, he had her top off and tossed it on the floor. "Hmm," he hummed into the skin on her neck. "Every time you wear scrubs, I wonder what you have on underneath. Had to find out. Like this red, babe. Like it better off, though." He dragged her bra down, exposing her breasts. "Fucking gorgeous. Can't get enough of this body, El."

"Jackson." She was lost in him. "Let me see you." She pulled away when they made it to her office and tried to tug his shirt off. "I need your skin on mine."

He peeled his shirt off and surrounded her again. "Is this where you sleep when you're here overnight?" he asked, indicating the cot.

"Mmm-hmm," she answered, but he didn't take them in that direction. Instead he backed her up *again* into the wall. My goodness, he could back her up anytime with his hot body against hers. Devouring her lips, he shoved her scrub pants down then...he stopped, and studied her as if she were a finished sculpture revealed for him. His gaze followed his hand down her body, along her panties. Everything about him went still, aside from his heavy breathing and the flutter of his finger caressing along the lace edge, studying it. She couldn't stand it — it was torture.

"Jackson," she panted, when he reached the thin straps by her hips and teased. How could she stand it? His hands moved the silky lace down her legs, dragging his knuckles against her super-sensitive skin while he did it.

"Mmm, love how wet you get for me, beautiful girl." He slowly, so slowly pushed two fingers inside and her entire body shivered. "Don't think that cot's strong enough to hold us."

"What?" She floated on a cloud of lust and he was talking about a cot? Then she whimpered when he took his fingers away. "Wait, don't..." All she wanted were his fingers back. But he unzipped his jeans and freed his cock and oh, she wanted that. "Please," she begged.

"Put this on me, babe." He handed her the condom.

Before she could even catch her breath, he wrapped his hands around her, lifted her and said, "Hold on."

"Hold on?"

"Gonna fuck you against the wall, El," he said and, holding her tight with one arm, reached around with his other and placed his cock right at her entrance. "Fucking dripping for me." And in one push he thrust into her.

Grabbing him around his shoulders, she held on. She held on tight while his slow torture flipped into powerful need. She mirrored his fierce motion by squeezing him tight. She held on when he stilled, deep inside her, and kissed her like it was his last breath. She held on as he roamed over her skin, causing fireworks to burst all over her body. She held on until she couldn't hold on anymore. They both let go and thundered through the storm together.

Ellie was lost, floating down from the Jackson Kincaid high. Half-naked, pressed up against *and* in her. Her head rested on his shoulder when he said, "Never had something so precious in my life before, El."

She smiled into his neck and hugged tighter around him. "You slay me, Jackson Kincaid." *I'm in love with you,* she wanted to say. *Is it too soon?* She wanted nothing to break this spell she was under.

He rested his lips on her neck, a featherlight caress, then set them apart. It was a good thing he steadied her boneless body still on a high from him. Then he helped her get dressed and set the food out in picnic style for them.

"This is the best dinner ever," Ellie said ten minutes later. She put a bit of chicken in her mouth. They were sitting against the wall of her office, eating chicken curry and drunken noodles out of cardboard containers with chopsticks.

Jackson nudged her shoulder with his. "See? Easy."

"What?" She smiled up at him.

"Eating takeout at eleven o'clock at night on the floor and you think it's the best dinner ever. You, El, are easy." He put his container down, leaned over and left a gentle but lingering kiss on her lips.

"Well," she whispered, "you did just give me a pretty fabulous orgasm."

"It's all part of my evil plan, babe." He winked at her.

"Your *evil* plan?" she teased.

"Making you happy, keeping you happy. Whatever I have to do to make sure you want to stay with me."

She put her container down, climbed on his lap and straddled him. "I'm not going anywhere," she said and kissed him. He wrapped his strong arms around her and he took the kiss deeper.

"Oh!" Ellie screamed and jumped back. Chewie had woken up and bounded in between them, barking and licking both of them. He tumbled off and raced headfirst into the knocked-over curry container.

"See, there are desperate forces trying to keep us apart," Jackson said before he placed Ellie to the side, grabbed Chewie with one hand and tossed the takeout container in the garbage with the other. "Time to get you home, crazy mutt. Here, babe." He reached out a hand for Ellie.

"Hate working overnights," Ellie grumbled, wrapping Jackson up in a hug.

"Me too, babe. Want you home in our bed."

Our bed. She loved the sound of that. "Mmm, bed." She yawned, thinking of how tired she was. Deliriously happy, but tired.

"Hey." He lifted her chin and gave her a smoldering look. One of her favorite views in the world these days. Boy, she couldn't wait to climb back into *their* bed together. She missed bed. She missed his naked body next to hers, even though she'd had it wrapped around her last night. A body as beautiful as his — she missed it the minute he was gone.

"Need to get these mutts home. I have a surprise for you. I have to go to New York City in two weeks, and I want you to come with me. I want to spoil you. I chartered a private plane and we have reservations at the Four Seasons. Thought maybe your techs could handle your crazy schedule for a weekend."

"Huh?" she said, startled out of her sleepy daze.

Jackson took her hand. "Buffy. Here, girl." He whistled, but Buffy groaned on her bed and didn't move a muscle. "I'll leave her here with you," he said.

New York? He's joking, she thought and slipped her hand from his. Her pulse kicked up and an image flashed into her mind. Ten years ago, Ellie and her few belongings in the used car she'd paid cash for. She'd driven across the New York State line into Pennsylvania. She'd had to pull over at the first rest stop because tears had flowed unbidden, threatening to choke her. For almost an hour, she'd cried. Cried and breathed. And those breaths had felt like the first safe, healthy ones filling her lungs after almost drowning. *Painful, fresh, necessary, new.* When she'd continued driving, she'd made it all the way across the country without another tear. And she'd sworn she'd never go back.

"Taking you on a mini-vacation," he said, oblivious to her heart racing and the shock on her face.

"Also, forgot, Katie wants us over for dinner one night next week. She said she'll give you a call. Lock up when I leave, all right? Get some sleep and sweet dreams, babe," he said and kissed her one last time before he took the dogs and walked out.

Like a robot, Ellie locked the door, watched them drive away until they were out of sight, then crumpled over the garbage can as all her delicious dinner came right back up in a heap of panic.

Chapter Twenty-Six

"Hey." Ellie rushed into Ruby's spa.

"Lord, this is the best fundraiser you've had, Ruby." Natalie had a glass of red wine in one hand and one of Ellie's chocolate-salted-caramel brownies in the other.

"Mm-hmm," Ruby agreed, and fanned her face with her clipboard.

"It's almost too much hotness for me to handle all at once. Almost." Natalie took a gulp of wine. "I mean, my man is beautiful over there getting his beard trimmed, but those three together? I. Can't. Even. How in the heck did you convince those broody, all-man hotties to get pedicures?"

"I don't know." Ruby sighed. "I mean, I know I have superpowers, but even I'm not that good. El?"

The girls glanced at Ellie for answers. "I have no idea," she said, and took in the scene before her. Jackson Kincaid, Lachlan MacGregory and Connor Duggan sat next to one another in the huge massage chairs with their pants rolled up, except for Connor who wore shorts, getting pedicures. *Pedicures!*

Spa La La was packed with people and noise. David Gray's voice came through the speakers. Glittery pink streamers, gorgeous dahlia bouquets and balloons decorated the shop, Ruby's employees and friends who'd volunteered were cutting hair, giving manicures and taking donations. And a large, pay-for-a-plate table of food and drinks lined one wall. But the focus was on three huge men looking ridiculous *and* ridiculously smokin' hot getting their feet massaged.

Ellie had almost forgotten—okay, she hadn't forgotten, she'd tried to pretend she'd forgotten—that she'd invited Jackson to the annual fundraiser Ruby held to raise money for breast cancer every year since her mom's death. But Ellie expected, if he even showed up, that he would drink a beer, maybe make a donation and hang out with the guys. And by hang out, she'd never in a million years have imagined him getting a pedicure, let alone Lachlan and Connor joining him.

Unlike everyone else here, she was still dressed in her scrubs from work—at least they were pink to fit the theme—and she almost hadn't come. Things had been going so well with her and Jackson. She'd let her guard down, opened her heart and started to believe that she deserved the love of a man like Jackson Kincaid. Four weeks had passed since her apartment had flooded and he'd not only shared his demons and vulnerabilities with her but told her, *showed* her every day how much he liked her. He'd made his home her home. Her emotions for him overflowed, happiness, warmth, safety, lust—all these things she felt in his presence. She'd almost blurted out several times that she loved him.

Thank God she hadn't.

Because, last weekend, reality had slapped her in the face. All it took was Jackson asking her one question, and her warm comfortable emotions were stomped out by sickness, depression, self-disgust and, worst of all, fear. All her old memories and terrors broke out of hiding to taunt her. She'd sensed them resurfacing since the night she met him, but she'd tried to ignore them, bury them back in the pit where they belonged. Now she realized she shouldn't have. They were a warning she'd ignored. She did not belong in his life.

"Did they pick their color?" Natalie asked and giggled.

Ellie watched her friends laugh and tease. She couldn't even fake a smile.

"In the words of Lachlan MacGregory, 'Hell. Fucking. No.'"

"I think Lachlan's trying to impress you," Natalie whispered to Ruby.

"What?" Ruby hushed her friend. "Why would he do that?"

"Uh, because he's had the hots for you for the past year, at least," Natalie said as if the entire world was aware of that fact.

"Don't be ridiculous," Ruby said.

"Hello? Get a clue, girl. Am I the only one around here with an ounce of intuition?" Natalie rolled her eyes.

"He's dating someone," Ruby said.

"Maybe he thinks you're not interested."

"I'm not."

Natalie took a sip of her wine. "Uh-huh, keep telling yourself that," she said into her glass. "At least we can all agree on the fact that Jackson is head over heels for Ellie."

"True." Ruby sighed. "It's adorable, isn't it?"

No, no, no, you're wrong, Ellie thought.

"Here, you need wine." Natalie pushed a glass into Ellie's hand. "And these brownies are the best thing I've ever tasted, but nothing compares to that scene," she said and they all glanced at the guys. "Please tell me someone's getting pictures."

"Natalie," Ruby said. "You're married to your own hottie."

"Thank the Lord." She blew Gage a kiss from across the room. "But you have to admit, that" —she pointed toward the pedicure chairs— "would make one fine photograph. Maybe eight by ten, or larger. I'm not sure where I'd hang it. The kitchen, where I spend most of my time, or — "

"You're killing me," Ruby said and laughed.

"Hey." Natalie nudged Ellie. "You gonna go say 'Hi' to your man? He's piercing you with his come-hither look. Go, kiss him, then come back and tell us why you were late and what the hell's going on with you."

Ellie tore her eyes away from Jackson. "Piercing me and come hither? You sound like a historical romance novel."

"I do, but it's the truth. I mean I've never seen eyes pierce the way his are right now. It's like he wants to tackle you right into bed and keep you there while he does delicious things to your body. But that's beside the point." She poked Ellie in the shoulder and stared at her. "Don't change the subject. You've been acting weird for days, maybe even longer. Yep, more like the past eight days to be exact. So, what happened eight days ago?"

Ruby faced them. "Wow, you're good, Nat." She crossed her arms, studied Ellie and said, "I was thinking it had only been a few days, but you work with her. You'd have a better idea."

"What are you two crazies talking about?" Ellie said. She tried to play off their interrogation, but her skin always gave her away. *Stupid, pale, freckled skin!* She could feel her cheeks getting hot. Couldn't they ignore her and go back to talking about Lachlan's apparent infatuation with Ruby?

Her friends weren't crazy. In fact, she was the crazy one. She'd felt off balance. Worse, she felt sick. Ever since Jackson had asked her to go to New York City with him. She should have known Natalie would pick up on her nerves.

"Twice this week you walked by on your way to get coffee without stopping to say hi to me."

"I did not," Ellie said to Ruby. But Ruby raised her eyebrows at her.

"And," Nat began, "you've been weirdly quiet, like back-in-your-head quiet how you were when I first met you. Plus, that happy glow beaming from you, ever since you moved in with Jackson, seems darkened by storm clouds."

"I didn't move in with him. It's temporary," Ellie said and put her wine down. It tasted like vinegar. Her mouth felt harsh and dry. She hadn't moved in. Her apartment would be fixed in two weeks, and she'd move back home. That was what she'd started telling herself ever since he mentioned New York. He'd brought it up again, said he wanted her with him for a special event he had to attend. He kept saying he wanted to spoil her, give her a vacation. He'd pay for everything, treat her like royalty. She didn't need a vacation, and she did not ever need to be treated like royalty.

His invite had turned a switch inside her, and all her old fears flooded her gut. New York alone freaked her out, but attending an event with him, at the Four Seasons? *No, no, no.* She was not part of that life, those people who hid monsters behind their wealth and perfect appearances. She couldn't do it. The only way she could cope was to tell herself their arrangement was temporary. She shoved those atrocious memories of her past, along with her feelings for Jackson, into the deepest hole and pulled the cover over tight. "He's letting me stay there until my apartment is fixed."

"Ellie Blevins, you're being snotty and flippant. I have never seen you act flippant in all the years I've known you. Does *he* think it's temporary?" Natalie asked. "Do *you* think that?"

"You're the one who warned me not to go too fast," she snapped at Natalie. God, she was hot. Her scrubs stuck to the sweat on her back.

"Honey." Natalie put her brownie and wine down and took Ellie's hands. "I was worried at first. But I've watched him, how he treats you, how happy he makes you, how kind he's been to all your friends. Lord, he changed his mind about his billion-dollar development for you. That man is devoted. What has you looking like you want to run from the monster in a horror movie? Did something happen? Did he hurt you?"

"No." Ellie shook her head and pulled her hands away, wringing them out as if that would help her racing heart. *God, I'm an idiot!* She'd known from the beginning he lived a life she could never be a part of. What had she been thinking? "He's... You're right.

He's wonderful. But we're just enjoying each other's company. That's all. It's not going anywhere."

"Ellie." Ruby glared at her. "Don't lie to us. More importantly, don't lie to yourself. Tell us what's going on, honey."

"Here." Natalie pulled them out of the front door of the spa. "Sit down." She pushed Ellie down on the bench, and she and Ruby sat down on either side of her. "Talk to us."

Ellie couldn't look at her friends, so she faced her lap. "He asked me to go to New York with him for a trip," she whispered because she could hardly spit the words out. It took saliva to speak and her mouth was desert-dry. She could not go to New York. She felt it in her bones.

Ruby and Nat glanced at each other and back at her. "And?" Ruby said. "That sounds awesome."

"No." She squeezed her eyes shut. God, her head ached, a pulsing right behind her forehead, a sharp knife stabbing her. "I can't go to New York. I can't ever go back there." Her hands felt like they'd fallen asleep and were tingling with pricks of pain. She rubbed them on her legs. If she'd had any food in her stomach, it would have come back up by now, if the harsh taste of bile in the back of her throat was any indication.

"I have to go." *What is happening?* Not another panic attack. She'd had more panic attacks in the last six weeks than she'd ever had in her life. This one, though...it... This one felt different. "I have to get out of here," she said, and shot up.

"Ellie." Ruby tried to take her hand, but she tore it away.

"I have to get back to the clinic... There's a... I'm going...check...a patient...dog—"

"Ellie, something's wrong. You're not making any sense. We're worried about you," Nat said. "Please sit down and talk to us. What is it about New York?"

"I can't...right now. Tell Jackson... Tell... I...have to go." And she did what her gut had been telling her to do—she ran.

Chapter Twenty-Seven

"Well, I feel like a complete fool, and I never thought I'd say these words, but you were right, Duggan. My feet feel awesome," Jackson said. He took a sip of his beer and relaxed into the massage chair that dug into the tight muscles on his lower back.

"Genius, isn't it," Duggan said and clinked his beer with Lachlan's and Jackson's.

"I worry about the kind of info you have in your head, Duggan."

"Have I ever steered you wrong, my friend?"

"Not answering that one," Jackson said.

"Lachlan, don't know you well, yet, but what about you, enjoying your pedicure?" Connor asked.

"Fuck off, asshole," Lachlan said.

Connor laughed, and Jackson knew his friend was enjoying the heck out of embarrassing him and Lachlan. He hadn't known what to expect when he'd shown up tonight, but he had to admit he was impressed at the spread Ruby had going on. Her spa was packed and people were having a great time. As soon as they'd entered, Duggan had bet them they weren't brave enough to get pedicures. Apparently neither he nor Lachlan was a fan of being called a coward because here they sat, paying a few hundred dollars, or donating it, so a stranger could soak their feet in bubbles and massage them. Although all three men had shut Ruby down when—trying to control her laughter—she'd asked what color polish they wanted.

"It's a good way to impress the ladies," Duggan said. Ruby, Natalie and Ellie were grinning at them. Correction, Ruby and Natalie were grinning. Ellie had that veil over her face again. That fucking veil. He had no clue what was going on with her, but something had happened. Like an invisible snake had slithered into her mind and shut it down. Most of the time his ability to solve puzzles was awesome, but this time he couldn't put his finger on what had happened.

One minute she was opening herself up to him, warm and happy, as free with her heart as she was with her body. And he cherished both. The intimacy she shared with him. The little ways she took care of him. Calling to check in during the day. Leaving him notes on his pillow when he got home late. Wrapping her warm body around his every night. Like she was trying to infuse him with goodness. Fuck, she'd flipped his life upside down and cracked through the anger and guilt he'd been holding on to for decades. For the first time in his life, he saw an incredible future full of love and happiness. Love and happiness were two things he hadn't even believed in until he'd met Ellie.

Until last week, when she'd sewn herself up. Three nights in a row she'd worked late, which he understood. But she hadn't woken him when she'd gotten home. And she was gone before he got up the next morning each time, which also meant they hadn't made love in days. And she'd started answering his texts with normal shit, like, "Okay." Or a fucking kiss emoji.

Even after he and Duggan had decided to cancel their condo plans, and instead revitalize the buildings with the help of a historical architect, she'd still answered his good-morning texts with silly facts about the old buildings, or a cute story about a family who'd lived in the Corvallis neighborhood for generations. She teased him, and he fucking loved it. For the past month it had been like watching the most beautiful, exotic flower bloom while she came out of her shell and showered him with her goodness.

A switch had flipped and she'd begun to wilt. She was pulling away. He didn't want fucking kiss emojis — he wanted her ridiculous facts and data about how to apply for historical registry status, because it meant something to her.

"Hey, I meant to ask you, what's up with you and Ellie?" Duggan said.

Fuck, even Duggan's noticed. "Why?" Jackson braced.

"Yesterday she called and asked me when her apartment would be ready to move back into. I thought maybe she had a friend in mind for it," Duggan said.

"What the fuck?"

"Careful, man," Lachlan said. He took Jackson's beer from his hand and gestured to the water Jackson had splashed all over the basin and floor when he'd jerked his feet out of the soaking tub.

Why in the hell would she call Duggan instead of talking to me? And why in the fuck does she want to move back to her apartment?

He stood and got out of the tub and focused on Ellie, in time to see her through the spa windows, ripping her arm from Ruby's and running from her friends.

"Jesus. What happened?" Lachlan asked. All three men stood up, grabbed their shoes and walked to the front.

"No fucking clue," Jackson said. He pulled on his running shoes. "Natalie, Ruby, what the hell's going on?" They reached the two shocked-looking women.

"You have to go after her, Jackson," Natalie said. "She's freaked out. I think it has to do with New York. What's going on? I've never seen her like this?"

"I don't have a clue, but I'll find out." And he took off after her.

Fucking New York, he thought, racing after her. She'd beaten him to her clinic, but left the door unlocked, again. New York was the connection. That was when she'd started shutting him out. But no matter how many times he'd asked her if she was okay, she'd shoved a brick wall between them and changed the subject or said she had to get to work. And she wasn't subtle about it. It might have been funny if it hadn't been breaking his heart.

He found her behind the reception desk, sitting on the floor with her head on her knees, her arms wrapped tight around her legs. "Ellie?"

She whipped her head up and her expression was pure torment. All the color had drained out of her skin and sweat beaded her forehead.

"Jesus Christ, babe," he said, and sat down next to her. "What's going on?" He tried to take her hand, but she pulled it from his and scooted away.

"Ellie." His voice was harsh, but he was a boiling combination of pissed off and alarmed. He hardly recognized her. Little by little this week she'd packed parts of herself away. The sweet, the loving, the embarrassed, the laughter, the fire. Her fire was gone, and he wanted it back. He wanted it all back. He forced a calm into his words. "Talk to me. It's about New York."

"I can't go. Don't ask me to. I can't."

"El, tell me what is going on. Is it the flight—are you scared of flying? I know you don't like to shop. Is that it? I have a person there who can help you find a dress for the event, if you want, if that's what's freaking you out."

She shook her head at his suggestions, but she wouldn't make eye contact with him.

"I'll get my things...from...out of your house so when you come home, we can...we can... It'll be easier to go back to the way things were."

"You'll what?" Jackson stood up. He needed space. "What is going on? I can't help you if you cut me out."

"I'm not right for you," she whispered. "You want someone I can't be."

"Please look me in the eye and tell me that." He leaned down into her face. Her eyes never lied to him.

"We don't fit, Jackson."

What the hell? "How did inviting you to spend the weekend in New York with me equal us no longer being a good fit?" Jackson fisted his hands at his side. He wanted to put his hand through the wall. Maybe that would release the vise squeezing his chest.

"I can't do that life, your...life... New York... I don't belong there."

"My life? What is that supposed to mean?"

"All the pomp and expensive stuff, people with more wealth than they know what to do with. I don't need a servant to help me find a dress," she spit out. "I left that life a long time ago. And I'm never going back."

"Never took you for a snob." The words were out before he could stop them, and her shoulders flinched. *Good. Fucking show emotion.* Jesus Christ, what? "I'm sorry," he said and rubbed his eyes. "I didn't mean that, but I have no clue what is happening."

This was a side of her he'd never seen, except maybe a glimpse that night when they were dancing, and he'd called her 'easy.' Something was seriously wrong.

He studied her pale face and her blank eyes. She was full of fear, but he didn't know why. "Ellie, Jesus. Please don't hide from me. Whatever is hurting you, whatever is in New York that you're afraid of, let me help you. I will do anything for you."

She hung her head over her knees, and he knew she was lying when she said, "I'm not afraid."

"Bull," he said.

"Quit swearing at me," she cried.

"I'm sorry." He tried to steady himself. "I'm trying to figure out what the hell happened to the bliss we had, why you're shoving me away." He went from pissed off to begging.

"Not every moment is bliss," she whispered.

"I know, darlin'. Pretty certain we've both had our fair share of crap. But, when you're in a relationship that matters, you talk and lean on each other."

"You don't want to know," she yelled.

She's fucking petrified. "Yes, I do. I want to know everything about you! I want you by my side. I can help you. Let me help you. I want everything with you."

"You don't." She shook her head and looked everywhere but at him. Her face was rigid, void of emotion. She'd shut down.

"I've never wanted anything more, El."

"Fine... I don't. I don't want what you want...and, and I can't go to New York."

"Can't or won't?" he snapped. He lost it. She was lying and nothing he said made a difference. And the metal clamps around his chest squeezed tighter while someone slammed his head into the concrete.

"Don't make this harder, Jackson, please."

"Hard?" he rasped out. "Sorry, I invite you on a vacation and you decide to end this?"

She blinked and her eyes filled with tears. "Don't do that, don't throw your money at me. That's exactly what—"

"You're the one using money as an excuse to hide behind whatever's scaring you enough to break up with me."

Silence. And he realized that was worse than the garbage spewing from her mouth. He waited for her to speak, to contradict him. When she said nothing in return, his heart fell. Maybe she needed time. If he gave it to her, would she ever decide to trust him? He had to get out of there, before he did something he'd regret. Maybe he was having a heart attack. Fuck, even that was preferable to how he felt right now, his insides being torn apart. He forced himself to walk toward the door.

Taking one more chance before he left, he said, "You're wrong. That *life* you think I live, that pomp and whatever you have going on in your head means nothing to me. You, *you* are my life, Ellie. You're what matters. You opened the world up to me with your warmth and goodness. And I invited you to New York… I thought… I wanted you by my side at a fundraiser I started in my mother's name. I need you too, Ellie."

"What?" She snapped her head in his direction. And the tears were the last thing he saw, because he couldn't stay and listen to her shut him out. Instead, he walked away with the shattered pieces of his heart littered behind him.

Chapter Twenty-Eight

For four nights, Ellie slept on the cot in her office. Well, sleep was a lie. She crawled into her sleeping bag each night with Buffy on the floor by her side and Chewie tucked into a ball on her feet and tried to get warm. But sleep never came, and her body stayed cold. Instead, the horror movie of her breaking up with Jackson and him walking away played in a loop in her brain whether she closed or opened her eyes. The words she'd thrown at him, the ones he'd shot back. *You are my life. You are my life.*

The days were no better. She tried to use work to shut out the assault, but it was useless. Could a person call the agony of getting through the days *better*?

It was a good thing most of her exams were routine this week, because she was a zombie getting by on coffee fumes. Exhaustion and pain ruled her. Nothing made sense. She had no home. She'd thought pushing Jackson away had been the right thing to do, but now the emptiness and loss ate at her.

She shut off her phone Saturday because Natalie and Ruby had called a million times. Ellie had nothing to say. How did one describe that pain? Wretched? There was no way to describe wretched, no fitting metaphor. Her insides were hollowed out and the headache behind her eyes throbbed constantly. Even her bones hurt, like a malignant tumor was sucking all the nutrients from them. But, worse, once she'd turned her phone back on, the swift kick to her gut every time she studied the screen hoping it was Jackson calling or texting. Nothing. She hadn't heard from him since he had walked out. Not that she expected to, but she *wanted*.

Even though they weren't meant to be together, even though she'd shoved him away and tried to make it about his money, she wanted him.

Too bad neither Nat nor Ruby got the message that she didn't want to talk because they tried to gang up on her Monday. But the waiting room demanded their attention when a few dogs started a fight with a hissing cat. By the time they'd separated the animals, cleaned up and sterilized the scratches on one of the dogs and tried to calm down the owners, Ruby had to get back to work and Ellie was behind on appointments. After Nat left that evening, Ellie felt relieved she didn't have to face anyone who cared about her.

Being alone felt worse. Jackson was everywhere in her clinic. Images of him yelling at her that first night and Chewie peeing all over him greeted her every time she stepped foot in the front room. Her office, God. She tried to remember the feel of him holding her up against the wall while he pushed inside her and ravaged her body with his. She could still breathe in his smell—clean woodsy, sexy. It was last Friday night that burned into her mind, the anguish on his face.

He was everywhere she turned. Except he wasn't. She'd cut him out. She'd thought she was doing the right thing, but she'd never felt so miserable in her entire life, not even after one of her mother's rages. It felt like she'd cut a part of herself out and the bleeding wouldn't stop.

By Tuesday, Natalie quit checking on her. In fact, she ignored Ellie, and with everything that had happened—even the words *'You are my life'* broken-record repeating in her brain—Nat's indifference was what made her want to cry.

Tuesday evening, Ellie walked aimlessly around her clinic. Natalie called her up to the front. *Huh,* she thought, *wonder why she's talking to me now?*

"Someone's out front with a dog they need your help with."

"Oh." Ellie zombie-walked outside. The exhaustion messed with her mind. *Is that my dog in Ruby's car?* "What's Buffy doing in—"

"Get in." Natalie shoved Ellie into the backseat of Ruby's car where Buffy relaxed on the seat.

"Hey! What the heck?" Ellie said, but the door was closed on her. Nat jumped in the passenger seat and Ruby took off. Buffy nuzzled her hand, begging for scrubs. Ellie rubbed the scruffy fur behind Buffy's ears, still not comprehending anything.

"Buckle up. Chewie's in the back in his crate. Matt and Rosie are working for you and *you*, lady, are coming to my house," Nat said.

"Are you kidnapping me?"

"Let's call it a love intervention," Ruby said. "We're your friends who love you. We think you got your heart broken. We're intervening. One big fat love intervention all the way around."

"If you want to call it kidnapping, that's fine with me. Whatever gets through that stubborn head of yours," Natalie said.

"I don't understand," Ellie said, still not caught up. "All day, Nat…" Ellie blinked back the tears. She would not cry. "All day you ignored me. I thought you were mad at me too."

"I didn't ignore you. You wouldn't talk to me, and since Ruby and I had a plan, I wasn't worried. We're going to get you settled in my guest room and you, my friend, are going to talk. Don't even think of telling us anything but the truth."

"So, you're not mad at me?" Ellie said.

"No, honey," Nat said. "Worried."

Buffy slumped her head down on Ellie's lap and gave a loud sigh. Comforted by her precious dog, Ellie couldn't hold back anymore. She bent over, tucked her head into the comforting fur of her first love and let the tears come. "I think… I'm pretty sure… I messed up," she tried to say through the tears.

"Don't worry. Ruby and I are here. You're going let it all out and we're going to take care of you. We're going to fix that broken heart of yours."

Ellie shoved her face in deeper and sobbed because she was pretty sure even her badass friends couldn't fix what Ellie had broken.

Natalie was wrong. They didn't get her settled and let her pour her heart out, at least not immediately. When they got to Natalie's house, her daughters rushed Ellie and Ruby for hugs and had a million questions. Why was Ellie crying? How did Ruby get her eyelids to sparkle? Could they adopt Buffy and Chewie? And, if not, could they get a puppy of their own? Ellie went from crying to laughing in a matter of minutes. Not only at the silly cuteness of Natalie's six-year-old and eight-year-old daughters, but Gage Kovacs stood in the kitchen wearing Natalie's floral apron cooking. Aromas of tomato and garlic filtered to Ellie's nose and her stomach grumbled, reminding her she hadn't eaten in days, other than coffee and crappy power bars that tasted more like cardboard.

"I see you were successful," he said, snaking an arm around Natalie and bending her over in a movie-worthy kiss.

"I think she was too exhausted to put up a fight. But Ruby and I do good work," Natalie said when he let her go and pulled out a stool at the island for her.

"Ladies," he said. "Come sit, I have wine for you. Lasagna's almost done."

"I never turn down a glass of wine," Ruby said.

"Hey, darlin'," Gage said to Ellie. He gave her a bear hug and guided her to the middle stool. "My cooking's good enough to fix whatever is wrong."

"I'm not sure anything can fix this," Ellie said.

"That's where you're wrong. As long as that man of yours isn't dead or stupid, we have a chance. And I know for a fact he's not either."

After two helpings of lasagna, more wine, salad and chocolate lava cake for dessert, Ellie almost felt better. A good food coma could do that to a person, temporarily. Then Ruby filled the tub in the guest room, added a bubble bath and exotic oil combination and forced Ellie to soak. When she climbed out, there was a beautiful pair of cotton pajamas waiting for her. When she stepped into the bedroom, Natalie and Ruby pounced and dragged her to the bed. *Oh, wow, is this bed comfy.*

Nat and Ruby pulled the covers over her and formed a warm snuggle cocoon.

"I don't know what magic you put in that bath, Ruby, but it was awesome. And, Natalie, thank you for the PJs," Ellie said.

Natalie shooed her words away. "Quit procrastinating and tell us everything that happened, El."

Cuddled in a warm bed, full from a delicious dinner and a tiny bit tipsy on wine, Ellie thought she'd rather drift off to sleep.

"Jackson won't talk to us either. We know something happened," Ruby said.

Ellie sat up. "You talked to him?" She pulled the fluffy comforter up to her chin.

"No, honey. He won't talk to anyone. Even Connor doesn't know what happened. He was supposed to go to Connor's for dinner last night but left a message and said he had to work late."

Ugh. She was supposed to go with him to that dinner. Ellie had forgotten about it. "You talked to Connor?"

Natalie gave her a stern glare. "Yes. We're all worried about both of you. Now talk. We know you freaked out because he invited you to go to New York. Why was that bad enough to have you breaking up with him or him breaking up with you?"

Ellie closed her eyes and whispered, "I think I'm the one who broke up with him."

"You think?" Ruby said.

"I didn't argue when he yelled, 'You're the one using money as an excuse to hide behind whatever's scaring you enough to break up with me.'"

Ellie could hear *and* feel the collective gasp of her friends. She pulled the blanket over her head. Thinking back on that moment made all the wine she'd had tonight rush right to her head.

"What?" Ruby said.

"I did that. I... He... I told him I couldn't live that kind of life with that kind of wealth... I was a total bitch."

There was silence and when she peeked, both her friends were staring at her as if she'd grown a bright pink unicorn horn out of her head.

"Ellie." Natalie pulled the blanket down. "I think you need to start at the beginning and explain. Start with New York. What's in New York that scares you?"

Ellie took a deep breath. Then another. She didn't know how to talk about it. It hurt too much. But right now, the pain of shoving Jackson away, the wretchedness of it all felt worse than what she'd endured as a child. So she let it pour out of her. "My monster of a mother and a lifetime of her telling me I was ugly and irritating, or ignoring me, and..." Ellie paused and tried to calm her breathing before she whispered the last. "She also hit me."

Ruby gripped her hand tight.

"What?" Natalie practically screeched.

"You two, you grew up being loved. I didn't. I grew up with people trying to beat me down every step I took."

"Ellie," Natalie breathed. "No."

"I left the day I graduated from high school. I took all the money out of my account, bought a used car, packed a few bags, headed west and drove for days until I ended up here in Opal, about as far away from New York as I could get without falling in the ocean. I enrolled in the university, met the Heelys who helped me. And I started finding my way. I put New York and that entire part of my life behind me and I can't ever go back."

"I still don't understand," Ruby said. "Did you tell Jackson this? Did you explain why you couldn't go to New York?"

Ellie shook her head.

"Why not?" Natalie yelled, and Ellie flinched.

"Talk about it? No way. I can't. I…I've never told a soul what my mom did to me. She was, maybe *still is* a wealthy, famous model. I can't *tell* anyone, especially not Jackson." She covered her face and whispered, "She hurt me, emotionally, physically." It felt like knives scraped the fine cells of her heart. "I shouldn't even be telling you two. And Jackson, he wants to take me back into that life, and I can't."

"Okay, honey," Nat said. "There's a lot going on with everything you said. Let's break it down. I'm going to start with this— That man would never hurt you. He is not like your mother. You were abused by her. You survived, but haven't ever spoken about it to anyone. Not to your best friends, not a therapist or the man who is head-over-heels in love with you. You have lived through some serious shit and have *never* worked through it. I think him inviting you to New York triggered all this and you pushed him away."

"Like a volcano that lies dormant for years before it finally erupts," Ruby said.

"What?" Ellie asked Ruby, then looked to Nat. "He's in love with me? No… How could… Neither of my parents wanted me. How could he?" Her tongue dragged through her dry mouth, her head hurt, and she was tired, so tired of not feeling good enough.

"It's obvious how much he cares for you. And just because two idiots didn't love and take care of you the way parents are supposed to doesn't mean you're unlovable. We love you. Don't you know that? I tell you all the damn time!"

"Yes," she admitted and felt embarrassed that they had to ask her. She did know it, and she loved them back. They were the best friends a girl could find.

"And you can't bury stuff that shitty. It's unhealthy. I'm surprised you haven't fallen apart before this."

"I've been having these ridiculous panic attacks," she admitted.

"They're not ridiculous. Your body is trying to protect itself. But sometimes we need help to get through stuff like this, Ellie. I don't know anyone who could go through all that, bury it deep in the darkness and come out unscarred on the other side. It seems like being with Jackson has triggered your past trauma and this is your body's way of reacting. But you can't keep it hidden. It's going to get worse if you don't deal with it, honey."

Ellie leaned back into the fluffy pillows and took a deep breath. Natalie was right. Jackson would never hurt her. She felt it deep in her tired, aching bones. Her heart beat for him, her world brightened into gorgeousness when he was in it. She didn't know how she could have messed up so spectacularly.

"You're still afraid of her, aren't you?" Ruby asked gently.

Ellie burst out crying, because that was the truth and she didn't know what to do with that knowledge. "I'm stupid and afraid. Jackson was trying to do something nice for me, and I freaked out and lied and told him I didn't want him, didn't want his money. I'm scared of ending up back in that place, where she can still hurt me. And I screwed everything up, because I *do* want Jackson. I want to be with him. I want a life with him. Having it for these past few weeks, then being without, well I think living without him is the scariest thing of all."

Ruby and Nat wrapped her up in a huge hug and let her cry it out.

"How am I going to fix this?"

"You have to tell him how you feel," Ruby said.

"It's worse than you think," Ellie said. She took the tissues Natalie offered and blew her nose.

"Worse?" Natalie said. "I can't even begin to imagine how this scenario gets worse. Do we all need more wine?"

"Maybe," Ellie said. "Or chocolate?"

"There's my girl. You're feeling better already. Jeesh. You were ghostlike all week. We were so worried about you. I'll be right back." Natalie ran to the kitchen and returned with dark chocolate sea salt bars and the bottle of red.

"Okay," she said. "I think I'm prepared for worse. Hit us."

"The reason he's even going to New York is because he's hosting a fundraiser he created in honor of his mother, a victim of domestic violence." She wanted to share his whole horrible story with them, but she didn't want to betray Jackson's trust.

"No," Ruby said.

"Yes. I didn't know until he told me right before he walked out. I threw the trip, the stay at the Four Seasons, even the person he hired to help me shop for a dress—I threw it all in his face."

"He had someone ready to help you shop?" Natalie sighed. "That man knows you well, honey."

"I think you're right," Ellie said.

"Do you love him?" Ruby asked.

"God, yes," Ellie said without hesitation. "If feeling like a truck keeps rolling over my body right now is love, then yes, I do."

The girls laughed. "Love sure hurts like hell sometimes," Nat said.

"But what do I do? He hasn't called or texted. I tried to call him today and he won't answer my calls. I even talked about Chewie who I think might miss Jackson more than I do if that's possible. It feels unfixable, like he won't forgive me." She waved her hand in front of her eyes when more tears threatened. Maybe saving up tears for ten years hadn't been the brightest idea.

"Gage was right. Jackson's not stupid, but he is capable of being hurt. Maybe he's licking his wounds. Or maybe he's giving you time. You could do something big, something brave, something that shows him how much you love him."

"Something big?"

"New York," Ruby and Nat said together.

"Me? Go to New York?" she asked but already knew that was what she needed to do. "But how? My clinic, my patients... I—and all my clothes are at Jackson's house... I don't have a dress."

"Leave the clothes issue to me," Ruby said.

"I'll deal with the clinic. I'll cancel everything serious. We'll tell them it's an emergency and between Matt, Ruby and me, we can handle everything else," Nat said. She pulled her laptop over. "Now, let's get you a flight to New York City."

If anyone could handle clothes, it was Ruby. And Natalie could run the clinic alone. Ellie put her trust in her friends and, for the first time since Jackson had brought up New York, drifted off into a deep sleep.

Chapter Twenty-Nine

Jackson rested on the couch in his hotel suite watching the basketball game. The Knicks were up by twelve. His team was winning. And he couldn't give a shit. The sound was off as were all the lights. Bourbon sat untouched in his glass. He was listening to Ellie's message. She'd called on Tuesday. He hadn't answered because he was hurt, too fucking stubborn and scared, but now he wished he'd picked up. He wished he'd never walked out of her clinic that night. The fuming haze of her trying to cut him out of her life had made him stupid. Too stupid to realize she wasn't pushing him away because she didn't want to be with him, but because something had her so freaked out she'd drawn inward to protect herself. And he'd let her get away with it.

Now he'd had almost a week to be pissed. Pissed at himself, because instead of digging deep enough to help her annihilate her demons, like he'd promised, he'd lashed out and abandoned her. *Goddamned fucking pride.* Ellie was not the kind of woman he would let his pride get in the way of caring for. And he'd done exactly that. Acted like a wounded animal and escaped.

His phone had been off most of yesterday on the flight to New York and today while he'd worked with the event coordinator to help finalize everything. He'd waited until now, in the dark, to torture himself with her voice. Her soft, fucking broken voice, begging him to call her back, to talk to her. And if he didn't ever want to talk to her again, which she said she'd understand, did he at least want Chewie?

Fuck! He did not want her to fucking understand him not wanting to talk to her again. He wanted her to fight for him, but he hadn't given her a chance. And yes, goddammit, he wanted that mutt. He wanted everything. He should have ignored her bullshit about not wanting to be with him. He should have dragged her to New York with him, stripped them both naked and made love to her enough until she fucking understood how much he needed her, how devastated he was without her. That was what he fucking wanted her to understand.

God! He sat up and dragged his hands through his hair. He sounded like a Neanderthal. But he was going crazy without her, and there wasn't a thing he could do until he flew home. Tonight, when he'd finally listened and tried to call her back, her phone had gone right to voicemail. He switched off the game, got up to toss his bourbon down the drain, when he heard a knock at his door.

"What the fuck?" he said as he opened the door. And his heart stopped. For a second everything stopped. She stood there more beautiful than he'd ever seen her in jeans and an oversized sweater. Her curls danced all over the place. She gripped a suitcase handle like it was her lifeline and she looked vulnerable and scared.

"I...I wanted... Jackson—"

"Jesus Christ, Ellie," he said and he took a step, wrapped his arms around her and lifted her, crushing her to his body, and buried his head in her hair. "Jesus Christ, Jesus Christ."

"Jackson. I'm so sorry for everything." She clung to him as tightly as he clung to her.

"Shhh," he said, letting the door slam. He carried her into the bedroom, climbed onto the bed with her, tangled them together and kissed her. In that moment he vowed never to walk away from her again.

"Jackson, I am so sorry." Her voice cut out as the tears came.

"Babe..." He brushed the first tear away.

She closed her eyes and shook her head. "I was afraid you wouldn't want to see me, to listen to me. I was afraid you didn't want me anymore after how horrible I was. I'm so sorry, Jackson."

He kissed one eye then paid sweet attention to the other. "I know. Me too." He kissed her forehead and rubbed his thumbs over her cheeks. "Ellie, look at me." She opened her eyes. "I fucked up. I walked out on you. I knew something wasn't right and I should have stayed."

"I pushed you away," she said and her voice broke. "I think I had another massive panic attack and I shut down. I was scared to come to New York."

He braced because pain and fear filled her face. He'd fucked up worse than he thought. "What are you afraid of, El? Please tell me."

"I will. I want to tell you everything, Jackson. You know a little bit about my upbringing. It's hard to talk about. All these feelings of shame surge up in my throat." She buried her head in his chest. And her stomach grumbled loud enough for the entire state to hear.

Jackson chuckled. "I want to hear everything about you, I promise, and this is not me letting you get out of explaining. But for now, I think I should take care of my girl, feed her, let her sleep and spoil her since she dropped everything and flew across the country to surprise me. No one has ever done anything like that for me."

He kissed her. "Let's order room service. Then we'll take a bath." He wiggled his eyebrows at her. A beautiful flush filled her face. "We'll spend the rest of the time naked in bed taking care of each other." He kissed her again, long and deep, and she relaxed under his warmth.

"That sounds awesome," she said, the joy back in her voice and on her face.

* * * *

"My first memory of my mother is of her dragging me across the room and screaming that I ruined her life."

Holy fuck! "Babe," Jackson said and pulled her close in the enormous bathtub big enough for a party. They'd shared a pizza and cake, and although the cake was nowhere near as good as Ellie's, she'd eaten like a starved person. Now they were soaking in the tub while he washed her hair. They were relaxed and warm, but her statement jolted him.

"I spent so long forcing myself to forget my past. Nat and Ruby said that wasn't healthy, that it had to start coming up at some point. I think that's what happened whenever you asked about myself, little cracks started to form. And when you invited me to New York—this is where I grew up, and as far as I know, she still lives here—everything, as Ruby said, erupted, and I shut down."

"El, gorgeous." He breathed into her neck. "I am so sorry."

"No." She squeezed his arms. "I should have told you. I know you would never hurt me. I trust you. I... Something happened in my brain, like it sent a message screaming *run*. Natalie and Ruby helped me." She giggled. "Or, rather, they staged an intervention and forced me to talk about it. Jackson, I've never told a soul about my mother before."

"Here," he said, stood and set her out of the tub. He got out and wrapped one of the warm bath sheets around her. "Let's climb into bed where you can tell me everything." She gave him a small smile, which didn't hide the dark circles around her normally bright eyes. She was fucking exhausted.

He picked her up and she didn't even fight him. She wrapped her arms around his neck and leaned her head into his chest. When he got to the bed, he unwrapped the towel and gently pushed her onto the soft mattress. He pulled the covers over her. "I'll be right back."

By the time he got his boxers on, pushed the room service cart out into the hall and switched all the lights back off, Ellie was sound asleep.

Chapter Thirty

"Natalie."

"Ellie? You okay? Why are you whispering?"

Ellie stood in the bathroom, one of the most gorgeous she'd ever seen. Huge gleaming marble floors, an enormous shower, a sunken whirlpool bath she and Jackson had enjoyed last night and a gold and crystal chandelier that Ellie would not be surprised to find out was made of real gold and real diamonds. The large window behind her reflected the skyline of NYC in her mirror. Everything shimmered. And she was starting to freak out again. Jackson was downstairs and had said he'd be back for her in fifteen minutes, but she needed help pronto.

"Ellie? Talk to me. Where are you? Shouldn't you be getting ready for your gala?"

"The Presidential Suite." She could barely get the words out. When she'd arrived last night, she'd been more exhausted than stunned. Jackson had taken such good care of her. She'd passed out before she could tell him everything. This morning he'd woken her with his tongue, drifting lazy circles on her inner thighs, and all talk of traumas had flown out of the window.

They'd napped until noon and made love again, after which he'd sent her off to the spa. All of this should have been amazing, and she should have loved it. What normal woman wouldn't? To be wined and dined in one of the world's most expensive hotels? But her nerves kept resurfacing.

"Is Jackson okay? Did he welcome you the way I predicted with open arms and hot body?"

"Yes," Ellie said.

"Honey, you're still whispering, and you're kinda freaking me out. Take a deep breath and explain. You can't do what, the Presidential Suite? The gala?"

Yes! She wanted to scream, but she knew, even as her heart raced, that that screaming would sound ridiculous and irrational. She took a deep breath and tried to focus on Natalie and her own reflection in the mirror. "My dress. I need help."

"Okkkkaaayyy, is Jackson there?"

"Not yet. He's downstairs."

"So why are we whispering?" Now Natalie was whispering too, which knocked Ellie out of her weird, nervous, haunted memory place.

"I'm wearing the dress. You know, the sparkly one?"

"Yes, honey, I know. The one that was made for you, the one you were too chicken to buy, but, thank all the goddesses, was still at Nordstrom when Ruby went back to speed-shop for you."

"I'm not sure I can pull it off. I don't know what to do."

"Yes, you can. You can do this. You got on a plane and flew across the country to be with your man. Now, do you still want to be with him?"

"Yes?" Ellie answered.

"All right. Do you want to tell me what's really going on and why you're hiding in the bathroom whispering about your dress, which I'm certain Mr. Kincaid will die a happy death when he sees you in?"

"I don't recognize myself."

"Ellie, I saw you in that dress when you tried it on. Now, with a hint of makeup, your hair done and those killer shoes, I bet you look like a million bucks. You deserve to feel beautiful, honey. That in no way means you are anything like that horrible woman who shall not be named. Are you having a panic attack?"

"No." Ellie breathed. She wasn't tingly or over-sweating. "I think I'm normal nervous. I've never been this pretty before."

"You have. You *are* beautiful and sparkly every day. It's your kind heart that makes you sparkle, honey. The dress is an accessory to your beauty."

"Ellie, babe, you ready?" Jackson knocked on the bathroom door.

"Honey, that man adores you. Let him see how gorgeous you look."

Ellie gave her best friend an air kiss through the phone. "Okay. Love you, Nat."

"Love you too. I'm always here for you, but so is Jackson. And he is literally right there. Let him in. Let him in all the way," she said and hung up.

"El?" Jackson said.

"Yeah."

"You ready?" Was she ready to let him in all the way? She loved him. She trusted him. She wanted to spend her life with him. Difficult as it was, she had to face her nightmares. He'd taken such care with her last night and today, insisting that he wanted her to relax and

218

enjoy him spoiling her and that they had plenty of time to exorcise her demons.

"El, been looking forward to introducing you tonight. Need you, babe. You okay?"

Fuck! Now she was starting to swear like Jackson. He always said just the right thing. She needed him too and she wanted to be brave and stand by his side tonight during this important event for him. She couldn't deny him this and she didn't want to. She was a tiny bit nervous, but a lot excited. And she knew Jackson would hold her hand and take care of her. "Take a deep breath, El. You can do this," she said into the mirror.

He'd created this gala and auction to support victims of domestic violence five years ago. One more reason why she loved him. One more thing that made his heart huge. Taking one more deep breath, she opened the door. And anything she was about to say got lost in her throat at one glimpse of Jackson Kincaid in a tuxedo. Then she met his gaze and saw pure lust in his darkened eyes when he raked his gaze up and down her body.

"Jesus," he said, then let out a low whistle. "You could knock a man over with your beauty, babe." Ellie was a warrior goddess painted in some gold, silver and pink fabric that molded her perfect body and accentuated her curves like it had been made for her. Stiletto sandals, held on with small straps and made from shimmery stone in shades of silver, gave her several inches. Her curls were up on top of her head with a few hanging down to tease her neck, to tease him. He stepped right into her and wrapped one arm around her back where he touched her satiny skin.

"Wait," he said and turned her around. He placed his hands on her hips. "Where the fuck is the back to this dress?"

"Uhm," Ellie said.

He met her eyes in the mirror and gently pressed her hips against the counter. "You okay, El? You look like a princess waiting for her prince." Her wide eyes darkened as he pressed his body up against hers and nipped her ear. He snaked his arm around to her front and caressed her breast, feeling her nipple harden through the fabric. "So beautiful." He raised the hem of her dress and toyed with her ass. "So soft," he whispered, rubbing his nose against her neck then kissing her there.

Ellie whimpered and leaned her head to the side to expose more of her neck.

"Not sure I can let you go to the gala dressed like this." He moved his hands over her ass and pulled down her thong.

"Oh?" There was that breathy moan he loved.

"Have to fuck you first." He sounded possessive. "Want me to fuck you, El, in this dress? Want me to make you mine?" He kicked her legs apart and pushed her body over the counter with one hand and found her wet core with his other. *So fucking wet.*

"Yes," she said. "Please, Jackson."

"I'm clean, babe. Want to take you bare. You good with that?" he asked.

"Yes, Jackson, please hur—"

He had his zipper down and thrust in before she could finish begging.

"This," he said, caressing her back. "This body." He gripped her hips and began a furious pace in and out. "This is all for me."

"Yes, honey, yes."

"Not letting you go again."

"No, Jackson."

He reached around and teased her clit. "Want you to come on my cock."

"Yes," she screamed, and she pulsed around him, losing all control.

Chapter Thirty-One

Ellie was relaxed, that was for sure. She also had a flush on her neck from Jackson's hands and mouth. God, that man could kiss. Slow and soft. Hard and deep. Every way he kissed her seemed like the most amazing moment ever. After he'd helped her clean up, he'd held her hand the entire way down in the elevator and into the ballroom. Even when they entered, he didn't let her go. Jackson knew what she needed. The amazing bathroom sex had taken over any worries flitting through her mind, and now he hadn't left her side. She squeezed his hand while he led them to the bar.

"I'm proud of you," she whispered.

He stopped walking and glanced at her, and she took the opportunity to rise and place her lips on his. This night was for him and, whatever issues she had, he was making it a point to take care of her and she wanted to step up and support him. All her worries and past could come later. She put her hand on his neck to hold his head to her for a moment. "I know how much this night means to you."

He wrapped his arms around her and kissed her back. Then he leaned in close to her ear and whispered, "You trying to get me to play hooky and take you back upstairs and fuck you again?"

"Jackson!" Ellie laughed and stepped out of his arms. He chuckled and took her hand back so they could make their way through the people to get drinks.

The Jennifer Kincaid Annual Gala & Auction is huge, Ellie thought, taking in the ballroom.

Her beautiful man kept surprising her. And she'd almost missed this. Thank goodness for her friends who'd pushed her to be brave. The place sparkled, from the chandeliers to the candles on the tables to the amazing dresses the women wore. Jackson's mother would have been proud of him. Ellie swallowed back the sudden rush of tears at the thought of what his mother had had to go through, and that she couldn't be here to see her own son creating an event that raised hundreds of thousands of dollars every year for victims of domestic violence and their children.

She felt silly now, for her own worry over coming tonight. Over returning to New York for the first time since she'd escaped almost ten years ago. *Not silly.* She wasn't sure how to describe the feeling. She knew her fears and past trauma were not something to laugh about, but she took strength from him. If Jackson could create such goodness in the face of his horrible nightmares, then she could do the same. She had miles to go before she was fully healed, but she'd made it here and she considered that a small victory.

She'd met lots of people, they'd had a fabulous dinner, and Ellie had slipped away to the restroom.

Now she stood watching the glamorous people. A few danced. Others ordered drinks at the bar. Streams perused the tables of auction items. Villas in Italy, the latest Tesla, expensive wines Ellie had never heard of. *Luxury.* She didn't need it, but it helped for events like this that others desired it and had the money to pay for it. *Luxury, what an interesting word.* She smiled when she picked Jackson out of the crowd. All the way across the room and he pinned her with that intimate smile and heated look, all for her. All of him for her. She smiled back. *I've found my own luxury in the arms of that man.*

She weaved her way through the sparkling gowns. She'd been here before, among the rich and famous, the diamonds. For her, as a child, it had been her nightmare, her shame. Unlike when she was a child, now she held her head high. She wasn't that girl anymore. She'd made it on her own, and she'd surrounded herself with people who cared about her. That was the life she wanted. She'd carved it out for herself and, damn, it felt good.

As she rounded the last table, Ellie had been so focused on Jackson that she hadn't noticed the woman approach him from his side. That voice, a sound she would recognize anywhere. The sound of terror, and in an instant her calm and bravery shattered.

Still tall, still thin. Dark brown hair cascaded down her back in straight lines. And her creamy complexion—not a blemish or freckle to be found. *Perfection.* Ellie knew how much it cost her to wear that mask of perfection. Her addiction. But not her *only* addiction. Ellie saw the glass of champagne in her hand. Drunk. Another wave of memory swarmed Ellie. Her mother liked her champagne.

"Mr. Kincaid," the woman purred and plastered her body against Jackson's. "I've been wanting to meet you all night. The work you're doing for women." She pretended to wipe a tear. Ellie recognized that move too. "I'd love to join you in this endeavor. Perhaps we could go somewhere quiet and talk?" Ellie watched in disgust as her worst nightmare slithered over her gorgeous man.

Jackson unwrapped her from his body and set her away from him. Ellie bit out, "Mother?"

Jackson's entire body locked.

"What are *you* doing here?" her mother spat.

Ahh, Ellie thought, *how quickly the façade falls. Too much to drink already? Or a mixture of alcohol and pills?* Ellie braced for the abuse, for the smell of alcohol on her breath while she yelled. Her childhood rushed in and backhanded her.

"El," Jackson said, looking down at her. He had both her hands in his and she relaxed a bit with the soothing caress of his thumbs on her skin.

"Who let *you* in?" Her mother whipped her hand around, sloshing her champagne on her dress and the floor. "Get me a napkin, now, you idiot," she sneered at Ellie and stumbled on her heels, catching herself on the edge of the bar. Ellie stood in shock, her mouth open, her heart pounding like she'd had too much coffee on an empty stomach and the coffee was threatening to come back up. "Mr. Kincaid." Her mother's voice was sultry again. "She doesn't belong here. Call security and they'll escort her out. *Security*," she yelled. People around them had stopped in mid-conversation to watch.

Jackson wrapped his arm around Ellie's waist and tugged her close. "She's here because she's mine." Ellie leaned into his warmth, not sure if she could even hold herself up.

"What?" her mother said. "This stupid, fat cow? With a broken nose? She never did get it fixed, I see. Well, it doesn't make much of a difference anyway."

Ellie put her hand on her nose to shield herself as if she could feel the base of the ceramic lamp smashing into her thirteen-year-old face and knocking her out all over again. Jackson reacted like someone had kicked him. He let go of Ellie's hands and faced her mother.

"Bartender, I need more champagne, now," her mother said. She swallowed back the rest of her drink and slammed it on the bar. "My God. You should have seen her when I broke it. She was so upset, crying and crying, and the blood... I had to toss out both Persian rugs in the living room."

"What the fuck?" Jackson said. Ellie had never seen or heard him this angry. He stepped in front of her, his body partially shielding her from her mother.

"Jackson." Ellie pressed into him, trying to calm him with her own body now.

"Where is security? Security," her mother screeched again.

The entire ballroom grew silent.

"Get the fuck out!" Jackson yelled and started to pull away from Ellie.

"Jackson, no." Ellie tried to hold him back. "Please, she's not worth it." Ellie pulled around to his front and buried her head in his chest.

"No, but you are," he said into her hair. He tried to set her aside. *This man, her heart.* He wasn't running for the nearest exit to escape her crazy past. Once again, he stood by her, protecting her, supporting her. That alone gave her strength.

"You know her father left me when he found out I was pregnant." Humiliation and anger filled Ellie, another volcano ready to erupt.

"Did you not hear me? Get the fuck out of my event," Jackson swore at her mother.

"Me?"

"Stop." Ellie whirled to face her mother. "Stop talking. Stop. My whole life, all you did was tell me how much of a burden I was, how important you were. But guess what?" She pulled herself out of Jackson's arms and walked closer to her mother. "You don't get to do that anymore. I got away from you. And don't come here and hurt this man. You don't get near him. You don't touch his beautiful soul! You may have ripped me to shreds over and over again, but I built myself back up. And this man showed me what it's like to have genuine, unconditional love for another person. Something you, my mother, should have done."

Jackson's arms wrapped around her from the back. "Babe," he said. "Let me —"

"No." Ellie leaned forward, Jackson holding on to her. "You don't get to hurt me anymore," she whispered. All the energy drained from her body. She turned inward to his hard, warm chest and he picked her up.

"I'm so sorry," she said, realizing what she'd done. She'd ruined the most important night of Jackson's life.

Chapter Thirty-Two

"I'm so, so sorry," Ellie repeated over and over in her hoarse, ravaged voice.

"Don't apologize, babe. Getting you into bed. You were fucking magnificent, but you're wiped."

He'd never seen her face empty, ghostlike. And her body drooped like a ragdoll when he peeled her dress off. He untied her sandals and tucked her under the covers, made a quick call down to the gala coordinator, stripped, climbed into bed with her and made a mental note to plan another vacation with her, one fucking free of drama.

"Babe." He wrapped his entire body around hers. "I've got you. You're shivering. Fall apart. I've got you. Let it go. Let it all go."

"I ruined your night," she whispered into his chest. Her tears wet his skin.

He caressed her back and lifted her face. "My night was phenomenal until that witch walked in."

She tried to pull away, but he held her tight, caressed her head and loosened the pins holding her hair up. "I'm so embarrassed."

"Babe, you were fucking magnificent. You have not one thing to be embarrassed about."

"That was my *mother*," she said. And the anguish on her face made him want to find that bitch and rip her to shreds.

"You wanna know what I saw?" he asked her, and she studied his face for a few seconds before she nodded. *There she is. My light. My brave beauty.* "I saw a piece of trash who you might be related to by blood, but no mother acts like that. She hurt you." He tried to keep the venom out of his voice. Jesus, he'd almost lost his dinner when he learned how Ellie had broken her nose.

Ellie nodded again but kept his gaze. Her body warmed and relaxed against his. "I saw you hold tight, stand up for yourself, stand up for me in the face of someone who abused you, Ellie. Do you know how fucking brave that makes you?" He trailed his nose right along hers.

"Jackson," she whispered.

"You didn't ruin this night. You are what this night is about, to empower survivors. That was the most beautiful version of empowered I've ever seen. You are my hero, El. Jesus, no wonder you didn't want to come." He wiped the last of her tears away. "My fucking fault, bringing you here."

"No." She wrapped her arms around him. "Like I said last night, I was too ashamed to tell you." She smiled. "I fell asleep before I could get much of my story out."

"It's not your shame, El. She's the reason I had to burrow in to get you to see your beauty, why you always seemed shocked when I complimented you?"

He didn't wait for her reply. He could see her mind working it through. "You buried that shit deep, El. Had to, I bet, to survive."

"I fell apart at your gala."

"Yup, babe. You came face to face with your demon, battled that fucking demon and you won."

"I think I need therapy," she blurted out and wiped away the few tears that were left. "God, I haven't cried this much in ten years and all of a sudden I'm a crying fool."

"I'm thinking therapy is a good idea, babe, but don't discount what happened. You used everything you had to stand up for yourself and for me. Never seen something so magnificent, except maybe when I'm buried deep inside you and I'm making you come."

"Jackson!" He chuckled and held her tight again.

She snuggled in and said, "I won," almost like she didn't believe it.

"You won, babe."

"You protected me." She gave him a light kiss.

"Nope. You protected yourself." He took the kiss deeper. "And you fucking protected me."

"I didn't want the night to end like this," she said and trailed her fingers over his jaw.

"Like what?" He moved his lips to her neck.

"Me falling apart in a panic attack. You having to tuck me in again."

"You don't like me tucking you in, babe?" he rasped as she raked her fingernails across his chest.

"I had a surprise for you under my dress," she whispered, and brushed her body against his.

"You mean this?" he said, peeling the covers down. He ran his thumb over her nipple under the red lacy bra she wore. He leaned down and took the other nipple into his mouth through the fabric.

"Jackson," she said, pushing her hands through his hair.

"Or this?" He lifted and traced the edge of her matching lace thong which he'd already seen earlier. "Guess what?" he said, pulling her thong down her body. "Got two more days." He drew back over her and undid her bra. "With no commitments." He took in her creamy skin, naked and waiting for him. "To spoil you rotten." He leaned his head on one hand and watched his other one touch that body that was all for him, her hair spread out all over the sheets. She placed her hand on his heart. "You're beautiful, El. He kissed her waist, her belly button and listened to her moan. "Might not let you leave this suite. Might keep you right here in bed with me until the very last minute when we have to fly home to reality."

"Mmm," she hummed and roamed her fingers down his body. She wrapped them around his hard length and he sucked in a breath. "I think that sounds divine. You know what else sounds divine?" Her eyes were focused on his dick and the way he pulsed in her hands, and fuck but that was sexy, watching her eyes get heavy with lust.

"What?" he rasped out.

"You being inside me again, bare." And she smiled her siren smile. All the invitation he needed.

* * * *

"I had a good time, honey," Ellie said on the plane on the way home. They had ventured out of bed and out of the hotel on Saturday afternoon to walk. It had been a warm, perfect spring day in New York, and they'd strolled for hours, holding hands, window shopping, chatting. They'd eventually found a bar, where they'd cozied up next to each other, drunk wine and sampled the appetizers. Although, to be honest, Jackson couldn't remember what the fuck they'd eaten. All he cared about was how cute and free Ellie had looked in her white sundress. A sundress that had left her shoulders bare. And all he'd been able to focus on was how to get her back out of it.

"Thanks for inviting me," she said. They sat next to each other. Ellie had napped most of the way and now her head rested on his shoulder. "I know we didn't get to see as much as you wanted. Maybe we can go back someday."

"No way," he said immediately.

"Huh?" She raised her head.

He leaned in and kissed her hard. "Next time, no New York. Either a private beach where I can see you in a sexy bikini and make love to you with the doors open while the sound of the waves seduces us. Or a hidden mountain cabin, snowed in with a huge fucking fireplace so I can ravage you in front of it. And later, while we're tucked together under the blankets, we can watch the snow fall."

She smiled up at him and leaned in to kiss him. "I like the way you dream. Those both sound amazing." Then she pouted. *Fuck!* Her pout was cute. "Can we go now? Can we tell the pilot a new destination? I don't want to go home. Your trial starts next week. And I'm so over-booked. We'll never see each other."

"We'll see each other. I have no intention of letting you go. Do you ever think of finding another vet to join your practice? You could have a few hours a week off?"

She looked shocked and he braced. "I know, I work a ton too. I'm not trying to tell you what to do, El, I—"

"That is a genius idea, Jackson Kincaid. For the last year, I've let my work be everything. I love my work, but I think I also used it to hide. I don't want my work to be my everything anymore."

"Good, babe," he said and smiled.

"What about you? What are you going to do when the trial's over?"

"Not sure, right away. I think I'm going to help Duggan on the renovations for a while. Get my hands dirty in a different way."

"Now, that is a nice image. Maybe I'll come visit you at work. Bring you lunch. Make sure you have your toolbelt on correctly."

"Yeah?" he said. He unbuckled her seatbelt and pulled her over to straddle his lap. "You gonna help me with my toolbelt?" He pushed his hands under her skirt and found the smooth bare skin of her ass, and he was instantly hard again. Ellie gave him a constant hard-on. "Ellie, *fuck*, babe."

"Well," she said and licked her bottom lip. She undid his belt and drew him out. "I know how to unbuckle one."

She placed him at her soaking entrance and glided down on him. He almost lost control right then.

"Although, I think I need more practice with the actual tools."

"You think?" he said and rocked her up and down.

"Mmm-hmm," she said, moving with him.

"You already know what to do, babe."

"Practice isn't a bad thing, though, is it?" she asked, and her teasing smile bloomed across her face. "If it feels so good." He let her drift for a minute, his goddess, his mermaid, while he changed position a bit to go in deeper.

"Want a family with you, babe," he said, and she snapped her eyes open. He held her hips. "You want that?" She nodded.

"I want that so much," she whispered. He pulsed inside her and she moaned. And slowly, beautifully, she came, pulling him in deeper with her body until he couldn't hold on anymore either.

"Like talking about our futures together, babe," he said, hugging her to him as she rested her head against his with her hand on his heart.

"Me too, honey. Me too."

Chapter Thirty-Three

"And where were you on the evening of March fifteenth between seven p.m. and ten p.m.?" Jackson asked Anthony Lucciano across the conference room in the high-rise that housed Jackson's law firm. Otherwise known as his current hell. He'd been prepping Lucciano for an hour, but it felt like days. He couldn't wait to get back to Ellie, to their home. After spending the weekend with her in New York, the last fucking place on the planet he wanted to be was in the presence of a man who'd beaten his wife. *Christ!* The irony struck him hard. Two days ago he'd been raising money for victims of domestic violence. Now he sat high above his city, trying to follow his legal obligation and get Lucciano off.

"I was at the Annual Business in Technology Banquet at the Park Hotel, downtown."

There were hundreds of people who'd seen Lucciano that night. The man was nothing if not slick, making sure he had a tight alibi. His wife, Victoria, the victim, had been there too, at first. And the police couldn't pinpoint the exact time of her attack. They could only guess between eight-thirty and midnight. All Jackson had to do was leave the jury with enough doubt for a not-guilty verdict. Doubt was on his side. Doubt was always on his side as a defense attorney. The prosecution was the one with the difficult job of proving guilt beyond that shadow. But fuck if Jackson didn't find his job a sick kind of agony right now.

"When did your wife, Mrs. Lucciano, leave the gala that night?"

"Victoria? She wasn't feeling well. My poor thing. Said she felt a migraine developing. Such a wonderful wife. She didn't want me to have to leave too. She offered to go home without me. I believe it was after eight. Right before dinner."

"Did she leave by herself?

"Of course she did, aside from my driver." The freeze in Lucciano's eyes could have sliced through a lesser man. He wasn't acting now. "What are you suggesting, Jackson?"

The man had attacked his own wife and was upset that Jackson might be implying she didn't leave a fucking gala by herself.

"I'm not suggesting anything. I'm trying to establish a timeline of the evening. We've been over this before. State the facts. If I don't have every detail, I can't do my job to defend you." Jackson didn't even spare a glance. He kept taking notes and he moved on to the next question. "When did she arrive home?"

"My driver dropped her off at eight-twenty-five. She went straight to bed."

"You can't testify to that. The prosecution will object."

"Very well, she texted me that she went right to bed. I had no reason to doubt her," Lucciano said, his smooth voice back in play.

"And what time did you leave the event?"

Lucciano leaned back in his chair and studied Jackson. He smiled in that twisted way, a warning— *Don't fuck with me.* The temperature in the room dropped as he glanced at Lucciano. This battle of wills was fucking getting old.

"I stayed all night. Bored out of my mind with all the big players in technology trying to schmooze me. All these people who want my money, my investments. Everyone wants me. I'm a very powerful, very wealthy man. I hope you haven't forgotten that."

Jackson ignored his insinuations. "The time, Mr. Lucciano."

Lucciano smiled at the law clerk, Mary. "And what's a pretty thing like you doing working for a bastard like Jackson Kincaid?"

"Enough," Jackson said.

Lucciano laughed. "God, you're easy to play with, Jackson. You used to be fun. What's happened to you?"

"You were the one who discovered your wife, Mr. Lucciano. Is that correct?" Jackson tried to steer the conversation back to the facts of that night. His blood burned. How many times would he have to be in the same room as this sick fuck before he launched himself over the table and beat the shit out of him? Lucciano was the one who deserved a beating, not the innocent woman who happened to have been unlucky enough to marry him.

"Yes. Victoria, my love." Lucciano put his head in his hands and when he lifted it back up, the practiced look of anguish would have fooled most jurors. "They won't even let me see her, since that night. Some bastard broke into *my* home and beat her and this cruel system is punishing me by separating us. I can't imagine what she's been going through. All alone without me to care for her."

"What in the fuck are you doing?" Jackson seethed.

Lucciano plastered his face with fake surprise. "Why, practicing my speech, of course."

"All I need are the facts. Can we finish this fucking timeline?"

Lucciano smiled. "I know what your problem is, Jack, buddy. You haven't had any good pussy in a while, have you? What about Mary here? She seems—"

"I said *enough!*" Jackson yelled. He stood up, opened the door and barely kept his temper in check as he said to his law clerk, "Get out."

Mary didn't question him. She gathered her notebooks and left. No one could stand being in the same room with Lucciano.

"My name isn't Jack and I'm not your buddy. You do not harass my staff. You can't play me the way you play a jury." He put his hands on the conference table and got in Lucciano's face.

"How wrong you are, Mr. Kincaid. I think we're finished. We keep going over the same old details. I'm bored, and I have engagements tonight." Lucciano stood up and walked toward the door. "Is that blonde you're seeing not keeping your dick satisfied? What's her name? Ellie? You let me know. There are plenty of women who'd be happy to service a man like you."

Fuck! "We're done after this. This is the last time I do anything for you."

Lucciano stared for a moment, then smiled his sick smile. "Well then, Mr. Kincaid, you'd better hope this trial is your last win. Let my assistant answer any further questions." And with that, he was gone.

Fury raged in Jackson. He swept his arms across the table and sent all his notes and briefcase flying across the room.

Chapter Thirty-Four

"Guess what?" Ellie said in an excited whisper of a voice when she answered her phone.

God, that voice of hers. A kaleidoscope of layers and he fucking loved every single one. This one was new, though. "What, babe?" He'd called her the minute he left the office, which, since Lucciano had cut their meeting short, and Jackson's next deposition wasn't until the morning, meant Jackson had left work early for the first time ever.

"Braveheart got adopted, by somebody kind and good, Nat said."

Must be one of the strays.

"Jackson?"

"Right here, babe. Enjoying your soothing voice. I have to admit, as happy as I am for you about Braveheart, I have no idea who you're talking about."

She laughed. And he let that husky, sexy sound wash over him too. Let it calm his fear and self-hatred.

"Remember that first night you came in and I said I had been there late performing a surgery on a dog? That's him. He's a beauty. A boxer about four years old. He's been thriving. He never leaves Nat's side when she's working. Today a lady came in to see if we had any strays to adopt. Braveheart went right over to her and leaned against her legs. The woman bent right down and hugged him and started crying. Nat said it looked like two lost souls meeting."

Fuck. He wasn't the only one she worked miracles for.

"That's beautiful, babe. How 'bout I make you dinner to celebrate?" He was planning on cooking for her anyway, but he'd do anything to make her feel special.

"I'd love that," Ellie said. "Can't wait to see your skills in the kitchen, Jackson Kincaid." She'd started teasing him here and there and it was fucking adorable. Sexy as hell *and* adorable. He couldn't decide if it made him want to hug her or fuck her.

"Are you working late?" she asked.

"Nope. Done for the day," he answered. "Headed to the store now. Need anything?"

"Excuse me, is this Jackson Kincaid I'm talking to?"

"You gonna keep teasing me, babe? Or let me get groceries?"

She laughed again. "I didn't know you were capable of taking off early from work, Jackson."

"Never had a good reason to before."

"Oh." She sighed. And he was done.

"Gotta go, babe, or that sweet, breathy voice of yours is going to make me hard while I'm shopping for vegetables. See you at home."

"Okay," she said, and he smiled huge when he hung up the phone.

* * * *

They were lying in bed, after dinner, after he'd made her come in the shower. He was wrapped around her, spooning her while she traced his arms with her fingers. "When you said you were going to cook for me, I imagined you tossing steaks on the grill. I did not imagine the best homemade ravioli in a browned butter hazelnut sauce I've ever tasted in my life."

He tickled her side. "You think all I know how to do is grill? Isn't that stereotyping?"

Ellie squealed and tried to get out from under his arms, but he stopped tickling and pulled her closer. He'd had her twenty minutes ago and his body wanted hers again.

"Well," she breathed, she rubbing her ass up against him, and the mood changed from playful to hot. "You are pretty manly. Isn't that what manly men do?"

"No fucking clue what other men do, Ellie," he said, roaming his hands over her body and when he found her pussy ready for him, he slid two fingers in. "I like to cook and having you to cook for makes it even fucking better."

She arched back into him and moaned. "You can cook for me anytime, honey."

"Next time I'll let you help me." He removed his fingers and placed his dick right there at her wet opening.

"Please don't stop," she begged.

He nipped her neck. "You can wear an apron and nothing else." And he slammed into her.

She screamed. "So good, Jackson."

He pulled out and slid back in, while he teased his fingers across her skin, her nipples, the sides of her hips. "You're fucking gorgeous, Ellie. You like this?"

She nodded and moaned again. "Uh-huh. I think this is my favorite position. Or maybe that one you did in the shower. God, you make me feel amazing. I—" And she shattered in his arms. As her body convulsed around him, the motion pulled him right over the cliff with her. He let himself fall.

They stayed like that for a while, until Ellie went to clean up. When she climbed back in bed, he dragged her close again. Her touch healed him, and he was absolutely going to take advantage of having her in his bed.

"Jackson," she whispered before they drifted off to sleep.

"Yeah, babe?" He could hear the exhaustion in her voice, her relaxed, satisfied, quiet breath speaking in whispers even though there was no one else around to hear them.

"I love being here with you."

He kissed the back of her neck.

"I love it when you cook for me."

"Mmm-hmm," he said. He'd definitely cook for her more often. Maybe that was what he'd do when he quit his law firm, become her slave.

"I *really* love all our positions," she said. And he felt her sleepy laugh.

He nibbled at her ear.

"I love the way you take care of me," she said. "And I want to take care of you too."

"Babe." *Jesus.* She fucking slayed him.

"I feel like you and me, Jackson, that we were kind of two lost souls who were meant for each other too, who rescued each other." Too choked up to speak, Jackson tightened his arms around her. "And I'd be lost all over again if it meant I could find my way to you."

Chapter Thirty-Five

Something was wrong. Jackson felt it deep in his bones, like a heavy wave holding him under. The last time he'd felt like this was his ninth birthday. The day his world had ended.

'Dad's been calling. He's found us. Take care of your sister after school, but don't answer the phone. I don't know how to protect you from him.'

The storm, later. Lightning and thunder so close together. The phone ringing and ringing. Thunder crashing through the door. Not thunder. Dad.

'Jackson, call nine-one-one!'

The pop of the gun.

Jackson's voice, echoing into the phone. 'My mom shot my dad.'

Jackson looked at Lucciano sitting there, smug as ever, and he felt that same dread in the quiet of the courtroom on the first day of trial. A silence full of ghosts, full of foreboding. It hovered and buzzed like an angry hive overflowing with bees.

For a long time, he'd been many things — angry, driven, focused, successful. With Ellie flipping his world upside down, he'd felt joy, love, happiness as well as a surge of disgust at where he'd let his career path lead him. But fear like this was an old companion he hadn't met in almost twenty years. Today fear sat in wait for him.

Lucciano sat relaxed beside Jackson who stood at the defense table. The childhood memory surged away quicker than it had hit him. He sweated through his suit jacket. They were earlier than the prosecution. Jackson was always the first to arrive at court. He liked every advantage he could get on trial days. Every time the prosecution walked in and saw him sitting there like he hadn't a care in the world was a point in his favor.

But today, calm and in control were not to be found. *You can do this.* One last trial and he'd be done. He could wait for his partner to buy him out, but he was done working with guilty assholes who could buy their way through heinous crimes and out to freedom on the other side. Maybe he'd get back to helping people who needed his legal expertise. People like his mother, caught like fish in the plastic ring of the system when they should have been free. The only thing he knew right now was that he had to get through this trial, because he had a life to start with Ellie and their dogs. *Ellie.* Jesus, thoughts of her would get him through.

He brought his mind back to a state of focus. His body temperature regulated itself down from the inferno. He paged through the documents to his left and let the ticking of the courtroom clock steady him.

The prosecuting attorney walked in with her client, Victoria Lucciano, behind her. Jackson watched them. Nadia Malone nodded at him. He'd beaten her in court before, but she'd beaten him too. She was a force. But then his gaze met Mrs. Lucciano's. The woman had frozen mid-walk, her face white as a ghost. A face he could now see beyond the bruises and bandages and swelling, months after her attack. A face he recognized.

"Jackie?" she said in disbelief.

There was only one person in the world who called him Jackie.

"Sasha?" He could barely get the word out. *No! My sister? I searched for her. Sasha is Lucciano's wife?* He took a step. She lurched back, glanced at Mr. Lucciano, and all the color drained from her face. Then she fled the courtroom.

* * * *

"How in the hell could you have missed this, Mr. Kincaid?" Judge Temple demanded, tossing his glasses on his desk in his chambers where Jackson and Nadia Malone now stood.

Nadia smirked, and Temple railed at her too. "Or you, Ms. Malone? Two of the smartest damn lawyers I've ever seen in my courtroom and neither one of you put two and two together to figure out Victoria Lucciano was Jackson Kincaid's sister? Because this screws you both."

Thirty minutes since his life had been upended once again. It felt more like an eternity. Judge Temple was a good man, and the best judge Jackson had ever encountered. A kind man with a wife of thirty-five years, a wife he adored, six sons and eight or nine grandkids. Jackson couldn't keep track anymore. The huge, black teddy bear of a man had framed family photos all over his office. He was one of the few men in Jackson's life who, by his size, power and grace, had the ability to make Jackson feel small.

He didn't seem like a teddy bear now. Now, he was furious.

"Sit down, both of you, and explain."

"Mr. Kincaid failed to disclose, Your Honor," Nadia spoke first. An unwritten rule in Temple's chambers — women spoke first, unless otherwise instructed.

"I didn't know," Jackson said. He put his head in his hands, still reeling from the shock and everything that came with it. "My sister and I were separated when I was nine and she was five. We were put in separate foster homes. She got adopted and I never saw her again. I've been searching for her since I was old enough to figure out how."

"Italy," Nadia said. She shed her haughty lawyer tone. Jackson and the judge glanced her way. "She was adopted at age six. They moved to Italy. She grew up in Europe. That's why you couldn't find her, I bet. Not sure when they changed her name. Her adoptive parents died when she was eighteen. She's been married to Anthony Lucciano for five years."

"Didn't you see her before the trial began?" Temple asked him.

"Once, in the hospital. Right after the attack. She was —" Jackson choked back his shame and disgust and tears. "She was unrecognizable." He got up and paced the office.

Temple watched him. "Didn't think you took domestic violence cases?"

"I don't. Never have. Our father abused us. My mother got us away, but he found us. He always found us. The last time, she killed him with a gun she'd bought that week. She got sick and died in prison serving six years for manslaughter. The night she killed him was the last time I saw any member of my family. Until today. Lucciano's on retainer with us. I had no qualifying reason, as his lawyer, not to take this case. I've hated every minute of it, and now, I—"

"Now I'll have to call a mistrial." Judge Temple sighed and stared out of the window.

"Fuck," Jackson swore low under his breath.

"Although I happen to agree with your emotions, let's keep the foul language out of my chambers, please. Mr. Lucciano will still go to trial, but he'll have to start over with a new attorney. You're off the case, Jackson. Ms. Malone, you're excused. Once a new defense attorney comes to my attention, and your office is notified, we'll proceed from there. See to your client, please."

Nadia stood to leave. "I want to talk to her," Jackson said.

Glancing over her shoulder, she said, "I'll tell her, but you have to be prepared for her refusal. You were about to defend the man who beat her with a large metal object, kicked her with his boots on, raped her, strangled her then cleaned himself up in their shower while she lay there on the floor, partially conscious, bleeding to death. And that wasn't the first time she'd been abused. She's afraid, but she's alone, and I think for her, right now, alone is the safest place to be." Her parting words felt like someone had dug a knife in his gut and twisted.

"You're a good man, Jackson Kincaid," Temple said after a few minutes of quiet.

A strange thing to say to a man who'd caused a mistrial of the scum he was defending, scared a woman, *his sister*, half to death, nearly broken down in tears in judge's chambers and right now wanted to punch a hole through the wall.

"We go into law for all manner of reasons. I suspect from watching your career path over the years, you had a desire to help people like your mother. I'm also guessing, as young as you were when you were abused, and your life changing forever with the death of both your parents, regardless of how you felt about either of them, you carry the burdens of guilt and self-blame on your shoulders."

Jackson let out a breath and sat. Ellie had said the same thing to him. Judge Emmanuel Temple was probably the only other person in the world who could get away with speaking those words to Jackson.

"I hear you're done with law after this case."

"You sure seem to know a lot about my life," Jackson said.

"I know everything. This might be your last day as a trial attorney, but your duty doesn't end today. Many of your toughest moments are ahead of you. You will face both your client, who, no doubt with his history, will continue to act like the venomous snake he is, and, eventually, you'll face your sister."

Jackson swallowed back his emotions. "Yes, sir."

"But the most difficult task will be when you decide to face your nightmares and deal with them in a way that sets you loose from their harmful bindings. We cannot carry the sins of our fathers or mothers. None of what happened when you were a child was your fault."

"All due respect, Your — "

"Stop right there with the 'I-respect-you-but-not-really' bullshit," Judge Temple cut Jackson off. "The Boys and Girls Home downtown needs mentors, big brothers and big sisters. All kinds of young ones there from horrible backgrounds believe they need to carry the blame for things their parents or guardians did. Stories worse than yours, stories unlike anything you'd have the stomach to imagine. You might be done with law, but I'm suggesting you not let your experience and knowledge go to waste. I'm suggesting you use them for good. Now, if you'll excuse me, my calendar is freed up for the rest of the day. I'm going to take off and surprise my wife with lunch."

He stood up and grabbed his coat. "That's another thing. Find yourself a good woman and the world becomes a much better place. Sit here as long as you like. Good day."

Jackson sat in the chambers for a long time while he played the judge's words through his mind. Lucciano was livid, and Jackson did not look forward to that talk. His fears about Lucciano were shoved aside by the absolute horror on the face of his sister. *Jesus Christ, my sister.*

'*Find yourself a good woman.*' Jackson had done that, or, rather, she'd found him. Ellie and her ancient Rottweiler and ridiculous puppy and heart of gold. Unfortunately, he didn't know how he was going to face her after today.

Chapter Thirty-Six

Ellie was worried. Nat had said that the reporters mentioned a mistrial, but that had been at nine o'clock this morning. Now it was after five p.m. She'd been calling Jackson all day and he hadn't answered. *Straight to voicemail every time.* Ellie had never bugged him at work before, but this trial was one of the most important of his life, and if there had in fact been a mistrial, she couldn't begin to imagine what that meant for him. She needed to know he was all right. Even on his busiest days, he left her messages or texts.

"You okay, Ellie?" Nat interrupted her thoughts. Gage stood right behind her. He was picking her up on his bike and taking her out for date night.

"Hey, darlin'," Gage said, giving her a warm hug.

"Gage," Ellie said. "Where are you taking Nat tonight?"

"Nope, don't you change the subject on me, Ellie. You look awful and, knowing that today was the beginning of the trial, I suspect it has to do with that."

Ellie sat down and saw the worry on Nat's and Gage's faces. She had such good friends, but right now, she didn't know how to ask them for help, or if she even needed it. Maybe Jackson was still at work and couldn't talk to her. But all day?

"Spill it, girl," Gage said, taking a seat on the couch in her office. "Or I'm never getting *my* girl out for our date.

"I'm worried about him," she admitted.

"I bet you are, honey. Did he explain what happened this morning?" Nat asked.

"I haven't heard from him all day. Can't get a hold of him. He's not answering, not calling me back. He said he'd call me once trial was over for the day. My gut tells me something's wrong."

"That man hasn't called you all damn day? Jesus, but he needs major 'How to Treat the Love of My Life' lessons." Nat raised her eyebrows.

Ellie smiled at her friend, who never had one bit of trouble speaking her mind. "That's why I have a horrible feeling. You know how good he is to me. And since New York he's been even more amazing."

"I'm on it." Gage got up. "You two head to Lachlan's for a drink. I'll check a few places. Won't be long."

"What?" Ellie said, "No, I don't want to ruin your date. I'm sure he's working or has his phone off. I—"

"That shit wasn't good at the courthouse today. A mistrial for Anthony Lucciano is either a good thing for Jackson, or his worst nightmare. I know where his office is. He might be dealing with shit that he's trying to shield you from. Now, I know how tough both of you ladies are and you don't need a man shielding you from anything, but we men like to believe we're protecting you, once in a while." He kissed Natalie, said, "Humor me," and walked out.

"Whew." Natalie fanned herself with her hand. "My man is hot! Come on, let's go order wine and a huge basket of Lachlan's spicy French fries. Fried food and wine always help, especially if there are brownie sundaes to follow."

"I ruined your date, Nat," Ellie said.

"That man lavishes me with a life of goodness, honey. There'll be more dates. Plus, I love hanging out with you at the bar. I need to get a couple gin and tonics in you and you can tell me how good the sex is with your hottie."

Ellie burst out laughing. Nat was one hundred percent not shy. She was also trying to take Ellie's mind off the situation. "I'll stick to one glass of wine. The last time you plied me with fancy cocktails, I made a complete fool of myself in front of Jackson and I'm still living down the embarrassment."

She walked out ahead of Nat. "Besides, I don't need any alcohol to tell you Jackson Kincaid knows what he's doing in the bedroom. And in the kitchen, and in the shower—"

"Stop." Nat cracked up laughing. "Wait till I'm sitting down."

* * * *

Six o'clock at night and the office was still abuzz with activity. Jackson, his sore right wrist wrapped in ice, watched it all through the windows of his office. It felt like watching an action movie with no volume. A movie he'd seen over and over. A movie he never wanted to watch again. And he wouldn't have to. He hadn't even had to meet with Lucciano, because the man didn't want to speak with him. Instead, Jackson's partner Mark had taken over as lead attorney.

Not having to face Lucciano hadn't lessened the sick feeling in his gut. Unfortunately, his partner had to go and open his big mouth. '*Of all the fucking bitches in the world, his wife turns out to be your sister.*' Jackson wasn't sure if it was the words or the laughter his partner spewed along with them that had motivated him to slam his fist into the asshole's jaw.

Well, he might have ruined his chance of a good buyout price from his now ex-partner, but the punch had been worth it.

"You gonna sit there all night or get home to your girl?"

"Jesus, fuck!" Jackson turned in his chair to see Gage Kovacs sitting in one of the leather chairs by the coffee table in his office. "How long have you been there?"

"Question is how long have you? Heard court ended early today. This morning, as a matter of fact."

"You here for a reason or to wax on about my day in court?" Jackson needed to go home and talk to Ellie. He didn't know if he was scared or in shock, but the rest of the day since court had been like one huge out-of-body experience. Shit was about to rain down on him from all different directions. How in the hell was he supposed to explain everything to his beautiful, open-hearted woman who believed in his goodness? Believed that he could slay demons?

"Hurt your hand, I see. Punch out that sick client of yours?"

"What do you want?" Jackson asked, pulling out a bottle of bourbon, pouring shots into two glasses and handing one to Kovacs. This man was a good friend of Ellie's. Jackson didn't know anything else about him.

"Quit fucking around and go get your girl. Get on with your life. 'Cause you have a fantastic life ahead of you. All you have to do is grab it. Instead, you're sitting here stewing. Ellie, who's been trying to get hold of you all day, is now sitting at Lachlan's while my lovely wife, and date for the night, keeps her company so she doesn't freak out about where you are or what the fuck you're doing."

Jackson sat down in the other club chair next to Kovacs. Somehow Kovacs' temper didn't bother him at all. All he felt was cold and defeated. "It's not that easy."

"It's the easiest fucking choice of your life, man. What the fuck?"

"I respect your concern for Ellie, but one of the biggest Italian mob bosses in the city wants my body in the gutter." He stood up and slammed his glass down on his desk. "No offense, but you have no idea what this all means."

"I know a thing or two. Haven't always been a laid-back biker husband of a gorgeous woman and father of two beautiful girls. Ever heard of the Piťovci family?" Gage swallowed his bourbon.

Jackson stared at Gage. "The largest Hungarian mob family with ties in fifteen US states?"

"My mother's side," Gage said, as if he were ordering a root beer.

"You're fucking kidding me!"

"Who kids about that? From the time I could walk, I was groomed to be a part of it. Did my time. Hated every moment of my life. Got smart. Collected my own kind of information so I could get out and stay clean and away from that life forever. Good thing too, because the year I left, I met Natalie. Almost fell off my bike in love at first sight and set out making her fall in love with me. Haven't looked back since."

"This entire situation is fucked up, Gage. I was already leery of bringing this horrible part of my life into Ellie's. Now it's exploded. Who knows what the fuck Lucciano will do? We all know what he's capable of."

Gage leaned forward and clasped his hands together. "Here's the way I see it. He's not going to do anything. He still needs this firm to represent him, even if you're not the one doing it. He might be one sick fuck, but he is not stupid."

"And if he is?"

"You being with her is the best way to protect her. Can't protect her if you cut her out. You know that."

Jackson didn't know anything. He'd never been able to protect those he loved. Every single time he'd been faced with that task, he'd failed.

Gage studied him. "What is it? You're not just worried about Ellie's protection, are you?"

"I can't see, after I explain what happened today, how she could ever want to be with me."

"Why the fuck not?" Gage asked.

"Because Victoria Lucciano happens to be my long-lost sister."

Gage whistled and stood. "The reason for the mistrial?" he guessed.

Jackson nodded, waiting for Gage to agree with him and warn him away from Ellie. Instead, he walked around Jackson's office taking in the awards, the view from twenty stories up over the river and the mountains beyond.

"That is cruel. Must have come as a huge shock. It's a good thing Ellie can help you deal with this shitty day you had."

"What?" Jackson faced Gage, surprised at the easy tone of his voice and sentiments. "How can I ever expect her to look at me again? She brings nothing but light into my life. I'm covered in darkness and it keeps coming back. Fuck! I was about to defend the man who put my sister in the hospital!" he yelled. He needed something to punch. He was disgusted at himself.

"Did you beat Mrs. Lucciano?"

"Fuck no!"

"Well then that, my friend, is all you need to know in your heart. That's all that will matter to Ellie. Deep down, you know that shit." Gage started to walk out. "Oh, and, Jackson, the way that girl's blossomed, I'd say you bring plenty of light to her life. None of us are all light or all dark. And if we find the right person, that person helps us beat back the dark."

Chapter Thirty-Seven

Jackson had texted her to let her know he was on his way home. She kissed Natalie goodbye, left her sitting at the bar with two glasses of wine and half a batch of fries, where Gage would pick her up. She raced to get Buffy and Chewie from the clinic and headed home. The ride to his house was long enough that her emotions had time to swing the pendulum from relief that he'd made contact to worry about what had kept him silent all day to mad at him cutting her out.

When she pulled up to a dark house, her mad worked itself into a tornado. Why the hell *had* he ignored her calls all day? After their weekend in New York, she'd thought they were done hiding stuff. She'd thought they'd moved on to forming a strong relationship built on trust and care and lots of steamy sex. And love. She loved him and hadn't even told him yet. She'd thought he had enough respect for her to let her in, to let her know what was happening. Not only had he ignored her all day, but when he did contact her, it was with a text.

A text! Oh, hell no!

The dogs got to him before she even saw him. He stood on the back porch with the doors wide open. She let the dogs attack him with kisses. He glanced at her. "El."

"You're okay. Good. I'm glad you're safe. Thanks for letting me know that today by the way. Since I worried about you the whole damn day!"

"El," he said, walking toward her.

"Don't!" she yelled, surprising them both with her temper. "You said we were building an important relationship. One you wanted to last. I trust you to care for me, Jackson. I thought you trusted me to do the same."

"I do, Ellie—"

"You do? Well, that means not ignoring me all day, especially when something critical happens to you!" she yelled.

"I know. I… They called a mistrial."

"Duh, I know, that's why I've been worried sick. That and the fact that you ignored my twenty phone calls!" As fast as her anger had sparked, it faded. She was exhausted from the worry, the not knowing, the damn text from him at the end of the day. "You can't… Don't shut me out."

"I wasn't trying to shut you out, El. You don't understand—"

"Maybe *you* don't understand."

"Let me explain. Then you can yell at me all you want. I deserve it." He still stood on the porch but he felt ten miles away, not ten feet. She wanted him to come closer, but he kept his distance. God, how she wanted him to make the decision to close that gap.

"Okay, explain." They stood there in the twilight with scents of sweet, spring magnolia blossoms and damp rain surrounding them.

"Things were crazy after the mistrial. I wanted to call you, but I didn't know how to tell you." His voice was unrecognizable, lost and empty. His silence surrounded them. Fear crept in to replace her anger.

"What?" she whispered. "You can tell me anything."

In a quiet, defeated voice, he said, "Victoria Lucciano is my sister."

She blinked, almost unable to process his words.

Then he leaned against the deck fence. "I know it's a lot to deal with," he said. "I can hardly comprehend it, let alone stand myself right now."

His sister? "What?" she asked, the disbelief in her voice evident in the scratchy, high-pitched tone. "Oh, honey."

"Ellie, Jesus, don't you get it?" He sat on the end of the lounge chair, his voice full of scars. "I was defending the man who put my sister in the *hospital*. Who beat her to the point *where she was unrecognizable!* She still had a cast on her arm today, two months later. And when she recognized me, fuck, the shock and fear in her eyes… I can't even describe it. Then she ran." His voice sounded like glass shattering.

She sighed. No wonder he hadn't called her. He'd been in shock. All the anger drained out of her.

"Fuck. My mom, my sister, I couldn't protect them then and I sure as hell wasn't protecting her now."

Ellie walked to him, took his hands in hers and climbed onto his lap. She wound his arms around her back and put her hands on his face. She needed to get as close as possible if she was going to make a dent in his battered heart.

"Ellie?" His gorgeous eyes held all the pain of the world. She'd never seen such dark circles. *Haunted.*

"Shhh," she said, placing her fingers on his mouth. He looked as confused as she'd felt when they first met. *Good,* she thought, *maybe what I have to say will sink in.*

"Listen to me, Jackson Kincaid, and listen good. I love you, dammit!" She watched his entire body brace as if she'd hit him. But his arms clenched around her. "I am so in love with you, my heart explodes every day. It hurts. It hurts so much, and it is the most exquisite kind of pain ever. Maybe you don't love me back, although I think you do, but I'm trying to support you. I want you to trust that I can handle whatever shit happened today, whatever shit happens *any* day to you. I promise I won't leave you again, no matter what happens to you or me. I am sorry they called a mistrial because I know this has been weighing heavy on you. I am so, so sorry you found your sister in such a horrible situation. But you are not defending that man anymore, and, more importantly, you did not do anything wrong. Not twenty-one years ago and not today. I'm here with you, for however long it's going to take for you to get that. Like you promised to slay my demons. I need you to hand me yours. And you need to let me love you. I *need* you to let me love you."

"You love me?"

"Yes, Jackson Kincaid," she said. "I love you."

"Jesus Christ, but you are so fucking beautiful. You're made of steel. My strong beauty," he rasped out, tightened his arms around her and pulled her flush against his body. "Never thought in a million years I'd find a love as amazing as yours, Ellie." He caressed her back, pushing in deep with his hands.

Beautiful and strong. Never in a million years would she have believed those words belonged to her, but he made her feel that way.

"I love you so fucking much. Still don't know what I did to deserve you."

She placed her lips on his. "We deserve each other, Jackson. We fill each other up. We were made for each other. That's all that matters, not our pasts, not anything we did or didn't do, but how much we love each other. You are the most amazing man I know, strong, loyal, warm, compassionate, sexy as hell and —"

"Hard." He pulled her even tighter against his body.

"Jackson!" She snuggled closer, let out all the tension she'd been holding on to and swatted him on the shoulder. "This is not a joking matter."

He stood with her in his arms. "Not joking, babe," he said and walked her to their bedroom. "You, your body, your love, it affects me. I want you even when you're away from me. Love you so much." He peeled her shirt over her head, laid her back on the bed and followed, his body flush against hers. She loved the heat of him covering her. Her skin tingled like a hundred butterflies were kissing her.

"Fucking love this body." He unhooked her bra and tossed it behind him and kissed her right between her breasts. "Love this gorgeous heart of yours," he said.

And she nearly cried, her emotions overflowing and sensitive, but then he brought both hands up to cradle her head and kissed her, for minutes, for hours. She was lost. His tongue tangled with hers. He worked her scrubs and panties off. God, the feel of his big hands on her. "Can't quit touching this silky skin. Every part of you, so soft and strong at the same time. Fucking *love* how hard you make me." She loved it too, boy, did she love it.

Now she was naked, and his hard, jean-covered hips rubbed into her sensitive flesh, teasing her clit. His T-shirt brushed her nipples into hard peaks. She wanted him naked too, but she relished the knowledge that he could make her come like this with all his clothes on.

"Gonna make you come so I can watch you. Then I'm gonna make you come again. Show you with my body how much I love you," he said as if he'd read her mind. "Tell me what you need, babe?" He rubbed one nipple between his fingers and rotated his hips into her, agonizingly slowly. It was the best kind of lust-filled torture ever. He put his hot mouth on her nipple and tugged with his teeth.

"Jackson," she rasped out. "That. I need that."

He caressed the skin of her hips. She'd never known that spot could be so erotic. Everywhere he touched her sent sparks right to her core, building up an inferno.

He moved to the other nipple, flirting with his tongue before he grazed over it with his teeth. Then he moved up her sensitive body, rubbing his entire body over hers again. He nipped her lip and kissed her hard, possessing. Then he took her arms and held then down above her head while he rocked against her core, back and forth, the scrape of his jeans a sweet torture.

"Jackson. I need you. I need you touching me, kissing me, loving me."

"Most beautiful woman I've ever seen, Ellie," he said. She met his gaze, her arms still above her head. Her body relaxed, and she smiled, a smile she knew that bloomed with love for him. He stood and stripped, like he couldn't get naked fast enough. She wrapped her arms around him and with one thrust he pushed his way inside her.

"Oh," she sighed and angled her body into his, while arching her head back. It was too much and not enough together. He was everything. They belonged to each other.

"Look at me, babe," he said, taking his time sliding back out before thrusting in again. "Get ready. Because I'm going to love you for the rest of my life."

Chapter Thirty-Eight

"Hey, George," Ellie said and held the back door to the clinic open to let him in. "Raining hard out there tonight. You want to sleep on one of the cots in the break room? I've got coffee on."

"Appreciate it, girl. Like a banshee out there tonight. A river pouring out of the sky and the wind is relentless. Hate to bother you."

Ellie smiled. "You know you're no bother. Besides, I'm here overnight and I hate being alone. You make yourself at home, I still have work to do."

"Thanks, darlin'."

Ellie finished her charts and was taking notes on the way the new sutures were working when her phone rang. "Hey, honey," she said and smiled into the phone at Jackson, as if he could see her through the lines.

"Babe. Bringing you dinner and Chewie. He misses his mama and his Buffy. He's been like a lump for the past two days and glued to my side."

"That sounds awesome. I miss you guys too. I promise to find another vet to help me soon."

Since the mistrial, Jackson had started helping Duggan here at the renovation project, which was good because Ellie's clinic was crazy busy so she got to see him for lunch. And most mornings they came to work together, which she loved. She loved everything. A fool in love and she wasn't ashamed to admit it. Aside from the long hours she worked, everything was awesome.

Well, almost. Jackson had been unsuccessful at getting Sasha, aka Victoria Lucciano, to speak with him. The last time he'd put in a message to Sasha's attorney and had been turned down, Ellie had suggested maybe Sasha needed time. She hoped she was right.

"Be there in fifteen. Love you," he said. And her smile got bigger. Every Thursday or Friday, whichever ended up being her overnight, for the past four weeks he'd brought her dinner and stayed with her. Although, she'd prefer being in their soft king-size bed over the sleeping at the clinic any day.

"Love you too, honey." She put her files away and went to take the garbage bags out to the dumpster. Passing George, she could see him asleep on one of the cots and she reminded herself to cover him with a blanket.

Lost in a happy, tired daze, she pushed open the back door and had one foot outside when someone shoved her back with two hands. The force crashed her flat on her back, smacking her head against the cement floor. Pain shot through her skull, down her back, and both arms zinged from the force through her elbows. Before she could scream, a man climbed on top of her and pinned her down, smacking her head back into the hard surface again. She blinked and almost lost consciousness. *Scream,* she thought, but one of the man's hands covered her neck, forcing her down with enough force that she thought he might break her windpipe.

Choking, she brought her hands up, struggling to pull his hand away, and he laughed. "You want to fight me, bitch?" he whispered. Then he flipped out a knife, grazed it along her cheek, and she froze. "Bet Jackson Kincaid loves a bitch who fights. Mine always gave up way too soon."

Her stillness changed into shivers of dread. *What is happening? A monster is attacking me.*

"Such a disappointment to me how she'd quit fighting and cower." He trailed the knife down Ellie's neck. "Let's see what we have under here," he said. He slipped the knife under her scrubs top. Cold metal glanced against her stomach and she whimpered. Then he brought the knife up through the fabric and sliced it open in one savage thrust. His movement loosened his hold on her neck. Ellie bucked and tried to shove him off, but he laughed and slammed her chest down. She sucked in air but froze when he toyed with her bra and slid the knife over the lace fabric. "You wear this for Jackson?"

Ellie felt her stomach revolt. Tears weren't far behind.

"I asked you a question," he sneered and backhanded her across the face. Her neck snapped and her vision went hazy. "I don't think Jackson deserves such a luscious body. Not after he fucked with me."

Jackson? Jackson's coming.

"You know what happens when people fuck with me, sweet Ellie? I fuck back."

"Ellie?" George's voice came from the open doorway. "What the..." George lunged through the air and knocked the attacker off her. She scrambled back and watched them wrestle, the man momentarily surprised. But then he kneed George in the gut and rolled him over. "Get out, Ellie, go!" George yelled.

She scrambled to the front reception area, and had almost made it to the front door when the monster grabbed her leg and landed on top of her on the floor.

"No!" she screamed and tried to fight back. Blood warmed her mouth. He pinned her down. She felt the knife by her neck and turned slightly to see it covered in blood. "No," she whimpered. "You hurt George."

He ripped her pants down. "George your friend, huh? You think anyone can stop me? No one can stop me! And now," he said, roaming his hand over her naked back, "I'm here to take what Jackson Kincaid thinks is his. I'm going to fuck him up. He'll wish he was dead."

No, no, no, she whimpered in her head. "Stop," she screamed again and, despite the knife, tried to shove against him. *I'm not strong enough!* Ellie heard barking, angry, vicious barking. Buffy. Her bark became low growling and when the man paused, Buffy bared her teeth and lunged.

Jackson pulled up in front of Ellie's clinic and even before he opened the back door, Chewie went ballistic, growling, barking. The mutt's hackles stood straight up. He lunged past Jackson's hand that held his leash and raced to the clinic, barking like crazy. The inside lights were off in the reception area, but the few on in the back lit the scene in front of him in an evil play of shadows and light. Anthony Lucciano had a mostly naked Ellie pinned down.

"Fuck!" he roared and pounded on the glass. "Fucking no! You bastard!" He shoved his key in the lock and watched Buffy attack, grab onto Lucciano's leg and drag him off Ellie. Lucciano punched and kicked Buffy, sending her sliding away. Jackson heard the dog's whimper of pain. Filled with rage, he was through the door. He smashed Lucciano into the reception counter.

"You piece of shit!" Jackson yelled. He reared back and punched him.

"Warned you not to fuck with me," Lucciano said, calm, his words filled with menace.

"You're the one getting fucked now." Jackson's rage fueled him. Punch after punch. "You sick fuck."

"Jackson." Ellie's voice, raw and pained, came to him from across the room. "He's got a knife." He heard the word *knife* just as Lucciano raised his hand and lunged. Jackson caught his wrist and wrestled with him. Lucciano elbowed him in the gut and Jackson lost his balance on him for a split second. Lucciano took advantage, shoved his body up and rolled them.

"No!" Ellie screamed. Lucciano reared back with his knife hand and brought it down, but Jackson punched his fist into Lucciano's face, grabbed his knife hand and twisted, using Lucciano's weight against him, and he fell onto his own knife.

The bastard's face deteriorated from sick glee to understanding. Jackson shoved him off and Lucciano crumpled onto the floor with a knife sticking out of his chest. Blood seeped through his dark clothes. Adrenaline burned through Jackson. He stood and kicked him one more time.

"Jackson," Ellie said. He raced to her.

"Jesus Christ, Ellie." She'd crawled over and rested her head on Buffy. She ran one hand down her fur while the other one held Buffy's head down. Both hands were shaking. "She's hurt. Stay, baby. Shhh. It's okay," she cooed to Buffy. Clothes ripped off, beaten up and bleeding and she still took care of her animals. Jackson couldn't catch his ragged breath. He took his T-shirt off and covered her with it, dug his phone out, and called nine-one-one. This time he didn't hesitate when the person on the other end asked him to state his emergency.

"Assault at Corvallis Vet Clinic — 253 Corvallis Street. Need ambulances and police. Assailant is unconscious with a knife wound. One victim, hurt but conscious, and an injured dog."

"George," she choked out.

"What?" he asked, gently touching her back. He wanted to haul her on his lap and fuse her to him, but he didn't know where she was hurt or injured.

"George was in the back. They fought... I think he's hurt," she whispered. Jackson found George, unconscious and bleeding by the back door. "Jesus! Fuck!" he swore. The sound of sirens wept through the night.

Chapter Thirty-Nine

Ellie hurt everywhere. Every bone, every muscle, her head, under her teeth. God, the throbbing under her teeth, would it ever go away? It was like feeling her head being smashed onto the floor over and over again. Ellie pushed herself up in bed. The pain hadn't been this bad in the hospital right after the attack had happened. *The beauty of narcotics.* Three days after the attack, however, she didn't want to be doped up anymore. She wanted to be aware of everything, so she'd take the pain. A concussion, fractured jaw, two broken teeth that they'd removed, and she'd have to have a bridge put in. And the bruises. The bruises resembled a B-grade horror movie playing on her face and her back where she'd slammed into the ground when Lucciano had shoved her.

Anthony Lucciano was dead, and Ellie felt not one ounce of sadness. What broke her heart was that, before he died, he'd killed George, her friend. A kind, good man who'd tried to save her. Heartbreak and guilt hurt worse than her injuries. Jackson promised they'd have a funeral for George once she'd healed. George's death was another wound she'd have to care for. But she was learning one's heart could break in places and still function. Because her heart was also flooded with love and gratitude. Although it was a confusing and exhausting matter for her to understand the mixture of relief plus guilt plus anger plus love, it meant her heart was wide open. She never wanted it to be closed up again.

"Here, babe." Jackson came into the room with pain reliever and water, somehow reading her mind. She smiled at him, but his face was granite.

"Want to climb in and cuddle?" she offered. Their king-size bed was the place to be. Chewie slept on Buffy who rested up against Ellie's side, touching the length of Ellie's body with her own. Her brave dog was going to be okay.

And even though the emergency vet who'd treated her had said Buffy would be in pain and need lots of sleep, her dog maintained a vigilant watch over her. Where Ellie went, Buffy went. Same with Jackson. As much as she loved them, she had to admit, going to the bathroom with Buffy and Jackson hovering, along with Chewie flipping his body around demanding attention, got old fast.

"Mrs. Heely dropped pastries off while you were sleeping. Girls wanna come by later. Told 'em I'd think about it. Police are done with your clinic. Lachlan called in a crime scene cleaning lab to disinfect it. All your animals have been taken in by Bendel Vet Center in Norwood. And I made chicken and rice soup for you."

He took care of everything, was never a second away from her and cradled her at night. But that didn't mean he'd let go of his anger. From the tightness of his jaw and the dark circles under his eyes, she sensed he was hanging on by a thread. She wondered if the guilt she felt over George was anything like the guilt he'd carried his whole life and the additional pile of crap she'd bet he would carry over the fact that Anthony Lucciano had almost killed her.

"Honey. Please come lie down by me... I need you." He fisted his hands and sucked in a breath. "Please." She didn't care if she sounded desperate. She was. Desperate for him to let her in, to hold her tight despite the pain, because they were both alive and she needed to feel it.

"You're in pain," he said. His knuckles were white and his entire body taut.

"Yes," she said. His face contorted as if she'd smacked him. "But I need you. I need to feel you. You warm me. You make me feel safe and loved. I need —"

"He almost killed you!" he bellowed.

She couldn't help the tears. There were too many of them pouring down her face. She nodded. "But he didn't. You got there in time. You saved me, honey. You have to let go of some of that anger and guilt. Please. You rescued me. Please come be with me."

He shoved aside the covers, fitted his body in next to hers and gathered her to him. With his face shoved in her hair, he said, "I almost lost you. Fuck, Ellie, I almost lost you."

"I know, but I'm here. Shhh." She soothed him the same way she had Buffy after the attack. "It's okay. We're going to be okay, honey."

"Yeah?"

"Yeah," she said. "You and me and our dogs. We're going to get through this and we're going to have our beautiful life and that starts right now."

He held her tight and they stayed like that until Ellie fell asleep, warm on Jackson's chest.

Chapter Forty

"Hi," Ellie said to the woman who'd entered the clinic. "Can I help you?" Natalie was out today and things were quiet. Ellie sat on the bench by the window, basking in the sunshine.

It had taken a month for Ellie to get back to work. Her clinic had reopened after a week with the help of Natalie, Matt and Rosie, but there had been only so much they could do without Ellie, the vet.

She'd had a small surgery to fix her teeth. Her jaw and bruises were healing, but the worst part of her injuries was her concussion. That slick bastard frustrated her. She felt as if she was listing to one side, a one-man sailboat in a storm, and it made her seasick. Dizzy and nauseated at the same time was worse than wrestling an angry cat into a crate. The last two days she'd felt better and Jackson had let her go to work for a few hours. He was not happy, and he made certain she knew he was in fact *letting* her. She humored him because he was still tender and pissed off over the entire thing and because, in the end, she got her way.

The woman's huge brown and white boxer tugged at the leash to get to Ellie and her eyes got wide. "Braveheart?" The dog sat. Ellie knelt and let him slobber kisses all over her face. He lifted his paw, which she took. "Buddy, I almost didn't recognize you. You look amazing. So healthy. And you're huge." She rubbed the side of his head and when he'd had enough, he turned and went to sit right next to his owner, leaning his body into hers. Ellie looked from the dog up into the woman's face with a huge smile. "He — Oh, my God," Ellie gasped when her gaze met the woman's deep blue-green eyes that were an exact match for Jackson's. She stood up. "You're Sasha?"

"I... Yes, I mean I'm..." The woman glanced back and forth from the door to Ellie for a minute. "That used to be my name. I've been Victoria for a long... I... I'm not certain who I am really. Not anymore." She ran her hand down Braveheart's head and rubbed behind his ear.

Ellie couldn't imagine what this woman was going through. And she didn't have a clue why she was here. "Do you want to sit?" She gestured to the bench. "Would you like coffee?"

"No coffee." She shook her head. But she did sit. Carefully, Ellie sat next to her. "I wanted to see you. You're Ellie?"

"Yes."

"You, ah... You're with Jackson?"

Ellie nodded.

"My husband hurt you," she started. "I'm so sorry. I —" The attack had been all over the news. The kind of story that drew reporters from everywhere like rats to decomposed garbage.

"No," Ellie said, reaching out her hand and placing it next to Sasha's. "It's not your fault." Sasha glanced at Ellie's hand and, after a minute, gripped it tight.

"I'm glad he's dead." Sasha squeezed her eyes shut and nodded. "I don't know how I would have gone on, if he...with him still alive. The prosecution had me hidden. But until I heard he was dead, I knew in my heart he'd find me and kill me." She appeared to be swallowing back tears and ran her hand over Braveheart. "Do you think Jackson still wants to talk to me?" She glanced at Ellie. "I know he wanted to or tried to, but I..." She let out a long breath. "Well, I feel like it's safe now."

"Yes." Ellie smiled at her. "I know he does. He's been searching for you for a long time."

Sasha nodded. "That's what my attorney said. You know, I..." She swallowed and got so quiet, Ellie barely heard her. "I never searched for him. Not once. I thought everyone I cared about left me. And when I got adopted and we moved to Italy, I had a new life, a new country, a new language, and I never once looked back."

"You were young—any child might have acted the same. I understand a little. I left a horrible life behind me and started over too," Ellie said.

"You did?"

"Yes. And I'd do it again in a heartbeat to survive. We do what we have to to survive."

This time Sasha nodded. She set the leash down and wiped the tears that had fallen on her cheeks.

"But I also know the past never stays buried."

Sasha let out a cross between a huff and a laugh. "No, it doesn't, does it?"

"Jackson is working up the street. Would you like me to get him?" Ellie said. Sasha's face blanched. "Maybe he could meet you in the park with our dogs. I could come too if you want."

Sasha gazed out of the window for a few minutes in silence, then back at Ellie. "Okay, maybe I'll go down now, and you can...you can come in a few minutes."

Ellie smiled. "Yes. We'll do that."

"We'll be at the end by the river," she said right before she walked out of the door.

"Jackson, I need you to bring the dogs and come down here right now," Ellie squealed into the phone.

"El, you okay?"

She sighed. She was going to have to be more careful with him. Everything put him on high alert when it came to her these days.

"Yeah, honey. I'm good. Please get the dogs and come down here."

"Be there in five. Love you," he said and hung up.

"Rosie, I'm going to take a walk with Jackson."

"Okay!" Rosie called from the back.

Ellie waited outside for her loves and saw not only Jackson, Buffy and Chewie coming her way—Chewie still trying to bust out of his leash—but also Duggan and his puppy, Kitten. Unlike Chewie, she seemed content to walk right next to Duggan as if she'd aced doggy training and was bragging about it.

"What are you doing here?" she asked Duggan.

"Gosh, darlin', it's nice to see you too." Duggan laughed.

"Sorry," she said, waving her hands in her face. "You know I adore you. But you can't come with us."

"What's going on, babe?" Jackson asked. He had on dusty boots, jeans and a work shirt with the sleeves rolled up. His longer hair curled over his neck and he'd let his beard fill in a little. All that, mixed with the way his skin had darkened from the summer sun, and she wanted to jump him right then. Or maybe not with her head all wonky, but she could lean into him and he could carry her away. *Ahh, dreamy.* She lassoed in her lusty thoughts.

"Babe?" he prompted again with his hand on her hip, which sucked her out of her hazy daydream.

"You have to promise me you'll be calm," she said.

"Babe, what is going on?" He lost his patience quickly these days.

"Your sister's here." She stepped in close to him to press her body against his.

"What?" He snapped his head up, looking around.

She wrapped her arms around him. "She came in a few minutes ago with her dog. Remember the one who was adopted by a woman who'd also been hurt? The two lost souls?"

"Yes," he answered.

"It was her. Your sister adopted Braveheart. She wants to meet us in the park with the dogs."

"Safe place," he said, and she nodded her understanding.

"Listen to me. I don't think she's afraid of seeing you because you were Lucciano's lawyer, at least not anymore. I think she's worried because she never tried to find you, and it's been so long." An entire story played out on his face, confusion, surprise, understanding. She pulled him closer. "She wants to talk to you. Let's go talk to your sister, okay?"

"Yeah," he forced out, took her hand and headed for the park. Duggan and Kitten followed.

"Duggan," Ellie said, "you can't come, she's — "

"Not gonna scare her, Ellie. Me and my girl won't get close. I'll be there in case Jackson needs me."

"All right," Ellie said and smiled, grateful for the fact that she was surrounded by love. She felt damn lucky that she'd found Jackson. Someone who cherished her and showed her every single day. And she was grateful to know Duggan also had their backs and wasn't afraid to let them both know how important they were to him. They were family, the best kind, and she couldn't wait to get on with this precious life surrounded by people she loved.

Epilogue

Damn! He loved this yard. End of summer. His favorite time in this city. Hot and dry, a deep blue sky above. Healthy, freshly mowed grass. Flowerpots lined the deck. A deck filled with low, take-a-load-off outdoor furniture. Ellie had planted rose bushes along one side of the yard. They'd gone crazy climbing up the fence and Ellie cut buds every morning and placed them in vases around the house.

Today they were having a party. People spilled out from the living room onto the deck and mingled in the back yard. He finished flipping the chicken and corn, shut the grill lid and took a sip of his beer.

"What's the verdict?" Lachlan asked.

"I like it," Jackson said, sipping Lachlan's newest brew.

"Too fucking hoppy for me," Gage said. "Can't you make a beer that tastes like a beer?" Lachlan opened the cooler and handed Gage a Budweiser. A man of extreme contradictions, in the kitchen Kovacs could whip up a beef Wellington or soufflé blindfolded, and his knowledge of wine rivaled that of a sommelier. But he liked his beer simple and cold.

All three men glanced over when they heard laughter coming from one of the sofas on the deck. Natalie and Katie sat on either side of Sasha and all three must have found something hilarious. Nat and Katie let loose their laughter. Sasha, not quite, but she smiled. *Progress.* There had been a point when he'd thought he'd never see his sister again. And now she was in his life for good, hanging out, coming over for dinner. One more thing he had Ellie to thank for.

Ruby sat in a chair next to the other ladies and was braiding Molly's hair. Behind them in the doorway to the inside, Clare and Mrs. Heely stood chatting. Mr. Heely sat in one of the oversized chairs while Nat's youngest read him a book.

In the yard, Duggan tried to teach a gaggle of kids how to play soccer. As usual, the dogs were trying to play too, except for Buffy. She was with Ellie, who was late to the party. But Jackson smiled because he'd planned it this way on purpose. This way she wouldn't have to set anything up after her morning at work. She'd be surprised. It wasn't her birthday and it wasn't a surprise party. It was so much more.

Finally, Ellie thought and took a sip of her decaf caramel iced latte. She'd just heard from the new vet who'd accepted her offer to be partners. Even better, the woman had agreed to start on Monday. She couldn't wait to tell Jackson. He was going to be relieved and happy that she'd cut her hours. And *she* was happy, because she wanted to spend more time with him.

She'd been seeing a counselor once a week since she had returned from New York and it was good, but it also brought up a lot of ugly stuff. Her therapist was a big proponent of self-care, and Ellie agreed. And for her, self-care meant lots of pedicures with her girlfriends and being tucked into Jackson's side. Plus, he liked having her near. It was a win-win. He was healing too, because he'd decided to see his own counselor. As shocked as she'd been when he told her, she'd wrapped herself around him and said, *'Good, honey.'* Just because the past never stayed buried didn't mean it had to control them. They both needed help healing and learning how to deal with their emotions.

Now it was Friday. She didn't have to work again until Monday and she got to enjoy a cookout with all her friends and family. And she could not wait. As she pulled down their driveway, she blinked in shock. "What is going on, Buffy?" she asked her dog who was snoring in the back of her SUV.

Jackson walked out of the front door to meet her. He helped Buffy out of the car then came around to her. "Hi." She smiled up at him. "Everybody's already here," she said.

He didn't answer right away. Instead, he smirked, grabbed her around the waist and kissed the breath right out of her. "Yep," he said, his lips still against hers.

"Why?" she asked back, smiling again. She loved him this close, this playful, this relaxed. It had taken months for him to relax around her again, unless they were making love, and even that had a gentle intensity to it every time. Now, he still liked to be close to her, which was fine by her, but he wasn't nervous-angry hovering anymore.

"Didn't want you to have to worry about getting everything ready. Wanted to do it for you."

"You love me?" she said playfully.

"More every day, babe." She loved when he said that. It never got old.

"I'm still in my scrubs," she said and scrunched up her nose.

"Go change. I'll get you a drink and meet you out back."

"You know what I'm craving? The biggest, coldest glass of lemonade you can find."

He touched his nose to hers. That was another thing he did a lot, caress her nose, her broken, once-a-source-of-shame nose. "On it."

She changed into a pretty floral sundress Natalie and Ruby had helped her find last weekend. Sleeveless and gathered along her chest, it flared out at her waist. Cute and comfortable. She paired it with bare feet, her favorite on these summer evenings. She loved how the cool grass felt tickling her toes.

After she'd greeted everyone, she wandered over to Jackson by one of her huge rose bushes. He handed her an ice-cold lemonade. "Perfect," she sighed after she took a huge sip. Jackson stood behind her, wrapped his arms around her middle and leaned his head down on her shoulder.

"Love this back yard, babe."

Ellie gazed at their yard full of people and animals they loved. "That boy is forever going to be a goofball, isn't he?" She pointed to Chewie who was toe-tapping a tennis ball up in the air right in Buffy's face, trying to annoy her into playing.

"It's a good thing he's cute. He knocked down more of your poppies this morning."

She laughed. "At this point, I think I'm over the poppies. He can have that win." The air warmed her, and she was surrounded by love.

"Maybe we should add one more to the bunch?" Ellie said.

He kissed her neck and chuckled. "Whatever you want, babe."

She turned in his arms to face him. "I'm not the only one who's easy."

"What?" His smile animated his whole face as though he was seeing her for the first time or falling in love with her all over again. She couldn't help it — she leaned in closer to him, loved feeling their bodies touching.

"You agreed to adding another slice of hilarity to our lives without me having to beg. And it didn't even take me a month to convince you not to tear down my buildings."

He tickled her side and she giggled and struggled to get away from him. "What was it, my extensive knowledge of nineteenth-century Victorian architecture?"

He trailed his fingers over her shoulders and down her back. "Couldn't give a fuck about the architecture, babe."

"Jackson!" She laughed.

"Serious, babe. It wasn't any of that. Just you sharing your goodness and your community with me. Had a taste. I was hooked." He linked his hands around her.

"Really?" she said, her eyes getting shiny. "When were you hooked?"

"That first morning in the park, when I had to untangle you from the pups and you bought George a coffee and sat with him."

"Honey," she whispered, "that was only the second encounter we had."

He brushed her hair aside. "You're right. It was the night before when Chewie fell asleep in your neck after he peed all over me. Think I was in love that night."

Her words lodged in her throat, and she knew he wasn't teasing because his eyes told her his words were his truth. Then he placed his full lips on hers, one lingering kiss. A kiss that said she was precious and he aimed to take care of her.

"So," she said. "I don't want another dog." She paused and watched his expression. "I was thinking of a baby." He stiffened and tugged her even closer. "Surprise," she whispered and twinkled big happy eyes at him.

He stared at her for a moment then he threw his head back and laughed. Then he kissed her hard, hugged her and laughed again.

"Jackson," she said, caught up in his excitement. He let her go and took a step back.

"What happened? Did I miss it? Did he do it already?" Natalie yelled, walking onto the back deck.

"Huh?" Ellie said.

"Shhh." Several people shushed Natalie and when Ellie looked back at Jackson, he was holding open a small box with a ring in front of her. "Surprise," he said and winked.

"Oh!" Ellie said. And she couldn't stop the tears. It was breathtaking, a shimmering oval emerald surrounded by tiny diamonds in a rose-gold setting and rose-gold band.

He wrapped one arm around her and devoured her mouth in a kiss that took her breath away. When he pulled away, he said, "You are the life I want to live,

Ellie. You are everything to me. Your beauty, your fire, your generosity, your love. Will you spend the rest of your life with me and let me love you?"

She nodded and jumped into his arms. "Yes," she whispered in his ear. "Yes, yes, yes."

Want to see more from this author? Here's a taster for you to enjoy!

Graciella: Handling the Rancher
Sara Ohlin

Excerpt

Cruz stood at the edge of the bluff above the Pacific. The ocean brooded, inky-dark and dangerous, while the wind whipped it onto the shore. He let the cadence of wild, crashing waves and gusting wind wash over him. He loved the water in its fierce and powerful nature as much as he loved it when it was calm and patient. Wide and open, the beach stretched on, completely untouched by footprints, secluded and vulnerable all at the same time.

He took one lasting breath of the misty sea air and headed towards his farm. *His farm.* He still had moments when he couldn't believe it.

Wispy slips of fog teased and lifted around Cruz, revealing the morning dew on the grass as he made his way up towards the main house of Brockman Farms. Mornings on the farm were his favorite, the way the new light barely stroked the land, how the hues of everything were rich in those few moments of soft sun and leftover darkness. The salty air mixed with the scent of damp earth as it rose up. Home—Cruz was finally home—a place most people took for granted.

He'd been back in Graciella for five weeks after more than a decade away. His relief on hearing that his father, T.D. Brockman, was finally dead had been such that he'd nearly wept like a baby when his brother Adam had called with the news.

Thank goodness no one had seen his near breakdown. And that it hadn't lasted long. He could finally breathe clear and easy here on this land he loved, knowing the monsters were gone. He aimed to do more than breathe easy, however. It was his time to take care of the farm and all the people who depended on it — and to put his stamp on something valuable.

As much as he liked helping out at the barns, this morning dictated that he make a dent on the estate paperwork and duties. That didn't mean he had to do it without a fresh cup of coffee. Cruz entered the main house through the back to grab a mug of their housekeeper Elena's rich espresso brew in the kitchen before he got to work.

Fueled by caffeine, he sat at T.D. Brockman's old desk, going through bank statements and employee schedules. Since he'd returned, the phone hadn't quit ringing with condolences for his father's death and calls from the press. He wasn't sure which group won the award for insincerity.

Who could blame them? T.D. Brockman had taken pleasure in his ruthless way of doing business. But he'd been a wealthy bastard, owning most of the commercial properties in downtown Graciella. And the farm was spread out over two hundred and fifty thousand acres, nestled between Oregon wine country and the prized breathtaking Pacific coast. Money was involved, and where money was involved, people were curious. What would happen now that he was dead? Everyone wanted to know.

The phone rang again. "Brockman Farms," Cruz answered, the words clipped at one more interruption.

"Mr. Brockman? This is Ms. Selby from the *Oregonian*."

Another reporter. "The family has no comment at this time."

"Please, Mr. Brockman—"

"No comment!" Cruz said through clenched teeth and slammed the receiver down. The only reason he'd left the damn thing plugged in was because there were legitimate calls from banks and people regarding T.D.'s investments that Cruz had to deal with as executor.

"You must be Cruz Brockman."

Cruz looked up at the musical voice. Normally he wouldn't have to force a smile for anyone, let alone for an elegant woman. "Hello," he said and tried to punch down his irritation. "Can I help you?"

"Do you ever wait to see who's on the other end or are you that rude to everyone on the phone?" she asked as she walked into the room. Her body language might have said *cool* and *put-together*, but the haughty tone in her voice gave away one serious, pissed-off attitude.

"Excuse me?" He pushed his chair back and stood. "This is my office and if I remember correctly, I smiled and said hello. Perhaps you'd like to start over—"

"Mr. Brockman," she snapped.

He locked his gaze with hers and came around from behind the desk. "I said, perhaps you'd like to start over." His tone was sharp, no longer concealing his frustration.

"I'm Miranda Jenks, the audit accountant. I've been trying to contact you for days to let you know when I'd be arriving, but your phone etiquette made that impossible. The times you actually picked up the phone, you hung up on me before I could say more than three words. I finally got hold of your lawyer. He should have mentioned I'd be here today."

Gorgeous and haughty, what a combination, like a goddess rising from the morning's crashing waves. The image, unbidden, teased through his temper. Cruz half-listened as he studied her. In her charcoal-gray suit and black high heels, with that tone of reprimand in her voice, she reminded him of his finance professor in college, who'd believed Cruz's choice of photojournalism a waste of time. That was where the similarities came to a screeching halt. His professor had been in her sixties, very short and very thick.

The woman in front of him certainly wasn't sixty, short or thick. In fact, she looked more like she could stand to eat a good meal or two. Contradictions surrounded her. Deep, confident and extremely sexy, her voice was like a rich port. It also vibrated with indignation. But the rest of her seemed guarded. Her long dark hair was pulled back and held in a simple ribbon at her neck. Tall and stiff, she did a good job of trying to pretend calm. Gaunt cheekbones shaped her face and dark circles rested under her eyes. Very green, very frustrated eyes. That expressive gaze and sultry voice were at odds with the rest of her controlled, veiled demeanor.

"Mr. Brockman?" Impatience sliced the woman's words.

"Accountant? Jake never mentioned you were coming today."

"Yes, I did, Cruz." Jake walked in. "Sorry I'm late, Ms. Jenks, I'm Jake Burns. We spoke on the phone."

"Nice to meet you, Mr. Burns."

Cruz watched her almost-smile at Jake and enjoyed the way her face warmed and softened a hint. *Wonder what she looks like when she really lets herself smile?*

"Cruz, good to see you." Jake smacked him on the shoulder. "Ms. Jenks, thanks for your patience. Cruz, Miranda Jenks—the accountant I told you would be auditing the books if we plan on settling this estate." Cruz had a vague memory of the conversation. One of about five hundred he'd had about the estate since the funeral. "I apologize, Ms. Jenks," he said. "The phones have been on fire since T.D. died and I lost my patience with them days ago." He flashed her a grin in apology.

He held out his hand, and when she took it, his nerves sizzled. Every pulse point in his body awakened. He nearly tugged her closer so her entire body could touch his. She closed her eyes and quickly removed her hand, one that had trembled slightly in his and had such soft skin that he wanted to hold it again. She opened her briefcase to search through her paperwork.

"Excuse me, it seems my phone's busy today," Jake said. He took out his cell and walked into the hall.

"Ms. Jenks, thanks for coming all the way from...?" Cruz began.

"Houston."

"How was the trip?"

"The trip was fine. Shall we get to work? I'm certain none of us has any time to waste."

All business. Cruz sighed. From experience, he found accountants shallow and driven by money. But he needed one to handle the books. Cruz had lived most of his adult life traveling from one assignment to another, documenting the beauty and tragedy of the world, photographing and writing other people's stories. He had not been running a large company or settling estates, meaning he needed help to get things reconciled. Only then could he begin making lasting improvements and changes to Brockman Farms, fulfilling his dream of making this place something to be proud of.

"I'll need all the records your father kept. Bills paid, bills due, revenue, assets, expenses, wages, tax forms from the past few years, receipts, investments." She drew him out of his thoughts with her long list of demands.

Cruz looked around at the piles of paperwork covering the desk. "Most of it is here somewhere, but it's a mess at the moment, a mess I've been trying to sort through. Jake and I have some things to take care of. I know you've come a long way. How about if we begin in the morning? That will give me some time to get things more organized for you."

"Certainly."

Damn! The force of that word breathed at him like a dragon's fire. He could almost see the inner turmoil as she fought the need to roll her eyes at his incompetence. "But time isn't something you have a lot of, Mr. Brockman. I'm sure you're aware of that."

"I realize the importance of this, Ms. Jenks, but it's not exactly life or death now, is it?" He grinned at her again, trying to prod some emotion out of her. At the least he wished she'd relax. At the most he wanted to see her smile again. He liked the way it softened her face, gave her a bit of mystery, as though she was holding a special secret or two. He'd even take the fierce side of her — it showed her strength.

"That depends on how you feel about the IRS shutting you down for good."

"What the hell's that supposed to mean?" he demanded.

Home of Erotic Romance

Sign up for our newsletter and find out about all our romance book releases, eBook sales and promotions, sneak peeks and FREE romance books!

About the Author

Sara Ohlin has lived all over the United States, but her heart keeps getting pulled back to the Pacific Northwest where it belongs. For years she has been writing creative non-fiction and memoir and feels that writing helps her make sense of this crazy world. She devours books and can often be found shushing her two hilarious kids so that she can finish reading. When she isn't reading or writing, she'll most likely be in the kitchen cooking up something scrumptious, a French macaron, shrimp scampi, a fun date-night-in dinner with her sexy husband, or perhaps her next love story.

Sara loves to hear from readers. You can find her contact information, website details and author profile page at https://www.totallybound.com